CTHULHU'S DAUGHTERS

CTHULHU'S DAUGHTERS

STORIES OF LOVECRAFTIAN HORROR

EDITED BY

SILVIA MORENO-GARCIA

AND PAULA R. STILES

Published by Prime Books
www.prime-books.com

ISBN: 978-1-60701-467-6

Cover art by Isabel Collier.
Cover design by Sherin Nicole.

All material original to this volume.

"There are black zones of shadow close to our daily paths, and now and then some evil soul breaks a passage through."

—H.P. Lovecraft

CONTENTS

INTRODUCTION

THERE IS A paucity of women in Lovecraft's tales. Keziah, Lavinia and Asenath are his most notable women, even if they never take center stage. Some fans of Lovecraft's stories have even questioned whether Asenath should be considered a woman, since it is her father who inhabits her body. In a way, Asenath functions as a literary Schrödinger's cat: She can be interpreted as a man and a woman at the same time. Philosopher Judith Butler would have a field day discussing her and issues concerning the materiality of the body.

In a couple of his collaborations/ghost-writing jobs, Lovecraft seemed to give women more prominent roles. Whether it was because ghost-writing client Zealia Brown-Reed Bishop asked for this is unclear. At any rate, collaborations with Brown-Reed Bishop yielded Marceline and Audrey, the latter the only point-of-view woman Lovecraft ever dealt with. However, in general, whatever women appear in Lovecraft's stories lurk distantly in the shadows.

The present volume assembles stories about women, by women. Why an all-woman volume? The first spark was the notion, among some fans of the Lovecraft Mythos, that women do not like to write in this category, that they *can't* write in this category.

Though, for a long time, the Lovecraft Mythos was a male-dominated field and tables of contents by men were commonplace, we have seen in the past decade an increasing number of women creators and fans joining both the Weird fiction and the Lovecraft scene.

Beside long-standing authors such as Caitlín R. Kiernan and Ann K. Schwader, we can find relative newcomers like Molly Tanzer and E. Catherine Tobler. In the arts, Liv Rainey-Smith has distinguished herself with her woodcut creations. Editors such as Paula Guran and Ellen Datlow have assembled more than one volume of Lovecraftian fiction. This year saw the release of the first South Korean film adaptation of a Lovecraft story. "The Music of Jo Hyeja" casts women as the leads, with a woman—Jihyun Park—also directing.

Yet, the perception that women are not inclined towards Weird or Lovecraftian fiction seems to persist. We hope this anthology will help to dispel such notions. We also hope it will provide fresh takes on a number of characters and creatures from Lovecraft's stories, and add some completely new element to the Mythos. Most of all, we hope it will inspire new creations and inspire more women to write Weird or Lovecraftian tales.

Women have emerged from the shadows to claim the night. We welcome them gladly.

—Silvia Moreno-Garcia and Paula R. Stiles

"Sea" by Diana Thung

AMMUTSEBA RISING

ANN K. SCHWADER

At first, a spectral haze against the darkness,
some apparition less of mist than hunger
made visible afflicts our evening. Stars
within it flicker, fettered by corruption
we sense but dimly. Terrible & ancient,
it murmurs in the dreams of chosen daughters.

Not *it*, but *She* . . . Chaos Incarnate's daughter,
thought-spawned at random from that primal darkness
past memory or myth returns. What ancient
sorceries survive to wake such hunger
in times like ours? What spirit of corruption
endures to threaten these well-charted stars?

Minds blind to science, doubtful of the stars,
accustomed to dominion over daughters
& wives alike, defy this world's corruption
with ignorance. No curse, but blessed darkness
obscuring every sin—or any hunger
for truth beyond the authorized & ancient.

Above us now, authority more ancient
than mankind manifests. As fading stars
surrender up their essence to a hunger
yet unsuspected by our science, daughters
of ignorance awake. Unveiled from darkness,
they lift their faces. Savor sweet corruption.

Arched like a crime-scene silhouette, corruption
assumes the form of female. Feral. Ancient
opener of all the ways to darkness,
Her mystery eclipses tarnished stars
we kept for wishing on. Perhaps our daughters
will walk in shadow gladly, holding hunger

inside them for a weapon. Nameless hunger
reshaped their spirits: should we fear corruption
in doing likewise? All of us are daughters
denied some truth or other; craving ancient
wisdom like the bitterness of stars
against Her tongue, expiring into darkness.

No dawn remains. O daughters called by ancient
hunger, know the truth of your corruption:
Devourer of Stars, perfected darkness.

TURN OUT THE LIGHT

PENELOPE LOVE

A re-imagining of the life and death of Sarah Susan Phillips Lovecraft.

"THE OPERATION WAS a success," the voice said. "Everything was done to ensure her comfort. Then, during the night, her condition deteriorated. I'm sorry, but early this morning, she died." The telephone line buzzed and clicked mechanically.

He stood, wrapped in his dressing gown, bare feet on the cold linoleum of the rooming house hall. It was late in the May of 1921.

He had been roused by the ringing of the telephone from lucid and horrible dreams. The dreams were forgotten on waking, but the nightmare aura still clung. He could not take the news in. He became convinced that there was no human on the other end of the line. This was an alien voice, something that only pretended to be human, that stole a human face to speak and human hands to feel. *Prodigious surgical, biological, chemical, and mechanical skill . . .*

"Everything that could be done was done. My condolences. You'll want to see her, of course."

The voice stopped.

"No, not at all."

The negation shot out before he could think.

"No." He shrank back, appalled.

He had never ventured inside the building, not even when she was alive.

15

"Last night," he blurted out, "the lights were left on? All the time, as per our instructions?"

"Everything was done to ensure her comfort," the voice mechanically repeated.

"Of course. Yes. My Aunt Lillian will make the arrangements," he said.

Afterwards, he went back upstairs to his small room. The news sank in at last. His hands shook. They had argued when they last met. He had been angry with her and she had wept. A harsh mechanical voice buzzed in his head. The distance they had struggled with all their lives was now made infinite by death. He took an old, brown and creased paper from his pocket. He hesitated. He examined the childish scrawls. Then he crumpled it and threw it in the bin.

He sat at his desk. He drew pen and paper towards him, and wrote. He wrote as tears blotted paper and blurred ink. He wrote with sudden and desperate furious intensity. He wrote as if words, *mere inconsequential scribbles*, could bridge the abyss between life and death.

✣

"Supper!" Sarah squinted out the front door. "Come in, son."

It was a bright, hot day, Summer 1910. The rooming house on Angell Street was far from the green shade of College Hill. The glare outside threatened to bring on one of her headaches.

She glanced at herself in the hall mirror, but was aghast at her reflection. She saw an ageing face with a wan prettiness that was fading fast. Her clothes were dowdy. Her hair was merely neat. Her hands, though, were still long and white. They, at least, were still beautiful. "If only I could have run a little business," she said to her reflection, "I could have supported us." A shiver ran down her spine at her own daring. She leant closer. "An interior decoration business," she breathed. She was an accomplished painter, with an artist's eye. She could turn any house into a stylish nest. The shiver became a frisson. She retreated in fright from herself.

Her crowning rage, however, was that she was not a man . . .

She should have been born a boy. A man's brain was figured differently. If she were a man, she could have taken charge of her inheritance instead of being sidelined by her sister Lillian. As it was, the money vanished when her father died, like a malignant conjuring trick. It was no use wishing. Lillian would never let her work for a living. She was more frightened of Lillian than dying.

She hesitated at the threshold, shading her eyes against the harsh light outside. A slow throb built behind her temples. What was the boy doing? He had such terrible nightmares when he overexerted himself. She had taken him out of school as study took its toll on his delicate health. If he had gone far in this heat, he would be sleepless for weeks.

Anger had bubbled in her ever since her father died and it was decided that only the sale of the house could give them anything on which to live. Now the knot of anger in her belly twisted tight, as though the boy's absence were a purposeful insult. There was a straight line drawn between the boy and the grandfather, which gave distance and death equal weight. They had always had an understanding she could not fathom. In her traveling salesman husband's absence—philanderer, *snob*, spineless, *whore*—her father had spoiled his grandson, told him stories, given the boy the black cat, then given it such a vulgar name.

She had never liked that cat. The one blessing out of all that loss was that the rooming house would not let them keep it. She arranged for it to be drowned, although she told her son it ran off.

She had married beneath her and got what she deserved. Her husband was absent to the end, locked away in Butler Hospital with that disgusting disease that she could not name, not even to herself and never to the boy. No, the son was told his father suffered from nervous exhaustion. The traveling salesman reaped the dirt he had sowed. He died a helpless paralytic, his brain tunnelled through and through by disease, as if by worms, the bones of his face crumbling and melting away.

She bit her lips down hard over the scream, shoved it down hard, but it bobbed right back up with redoubled force. It threatened to burst from her skin. "Your supper's getting cold!" she called.

She took a few steps outside. Her son might have gone up to the observatory. The astronomers had made a pet of him. She was so proud. Why, he studied the stars. He told her he was going to be an astronomer when he grew up. He wrote charts and scrawled calculations that made her head ache with their strange patterns. She carefully preserved even the ones he abandoned and crumpled up.

She squinted up and down the street. Some children, walking home from school, looked at her and laughed. The mocking sound swung and skittered in the summer heat. It echoed in her hurting head. A cold chill squeezed her heart.

He hadn't gone back? Not after she had forbidden him. The thought, *the fear*, was enough. She snatched up her hat and headed out, turning right. By the time she had walked the length of Angell Street to her father's house, she was limp, but her fists were clenched. She didn't clench them. The muscular spasm was brought on by something outside herself. She watched as her fine, white fingers gnarled and turned ugly, all of themselves. The knuckles showed red and taut and prominent. She dragged her eyes away. Her head pounded.

This spacious house, raised on a high green terrace, looks down upon grounds which are almost a park, with winding walks, arbours, trees, & a delightful fountain.

The boy was camped out on the front steps of the house, under the shade of the trees. Just as she had feared. He had a paper in his hand and was copying from it onto the front steps with chalk, great circles and scrawls, dark head bent over his work, too intent to hear her approach.

She pounced, snatching up paper and chalk. The paper had circles and diagrams and calculations in her son's neat hand. Strange meaning oozed from the signs. She crumpled the paper up and thrust it into her pocket. Her head pounded, and dark things crawled and snatched at the edges of her vision. "What have you done?" she whispered, appalled.

His white face looked up at her, the bony length of adulthood already breaking through the childish roundness; deep-set eyes, dark-ringed with lack of sleep, gazed, solemn and intent.

"I returned for the cat," he said, with his peculiar, particular confidence. "I dreamed he came back and was waiting for me on the steps of our residence."

"This is not our house," she said softly, because to speak loudly would jar her head. "We can"t just do what we like here. You have made a dreadful mess. Oh, I'm ashamed."

"It is Gramps' abode," he asserted.

"Do not use the word, 'Gramps.' It is common. Call him Grandfather," she said. She reached out a hand to lift him. He evaded her grasp and ran up to the top of the steps. "Come down at once," she snapped.

He turned to face the street. He filled his lungs.

"Niggerman!" he bawled.

A colored man was walking below. He snapped around as the boy called. His face was a mask, shadowed under the hat's brim, concealing his true feelings.

Her son's vulgarity gave her the impetus to climb the stairs. She dragged him back down.

"No gentleman would use that word," she hissed. "You just apologize." She looked up, but the man was gone.

"That was the cat's name," she said, too late, to empty air. "He didn't mean—"

"Gramps gave the cat that name," the boy said, unabashed.

"Your grandfather was not a gentleman. He made his own fortune and was never able to shake off his youthful habit of vulgar speech. I expect better from you," she snapped.

She hauled her son away, walking too fast for him in this breathless heat.

"But Gramps will require his habitation when he returns," the boy protested.

"Your Grandfather is not coming back. He has passed away. He is with the Lord."

He gazed at her pityingly. "The idea of a benevolent all-knowing deity is but a pathetic illusion of the rabblement."

He had taken to using archaic words he read in his grandfather's 1828 *Webster's Dictionary*. It was part of a long game he played at being an eighteenth-century gentleman. She normally took pride in his game, but now, she was filled with fury at his pedantic speech. She took a fresh grasp on the small, sweating hand and hurried.

That was when she realized she was muttering to herself, fists clenched, eyes staring and mouth square and wide. People took one look at her and crossed the street. She forced herself to calm down. Colors of strange shape and brightness blotched her vision. She forced herself to let go of her son's hand.

She slowed her step, glanced down at her son, and smiled, willing to pretend there was nothing wrong. Unfortunately, he took her gesture as encouragement.

"Are you recomposed, Mother?" he inquired politely. "Remember I used to climb in the old tree above the family plot in the cemetery? I watched Gramps' grave. I know Gramps is destitute of life. He is decomposed. That is a jest. He is eaten by worms. They have burrowed into his brain. It is riddled through and through with worms. I watched Father's grave, too, pretending he was still alive and would try to claw his way out. But he never did. He's dead, too, I expect. And the cat," he finished.

Shock swelled in her throat. "I told you that cat ran off. Even a dumb brute had more sense than to stay with poor folk like us."

"He drowned," the boy said. "Poor old fellow. He is deceased."

"Where did you hear that?" Had Lillian told him? Had she talked in her sleep?

"I saw it in my dream," he said. "But I will bring them both back. With that paper you took. I saw the straight lines between the stars. I worked the calculations. If they follow the lines, they will come back, Gramps and the cat. They will undergo a rejuvenescence."

She knelt and took his shoulders. "You stop this nonsense," she said frightened.

"It is not nonsense. It is a real word. It means they will become young again," the boy said, mistaking the source of her concern.

Now, the first odd thing about Joseph Curwen was that he did not seem to grow much older . . .

She put her hand to his forehead. His father had babbled like this before they took him away, babbled in Butler Hospital for years as his brain and face rotted from within, not that she'd ever let the boy visit him.

His brow was hot to the touch and damp. His eyes were too bright, feverish, and sweat shone on his face. "There, look what you've done. You've brought on one of your nervous fits," she said.

He couldn't eat any supper. She put him in his truck bed in the tiny bedroom they shared. His hair was damp and his face shone. His too-bright eyes, unsleeping, bored into the roof overhead. She sat down beside him and watched him, bathing his forehead.

Something crinkled in her dress. It was the crumpled piece of paper with his calculations on it, the circles and scrawls meant to call back his grandfather and his precious cat. She almost threw it away, but instead, she smoothed it out carefully and stored it with the others in the drawer beside her bed.

As she straightened, a lance shot through her head. She clutched her temple and muffled the cry of pain. She sat, quickly. She looked down at her hands, sick and dizzy. Her hands swirled in and out of her sight. She screamed.

"Mother!" the boy called, sitting up.

"Never mind; just sleep," she managed.

Her hands were not the hands of a lady. They were clawed and knotted and red. She shoved both monstrous paws under the pillow, then collapsed.

They lay, each in their own beds across from one another as the night lengthened. *The way they screamed at each other from behind their locked doors was very terrible.* A tomb herd rolled across the floor, first one way then the other, and bony hands reached up to claw at each restless dreamer.

It was early Spring in 1919. He had been visiting his grandfather's grave in Swan Hill Cemetery, although he had grown too old, and too unsure of his dignity, to attempt to again climb the tree above the family plot. He had grown tall and gaunt, and his legs seemed always too long for the modest chambers in which he and his mother lived. The rooms had grown smaller and meaner. His poor health had prevented him from finishing school and the dream of being an astronomer had crumbled to dust. He fancied the dust was gray and brittle, the dust of lost dreams; *the essential Saltes of humane Dust*. He was only at ease when he was moving. He took great walks out over the New England countryside, visiting cemeteries and ancient places.

He had grown pale and somber, with deep-set eyes, a long face, and a square chin: a tombstone face, he joked with his relations. His mother was proud that he looked like the portraits of his New England ancestors.

"None of your father there," she said, with satisfaction.

He was heading home from Swan Point along Blackstone Boulevard when the black car swept past in the opposite direction. He knew the car. Aunt Lillian's doctor. He recognized the profile in the back seat. It was his mother. He could imagine her drawing on her shabby gloves and checking her hat, delighted at this reminder of their old affluence. But why was she travelling down Blackstone Boulevard? There was only one possible destination. . . . He shouted "Mother!" as the car turned the corner onto Butler Drive.

"No!" he shouted. He ran after her. The gates of Butler Hospital came into view. The car swept through.

"There has been a mistake!" he shouted.

His mother had been staying with Aunt Lillian for a few days. That was all. Her poor health had got the better of her. Aunt Lillian had taken over her care.

His mother had fits, spikes of terror in which she insisted the lights must be left on or *They* would get in. She'd had a fit during a blackout several nights ago. He was writing when the blackout occurred, so he was able to look at his fob watch, his gentlemanly affectation, and note the time precisely: *2:12 am.* He often stayed up all night working on his poetry. It saved bad dreams—the night terrors had never given up. His mother woke screaming for the light and the police were called by a neighbor who was sure they were all being murdered.

"They come out of corners, of course," she told him when she calmed down. "I am sure you could calculate the angles yourself from the straight lines between the stars. But they only come out when it is dark. I am perfectly safe as long as the lights remain on. Oh, you understand. Can't you explain to these kind gentlemen?"

It was dawn by the time he had soothed her, dismissed the curious neighbors, and reassured the disgruntled police. His night of writing was ruined. He remembered, with a bleak wash of guilt, that he had been glad to hand her over to Aunt Lillian.

He arrived at the gates. They were wrought iron and very grand. Overhead was printed in iron: *Butler Hospital for the Insane.* The car stopped at the end of the long, white, gravel drive, before the stone steps that led to the wide, glass doors. His mother got out, courteously assisted by the doctor. There had certainly been a mistake. But it was all right. He was here. He could save her.

He tried to leave the gate behind, to go inside the grounds. His feet refused to move.

Butler Hospital was a beautiful red-brick building. Its mellow curves glowed amber and the windows flashed in the weak sunlight. The trees were budding new leaves. A plaque read, *For those bereft by God's providence of their reason.*

"She is not mad!" he shouted.

He could not stir. He watched as his mother was helped inside by two white-clad nurses. He could not follow. He clung to the cold stone of the gateposts to prevent falling. He could not take one step inside.

He had a horror of the place since he was a child, since he had over-heard the whispers in darkness. Behind the scientific ranks of windows that let the sunshine in, he saw his father lying paralyzed and aware, with worms crawling through his brain.

He rang Aunt Lillian as soon as he reached home. She told him his mother had another fit of terror, at 3:00 am, this time. Aunt Lillian had decided it would be best for Sarah to have a good rest. Thanks to their family name, she was able to secure a room in Butler Hospital for a fortnight.

"But what about the lights? They must be kept on," he protested.

His aunt's voice was crisp and decided, yet she evaded a direct answer. He knew she thought he was only humoring his mother.

"She needs a rest and good care," she reassured him. "Now let me go, dear. I am packing to come over and look after you."

He could never argue with Aunt Lillian. He carefully put down the receiver.

✻

They walked in the grounds of Butler Hospital on that May morning, 1921, along meandering paths through green lawns. It was too cold, but, as always, he refused to go in. He had to shorten his long stride and stoop over her, and she had to hurry to keep up with him. They looked as if they were locked in an awkward dance.

His eyes were dark hollows. The night terrors never dimmed.

She had been in Butler Hospital two years.

"I am very concerned about this operation," she said to her son.

"You will be free from all pain once your gall bladder is removed. You will receive the best care," he replied.

"What about the lights?" she asked.

"The surgeon requires bright lights," he reassured her.

"But afterwards, when I am still under the influence of the

anaesthetic. I won't be able to wake up. What if the nurses leave me alone in the dark? *They* will get in. I do wish you would sit with me afterwards," she appealed.

"You know I cannot," he said.

"Only for a little while," she coaxed.

"Mother, you know I cannot go inside," he snapped. "I'm sorry," he said at once. "I do apologize for my abruptness. I do not mean to be unkind. But there is no need for you to be concerned."

"But I *am* concerned," she persisted. "The nurses say the lights are left on always when I am sure they turn them off as soon as I am asleep."

She watched as embarrassment, tinged with disgust, flooded his stiff face. She had seen this look so often of late. It had been an insidious creep, almost unnoticeable at first, this flight from people's confidence, as loved faces became strangers. She had decided that they were wearing wax masks of familiar features, even though the person behind the mask had changed.

"Have you ever woken in the dark?" he asked.

"The nurses watch me through the spy hole in my door," she explained. "As soon as they see me stir, they whisk in and turn the lights on, then out again quicker than I can see."

"Mother! The nurses are wonderful here."

"Only you can understand," she pleaded.

She was lost in the dark. The only guide she had was the straight line drawn between the boy and his grandfather, the secret understanding between them that she had never fathomed, that they had celebrated in stories and games and such ungentlemanly nicknames. From all that, she had been excluded. If only she had been a man . . .

They arrived back at the entrance to the hospital, the stone stairs to the wide, glass doors.

"Goodbye, Mother," he said, stiff and embarrassed.

She climbed the steps, then stopped at the door. Her reflection in the glass showed an ugly old woman, ashamed and outraged at her own

25

mortality. She reached out her hand and touched the *cool, unyielding surface*.

Hot anger, as sharp as ever, pierced through her. She hurried down the steps to face her son. She held out the crumpled paper she had hoarded so long. It was brown with age, and had been folded and refolded so often that the creases were torn.

"If I should die, please mark the symbols on the front steps here as you did for your grandfather—and the cat. I know it is nonsense. Just do this for me, please. I would like to think that I could follow the straight line between the stars and come back."

He took the paper, smoothed it between careful fingers.

"Mother, don't tell me you brooded over this all these years? It is a bagatelle of infant fancy." He laughed ruefully. "I have got the calculations all wrong, anyway. I was an impenitent yahoo, wasn't I?"

He raised his eyes from the paper at last, awkwardly.

"Mother, you know I will always be here for you," he said, gently.

"You say that but you aren't," she said, bitterly.

She could not repress the anger. She could not hide her weakness. Hot angry tears spurted down her cheeks.

"Good-bye, Mother."

He retreated.

"I will see you tomorrow morning. After the operation." He turned away.

"Howard!" she shrieked.

He flinched, but he did not turn.

She watched his straight back and his long stride as he left her alone.

She looked up to see two nurses had responded to her scream. One stood at the top of the steps. The other came several steps down to meet her and held out a gloved hand, as if to help.

She raised her hands to wipe away the tears. To her horror, they were not the hands of a lady. They were clawed and knotted and red. She glanced with sick shock at the nurse's faces. They had waited only for her son to leave. They had swapped themselves. The shapes behind their white wax masks were all wrong.

She knew that as soon as she was unconscious and alone, they would turn out the light.

"Aya-Ig" by Pia Ravenari

BRING THE MOON TO ME

AMELIA GORMAN

THEY HAD NAMES like Herringbone and Honeycomb, or Tyrolean Fern. My mother turned yarn into thick forests and spiraling galaxies with luscious titles. I watched her fingers busy themselves for hours to produce squares of cloth. Sometimes, her hands faded away and the string had a life of its own. Like a snake or an eel, it raised its head then dipped it back down. It looped around itself, only to slip away and tie up its own tail. Eventually, a familiar pattern emerged.

In those days, our house smelled fat with lanolin and fish oils. Her customers stumbled in off the wharf, washed in grappa and mumbling at a frequency that made my head buzz. They put money in an urn on the shelf and my mother would dig some soft, thick sweater out of a basket. Sometimes, they would come back pointing out holes in the elbows or fraying at the edges. These woolen patterns were their defense against the dangers of the ocean.

I wasn't afraid of the storms or earthquakes that visited the bay. I wasn't afraid of the depths of the sea or the dark things that swam there. The shadows in our house made me anxious. They came out of the corners when my mother sang and knit, and flew across her face and hands. She sang about shepherds and Hastur and the sweet smell of lemon trees at night.

These were the days before quite so many lights had sprung up. There was a hole in the roof. When I lay on the floor, I saw moonlight shining through it. When it fell on my mother's hands, I could see every bone roving under the skin. A steady clicking went on forever, reminding me that patterns were filling the room.

. . . knit two, purl two, knit two, purl two . . .

. . . 11001100 . . .

My mother doesn't believe me when I tell her what I do. When I come home from the factory, she rocks in her eternally creaking chair. She asks me how my day was. She asks me about my coworkers, if anyone is getting married soon, if anyone is pregnant. If anyone has a nice brother to introduce to me. She says she can't remember if I weave blankets or rugs.

No, I don't weave blankets. I weave instructions for computers. They have names like Mercury, Gemini and, most importantly, Apollo. I'm like a fable character, threading shining metal on my loom. On each side of me are a dozen other women doing the same thing. Eventually, someone will take all of our work, bind it together, and put it inside the shuttle, where it will help a group of men navigate to the Moon. We're changing the world.

No, I don't weave rugs. I demonstrate my job at home with table runners and napkin rings. "See, when the cloth goes through here, it means one, but when it goes around the ring, it means zero. Enough ones and zeroes can stand in for complicated math." She squints at me while I stand with the contents of our dining room dangling from my hands. They feel warm and uncomfortably organic. I feel hot and embarrassed, and set down her nice things. I brainstorm other ways to get through to her. I light and blow out rows of candles. I get books from the library about Charles Babbage and George Boole, newspaper articles about Grace Hopper. It doesn't work.

At work the next day, I'm greeted by the daily stack. Pages are piled up as high as three of my fingers, covered in digits. By the 5:00 bell, I'll transform them all into sparkling strands. I try to be friendly, but it's hard not to absorb the numbers while I work. Sometimes, I even go out for drinks in the evening, but I'm always distracted by the numbers inside me. I'm starting to recognize patterns. These sixteen figures keep recurring, or these one hundred and twenty-eight. So, today, I take it even further. I breathe deeply and let the data into me. It's not so different from reading a highway map. I wish I were the one traveling along it.

My head is overflowing when I get home. I worry about the numbers turning into fat worms and eating holes in the side of my head, with all the zeroes falling out. I need to hurry if I'm going to bring them into the tactile world. I grab a pair of my mother's birch needles. They are slowly rotting.

My mother watches my hands while I work and I look at hers. They are swollen past the point of holding needles. She hasn't made anything in years. Those hands that made forests have become knotted branches. I see a painful future in them after a life of enabling a few to walk on strange lunar landscapes.

My finished product looks random at first glance. It's a screaming wreck of different types of stitches. Some patches are flat and others are rough. Here and there, a scallop rears its head and is abruptly cut off. I think I'm the only person who can read the calculations in it, and see the angles and velocity. I'm wrong, though. Recognition spreads over my mother's face for the first time. We finally have a common language to speak to each other.

She tells me about a night when she was younger than I am now. She tells me about a pattern she only made once. She gave it to a fisherman and told him her usual marketing ploy: It would keep him safe from all the dangers above and below the water. She lied. She sent him out wearing a beacon that shouted at the heart of the Moon. It made him see things. He still babbles about the underwater city and the sunken dead that drifted up from the seabed. Even that wasn't loud enough to bring something down from the sky.

She can't make it herself anymore, but she whispers all the stitches in my ear. I write them in machine language on the inside of my eyelids. I can visualize it in copper and cores. It will camouflage itself against the endless commands my coworkers weave day after day. When the time is right, the shining sign will call out to something that lives beyond here.

. . . knit one, purl two, knit one . . .

. . . 1001 . . .

The astronauts will return but not alone. They will bring the shadow from the Moon down, finally. It will be enormous. Its landing will send out ripples as large as the Pacific. Its hooves will trample the street lights and skyscrapers until there is nothing left but starlight. I will stand on the rocks by the bay and wrap my sweater tightly around my shoulders, knowing that I will be the last left standing. My work will change the world.

VIOLET IS THE COLOR OF YOUR ENERGY

NADIA BULKIN

ABIGAIL GARDNER *NÉE* Cuzak was sitting on the bathroom floor, thinking about the relationship that mice in mazes have with death, when a many-splendored light shot down from the stars like a touch of divine Providence. Abigail hurried to the bathroom window above the toilet, but just as she put her fingers on the smudge-stained glass, a loud noise—not an explosion, more like a diver's plunge—burst from the field and pushed her back onto her heels. The impact tripped the perimeter lights; she could see shockwaves rippling the corn. But there was no smoke, no fire, only the faintest tint of red-blue-purple now rapidly melting into night.

She heard Nate throw off the covers, muttering, "What the fuck?" And then, sharper, "Abby!"

The two of them rushed downstairs, a shadow of the team they had once been when they were first trying to forge a life together out of the money they'd saved in college, him at the chem lab, her at the campus store. "I bet it's our buddy Pierce," Nate muttered, barreling through the kitchen, running into a chair in the dark. If it hurt, he didn't show it. "He probably cooked up some radio-controlled boondoggle to mess with the crop. Probably aiming for the sprinklers. Or just trying to nuclear-waste the whole damn thing."

Abigail did not think that sounded much like him. Ambrose might have enjoyed eating up the little farms around him, counting up his tripling acres with a glass of whiskey, but he hated parlor tricks, didn't think he needed to lower himself to sabotage. She said nothing to Nate. It was better to let him cling to that bone if it kept him occupied.

Nate had his gun. Abigail had a fireplace poker. Her farm cats were skulking by the flower pots, making low, scratchy howls at something in the corn. Abigail followed him to the front as quietly as possible, her bare feet curling around dry stalks and kernels and poisoned insect corpses, but she had the feeling they would not find what Nate was looking for. They would not find any ruddy farmhand with a twistable neck, nor a small, broken, remote-controlled drone. Nate would periodically shush her and veer in a new direction, but Abigail knew there was no life out there. The field was so quiet, she could hear the cats' growling. Though the air sure smelled strange—pungent and tart with a hint of curdled sweetness. It prickled her skin.

Between the rows, Nate turned and whispered, "There's no one here."

She could have told him so, but Nate had to know for himself before he'd turn around. Had to go all the way to the state border before he admitted that maybe he had missed the turn for Salt Creek Road. That was just his way. He liked being careful; she liked that about him.

"Maybe it was something on the road," she said, so he would let them get back to the house. The thought of the road and the real world beyond the gravel driveway had reminded her that the children were alone. She had dreams about them growing up that way—little feral masters of the house, sunken and sullen and riding the dogs like wolves. "Maybe somebody blew his tire."

Nate seemed to be chewing the whole interior of his mouth. "That wasn't a tire, Abby."

"You can look again in the daytime," she tried.

"I'm gonna call up that son-of-a-bitch Pierce in the daytime, is what I'm gonna do," said Nate. "Teach him if he thinks he can intimidate me."

When they slunk back to the house, the boys were standing on the porch, the dogs at their heels. Zeke was trying to project his authority with his Little League baseball bat; Merrill was wiping his eyes. Teddy asked if a comet had crashed. Nate gave him a little push to the head and said, "Don't get too excited." Underneath the porch, the cats' diamond eyes were shining.

✳

Their harvest was surprisingly healthy that summer—bigger and greener than any others since they'd moved out of their south Lincoln bungalow three years ago and decided to make a more wholesome life in the country. Nate didn't have the nutrient content analysis back yet, but when he took bites off the blond-haired cob, he said he knew. Abigail thought it tasted off—sour, like the air in the field since the crash that wasn't a crash—but Nate said it needed processing and when was the last time she'd won any farming awards? Well, he was right about that.

And it was good to see Nate happy. She had never allowed herself to doubt him—before she married him she had asked herself, *Do I trust this man to lead this family?* and she had decided the answer was yes, come hell or tarnation—but it was still good to get good news.

"What kind of Frankenstein corn are you growing now, Gardner?" said Ambrose Pierce when they ran into him outside Horwell's General Store, sipping a Dr. Pepper. "I thought you were all about that hippie organic tofu living and here you are, pumping your crop with steroids."

"You're the only one growing Frankenstein GMO corn," Nate said, puffing out his chest. "Some of us haven't forgotten what it means to be a real farmer, growing real food for a real family." Ambrose wasn't married. Nate had suggested he was gay, but he was not. "Guess you Big Ag types wouldn't recognize real corn if it rose up and kicked you in the ass."

Ambrose made a guffawing sound. "Aren't you from Omaha?"

Nate shifted the bags in his hand and went to the truck and didn't answer. But Ambrose caught Abigail by the wrist before she could follow and said to her, "Abby, something's off about that corn. I don't like it. I don't know what *he's* been doing, but you gotta get that shit cleared by the FDA." A good wife would have stiffly told him he was just jealous, just sorry that he couldn't quite yet eat up Nate's land, but she must not have been a good wife. Nate unlocked the doors and shouted, "Abby! Let's go!" The *"go"* had a punchy desperation to it, probably because that was the moment he saw Ambrose touching her hand.

So, Nate was already in a bad mood when they started the drive home. Zeke and Teddy had been late meeting them at the truck, and Merrill had knocked down a chocolate display at Horwell's. Abigail understood. They were restless children. Sure, they had all the bicycling down country lanes that they could want, all the smashing of rotten pumpkins, but they needed people. They needed to look at things that weren't stalks or clouds. Teddy, especially. She could see the look in his eyes getting pounded in deeper all the time: the look of a cornered animal.

"Did you get that nutrient analysis back?" Abigail asked and she really shouldn't have.

Nate, chewing on a thumbnail, widened his eyes. "What?"

"For the corn."

"Why would you ask me that?"

A welt of worry in Abigail's stomach became a full-on ulcer as she searched the horizon—just corn and trees and ditch and road—for something that would answer Nate's question to his satisfaction. "I just was wondering." No, that wasn't good enough. The ache didn't stop.

"Did Pierce tell you to say that? Back at Horwell's? Huh?"

Her mouth was opening and closing, but only breath was coming out. She heard something constrict in Nate's ribs and he suddenly ripped the steering wheel to the right, pulling the truck to the shoulder of the road. She knew the boys were holding their breath, so she felt the need, then, to make some noise of protest on their behalf.

"Are you sleeping with him?"

"What?" Her voice broke. "Nate, the boys are right . . . "

His shout punched down like a hammer of God. "Answer me, Abby!

Was this some whore's bargain? Said you'd jump into bed if he'd just cut your poor idiot husband a break?"

The radio was playing a mellowed-out beach-pop song by a local band that had made it out. They used to get her dreaming about coarse California sand from the anarchic desolation of Sokol Auditorium. This song always made her think of breaking surf, of drinks with plastic umbrellas. Maybe they should go on vacation. Maybe they should never come back.

"No," she hissed. "You know I would never do that. You know I would never want to." She nodded toward the backseat. "Can we *please* talk about this later?"

For five minutes, they all breathed together. Then Nate changed the station with a sudden strike of his hand, muttered, "Hate that song," and drove back onto the road. So, the rest of the way they listened to Dr. Touchdown on KMKO out of Lincoln. "Wear them down," said Dr. Touchdown. "The key is to wear down the defense, go for the throat, and don't let up. Lights out. Bam!" From the backseat, Merrill echoed, very softly, "Bam!"

She was ready—no, not ready, never ready, but resigned—for a fight, but when they got home, Nate went into the field and started running the combine even though there was nothing to strip, anymore. He watched in a state of near-motionlessness. And Abigail watched him from behind the muslin curtain, and the boys watched her over the stained pages of their homework, and the dogs watched the boys with sad, bovine eyes. Boys and dogs alike asked for things—food, drink—and eventually, after the sun began to set, Teddy put down his American History book and asked for an explanation of Croatoan. When the Roanoke Colony disappeared, he said, they left that word behind. Yes, a sign post. Salvation, five miles south of Cripple Creek.

"Nobody knows," said Zeke. "They probably got eaten by an Indian tribe."

"Maybe they ran away," Abigail said. "Maybe they wanted to."

✳

The cats were gone. She waited for them by their little bowls of dirt-colored pellets for a week, but they weren't coming back. She had looked everywhere. She even peeked down into the well. She didn't know why, exactly. Cats didn't just jump into wells. Did a tiny piece of her think that perhaps someone—*who?*—had killed the cats and thrown them in? There was something down there, ding dong bell, but the flashlight revealed a collar, a yellow tag, a long nose. It was the dogs. She had last seen them the day before, pacing near the corn and whimpering. Nate had gone to tie them up and, she assumed, to untie them.

She was watching the kitchen clock tick toward, 3:30 and wondering how to tell the boys, when a silver Dodge Ram pulled up to the house. Like a crocodile, or a tyrannosaur, sidling up to its prey. Ambrose Pierce stepped out of the cab and she immediately calculated how long it would take Nate to get back from his meeting with Ticonderoga Mills.

"I haven't seen you and the boys in town much." Ambrose looked aside at the barely-tilting wind chimes. "Haven't heard from you lately, neither."

Abigail ground her teeth, head shaking slightly to the internal retinue of all the things she'd really like to say to Ambrose, to Nate. Finally, she conceded that "Nate's been acting a little different, lately. Since that light came down . . . "

"What light? 'Different' how?"

"Different" like standing in the sea of corn, humming at the sky? "Different" like telling Zeke he couldn't go out for Junior League baseball this year, because he was "needed" at home? "Different" like picking up the phone and telling her sister that she wasn't home when she was just around the corner, fixing dinner? No, that was more trouble than it was worth.

"Just different. He's stressed. It's hard, you know, worrying about feeding a family when your neighbor's lying in wait, drooling over your property." She gave him a look. He wasn't fazed. He'd long-ago reconciled himself to the vulture's life. "Maybe the water's gone bad. All the fracking they're doing out by the aquifer."

Ambrose clicked his tongue, muttering something about "hippie bull-shit," then leaned in, putting his right hand on the door frame as if he owned the place, as if she wouldn't have slammed the door on his fingers. His voice lowered. "Do you need help, Abby?"

"No, I don't need your *help*. What kind of *help* could you give me?" She grabbed the door. "Nate's coming home soon. I don't want to be a witness in a murder trial."

Actually, Nate didn't come home for another hour. She heard his truck pull up, but he didn't come in. When she ventured outside, he was standing and staring at the freshly scalped corn field with his keys dangling from his right hand, as if hypnotized by an inaudible sermon. She asked if he was all right, but her fingers wouldn't quite rise to touch his arm. His exhale seeped out like a deflating balloon.

"What did the guy at the mill say?"

"Max Beecham is a motherfucker."

"What?"

"Max Beecham doesn't believe in us."

Abigail hurried back inside. She called her sister's cell, but it was off; called her house phone and only got her five-year-old niece. "Will you tell Mommy to call Aunt Abby? Aunt Abby in Cripple Creek." She dropped the phone when she heard the porch squeak, but it was just the boys, who ditched their dusty backpacks, and started clapping and calling, "Here, boy! Here, boy!" Of course, no dogs answered.

All day, she'd been hoping that some vagabond, some wanderer, had snatched up the dogs in the middle of the night and dumped them in the well. Or that perhaps they'd been run over on the highway, or slain by a disease, or just spontaneously died—and that Nate had thrown the bodies in the well in an attempt to protect the boys from the reality of death. But when the boys were still mewling out in the field well after she'd called them in for dinner, Nate said, "Boys, I told you: They ran away. Told you we didn't train them well enough. Probably halfway to Colorado by now."

He turned to the little spoons tucked into the little chipped serving dishes, her meek attempts to ward off sadness. "Why aren't we eating our corn? Wasn't that the whole point of moving out here?" She thought they'd ruled out subsistence years ago. "Growing our own food? Living off our own land? Unless you think there's something wrong with it. You and Pierce."

She waited until after the boys were in bed, and she had promised Merrill that they would put up lost-and-found flyers all over town, to say something to Nate. That was how long it took to sculpt the nauseous worry in her heart into something spear-shaped. She lingered at the top of the staircase, rehearsing her words—*Did something happen to the dogs last night* or *I found something in the well*—when Nate rounded the corner at the bottom of the stairs and started laboriously climbing up.

"What happened to the dogs?" came stammering out when he reached the second floor.

He sighed loudly. She willed herself not to apologize. "They ran away. Like I said."

"But I found them in the well."

Nate's red eyes finally focused on her. Her poor husband was so horrified—so honest-to-the-bones horrified—by this revelation that he grabbed her by the arm, saying he needed to explain something to her—*explain*—then pulled the string on the door to the attic to drag her up into that spider-webbed lair of things unwanted, things unexplained. He pushed her down toward the boxes of books that they'd never bothered to cut open after the move and descended the ladder again, slamming the door shut behind him as she lay shaking in a cloud of dust.

�

❋

At the very beginning, she was relieved to be alone. The dark erased everything that taunted her in the light—the carved-up acres of a burned and spent, uniform earth; the harrowing passage of time. She made believe that she was nothing but a set of lungs, expanding and shrinking. She curled up near the door with her palm against the cold wood and slept.

But when sunlight leaked in through the tiny attic window and the attic door was still closed, the muscles around her ribs started to cramp. She tried pounding her fist and then a flashlight against the attic floor. She tried shouting—first at Nate, then at Teddy, then at Zeke. She avoided yelling Merrill's name until she had no choice. The boys' voices seemed so quiet, like they were many islands away across a great sea.

But someone was moving down there below the attic door. She tried everything to talk to it. "Nate?" she called. "Nate, please listen to me. Nate, I love you." When that got no response she started to scream—complicated accusations about his failure as a pharmaceutical sales supervisor and his need to maintain a sense of moral superiority that degenerated into words that degenerated into noise. She chewed off the tips of her nails; she dragged her fingers through her hair so many times that strands began to come off in her fist.

And then, after the sky's white-blue started turning to pewter, the door swung open. She was slow crawling toward it, but it was Teddy. Teddy, her wonder. Her savior. The only boy they'd named after a president. "Come quick," he whispered. "Daddy's in the field."

It did not work. Nate must have been waiting downstairs, because she woke up back in the attic with a welt and a throbbing pain in the back of her head. She resumed screaming because now the attic was drenched in fading amber half-light and that meant she had been locked in that room for almost an entire day. A child's voice screamed back at her from somewhere on the second floor. The *"Mom"* dragged like a serrated knife through the wood and the insulation, and she realized it was Teddy. He shouted something about *"Dad"* and *"crazy"* and *"room,"* and she thought at first that he was talking about her plight, but no. Nate had locked him in the spare bedroom, the one they saved for family—family that never visited.

She told Teddy to apologize to Nate. She told him to ask Zeke for help. But in the end, all she could do was press herself flat against the floor and sing, "I love you. A bushel and a peck. A bushel and a peck, and a hug around the neck."

That night, she stacked up broken furniture underneath the attic window and tried to signal Ambrose with the flashlight. His truck was hurtling by ten miles over the speed limit; he was probably on his way back from Cellar's Bar and Grill, and he was probably rushing home for another, but she didn't have a choice. She switched the flashlight on and off, on, off, on, off until his red tail lights disappeared behind the cottonwoods. Had the truck slowed? It hadn't stopped.

When the attic door was pushed open, she had to bite her knuckle to keep from calling Ambrose's name.

"You have to let the boys go," she said. She could not see Nate's expression, but his face had been a dark blank to her for months now. That light from the sky had come and eaten all the color off his face—all the variegation, the jokes he'd told her, the promises he'd made her. Every time he had shown her what a good father he was. "I'll stay with you. I'll help you through this, but you need to let someone else take care of them for a while."

"I need you to prove your loyalty to me, Abby. You and Teddy both." He pushed a cob of their corn—tiny shriveled kernels bounded their grotesquely swollen cousins like rings of baby teeth—toward her on a paper plate. The big, awful kernels looked like unblinking eyes. "Please eat it. Please show me I'm not wrong."

She picked out a little tooth-kernel and tucked it down between her lip and her gum. It immediately dissolved and filled her mouth with something that melted like pixy stix, something that tasted like bloody soap. "Let them go stay with my sister."

He nudged the plate with the long barrel of his gun. "More."

So, she ate more, but Teddy must not have, because his little voice dwindled to nothing but a whisper that Abigail eventually realized was her own ragged breath, tearing in and out.

It took Merrill hours that might have been days to speak to her. He would only push the door open by an inch. She crawled toward him in the dark, chewing another kernel—she was hoping they were poisoning her and was taking the fact that she couldn't feel her legs anymore as a good sign. "We have to be quiet so Daddy doesn't get mad," he whispered. Pale-blue eyes rolled down toward the light. "Teddy won't come out of that room."

"I know," she said. "Listen, baby. You gotta tell your daddy that you're going to the well. Tell him you're going to get water and then go to Mr. Pierce's, okay? Go. I love you."

Pale-blue eyes blinked, very slowly. In between, she saw her little boy smiling, crying, sleeping, dead. A great many colors passing so quickly they were all bleeding together into one monstrous, endless whole.

✳

When Abigail woke it was day. Rainbow sunlight filled the room with glitter, though she wore a cloak of shadow. The attic door was open and Ambrose was clambering up to see her. "Abby? Abby, are you in here?" He sighed green-mint toothpaste. "You're okay, now. Nate's downstairs; he's messed up bad. I don't think he can move. I don't know what's happened to him, he . . . I think he needs a doctor. I can't find . . . any of the boys."

She started to take off the shadow-cloak. The light started to touch the old useless leather skin she could no longer feel. Her hair wrapped around the sun and started to burn.

"Abby? Honey?"

The shadow-cloak pooled around the stumps that had once held her feet. All her cells looked at Ambrose, waiting to be embraced, but when his eyes and only his eyes looked back at her, they wept with horror and hatred, and he shot her with his unseeing fingers that cradled the gun like a baby. The pain was not a pain but a liberation. She rose as Ambrose fell, rose all the way to the ceiling and blossomed like a flower, filling the house's every nook. She saw Nate on the couch, dying and then dead and still shuddering, pieces of his mortal coil stubbornly struggling along on the floor. But he was fractured; she was whole.

The walls of the house peeled open like an onion for Abigail. Outside, the well was beating like a brilliant magenta heart, a small nuclear star. The boys were inside with the dogs; they were all waving to her. The many-splendored light was in there, too, curling and coiling as it prepared to spring-board off this world and into the next. It wrapped her in electric seaweed tendrils and promised her oceans. It promised her color. But when the boys weren't broken down into simpler matter, they were saying, "Mama," and for them, she floated down. Crimson and indigo and violet, for violence.

"Possession" by Kathryn Weaver

DE DEABUS MINORIBUS EXTERIORIS THEOMAGICAE

JILLY DREADFUL

De Deabus Minoribus Exterioris Theomagicae: Textual Criticism and Notes on the Book as Object, A Bibliographic Study by Donna Morgan, Ph.D. Candidate, Department of English, Miskatonic University

Reproduction of Title Page:

DE DEABUS MINORIBUS EXTERIORIS THEOMAGICAE:
A Diſcourſe on the Invocations of
the Lesser Outer Goddesses;
Grounded in her Creator's Proto-
Chimiſtry, and verifi'd by a practicall
Examination of Principles in the Greater Dimension.

By Septimia Prinn

The Voice of Idh-yaa:
She was a woman
with a tome.

Zoroafter in Oracul. (Zoroaster in Oracle.)

Audi Ignis Vocem. (Listen to the Fire)

(handwritten Elizabeth Breedlove)

LONDON,
Printed by E.B For H. Vondrak at the
Castle in Thorn-hill. 1650.

Binding:
1. 3"x5" in size.
2. Octavo binding (eight leaves per quire).
   a. Never seen an octavo so small; generally duodecimos are this size because of the folding of paper.
3. No evidence of rebinding; most likely not forgery; provenance unknown.
   a. Binding is intact but well-worn from frequent use.
   b. Cover in serviceable condition; leather is visibly weathered from repeated handling; dirty (oils from hands depositing in leather).
      b.i. Threads on back cover, where binding meets book structure, are raised; thick thread looks like "skeletal fingers" binding quires to cover.
      b.ii. Upon closer inspection, "skeletal fingers" are not just abnormally thick twine bindings; appear to be bound with articulated bones, with thread carefully sewn through the bone connecting binding to cover.

b.iii. Judging from shape and lightness of bones, I suspect they are wings from a single bat; search on library databases suggest that this technique has not been seen before; email sent to Professor Dane to confirm.

— A headache is forming with intense pressure behind eyes; artificial light in Special Collections is becoming painful.

4. Considering occult subject matter of text, small size, slim width: Binding suggests it was designed with secrecy in mind; could easily be concealed on body.

   a. I postulate this was a practicing occultist's grimoire.

Paper:

1. This octavo is printed exclusively on vellum, still pungent.

   a. Vellum most likely made of pigskin, although this does not have the same color or scent as the vellum commonly sourced in London during this era; perhaps chemically treated to achieve a whiter transparency, hence the remnant smell; possibly sheepskin.

2. On page 50, quire E, on the 7th leaf, on the face of one of the only decorative plates in the book, an illustration, beneath which these handwritten words appear (Translations are my own):

Idh-yaa Lythalia Vhuzompha

Shub-Niggurath Yaghni Yidhra (names of lesser outer goddesses)

Dare licentiam ad ut eam in servitium vestrum arma capere milites, (Give her permission to arm soldiers in your service.)

Septimia Prinn (proper name of author)

Deas à Conciliis, & Oracul Indiciarius, (Goddess' Council & Indicarius (?) of the Oracle)

Doꝗtor Utriusque Naturam & Divinam. (Doctor of Both Natural Laws & Divine)

3. At this site, a discoloration on the page. A watermark, perhaps; appears to be lettering.

a. Not aware of watermarks in this period using words instead of symbols.

b. Asked for a cold (fiber optic) light, but Carlo, the Special Collections librarian, claims they do not have one.

    b.i. Certain I used one in Special Collections earlier this week.

c. Carlo provides me with table lamp.

    c.i. Why is Carlo keeping the cold light from me?

4. Place watermarked leaf over table light, but nothing lights up beneath, meaning it is embossed.

a. Hold book at eye level, single leaf against overhead lights, read aloud: "*Eram quod es; eris quod sum.*" (I was what you are; you will be what I am.)

5. The book features deckled edges and is adorned with heavy speckling, most likely quill ink; the speckles are a brown, sepia tone.

a. Quill ink generally made with iron in this era, which oxidizes over time; same color of oxidization is on edges, as well as the handwritten portions of the text.

b. As Special Collections closed for the day, I placed tome on dissertation cart.

    b.i. Somehow tome ended up in my bag.

    b.ii. Will continue textual analysis at home; will return text to cart tomorrow.

6. The vellum is desiccated, making the edges of each page razor sharp.

a. Slit tip of thumb as I turned a page.

    a.i. Kind of cut that's so deep it doesn't bleed right away and looks as though the skin never separated.

b. Turned page, left bloody thumbprint.

    b.i. Went to get cotton swab and peroxide to lift stain out.

    — Blood is gone.

Illustration/Decoration:

1. Title page: encased in border depicting moon phases.

   a. Phases of moon include black circles that transition from black crescents into black, outlined crescents, representing shifting of new moon to full moon.

   b. Out of the corner of my eye, while I typed those observations on my laptop, the moons appeared to be actively shifting, as if animated.

      b.i. Possible that arrangement of the moon gradations are an optical illusion.

2. Page 51: single full-page woodcut featuring sextet of lesser outer goddesses.

   a. Above woodcut reads: *Supplication of the Unfathomable Ones*, beneath which the woodcut is printed.

      a.i. When I looked at this page to double-check the heading, the printed text was no longer in English, but what I can only presume is a cuneiform of Latin and Sumerian.

   b. Woodcut features worm-like Idh-yaa; sylvan Lythalia; Vhuzompha covered in multiple sets of eyes, mouths, as well as male and female genitalia; horned goat goddess Shub-Niggurath suckling infant devil at breast; many-tentacled Yaghni; and beautiful dream-witch Yidhra.

   c. Under woodcut, the following is handwritten: *Ungerent hoc in meo sanguine.* (Anoint this text in my blood.)

      c.i. Whenever I look at the book, the pages flicker and flash, like the popping lights of a camera.

         — I do not remember falling asleep, but I must have passed out from the headache because the next thing I know, I was lifting my head from my desk and it was after midnight. I'm so close to being done analyzing this book, I'm just going to power through.

3. Portrait of Septimia Prinn: aristocratic woman with square neckline, intricate Elder Sign necklace, long sleeves with embroidered cuffs. In one hand, she holds a "winged eye" symbol; in the other, a human heart, with her eyes fixed upon it. Vines are coiling around the edges of her illustration as she sits at a writing desk cluttered with miniature cauldrons and apothecary bottles.

    a. Both woodcuts are extraordinary for their level of detail and uniqueness.

        a.i. These woodcuts are contrary to McKerrow's supposition that Early Modern printers preferred woodcuts out of which they could "get their money's worth" from repeated use.

        a.ii. These decorations are too specific to be commonly used in other printmaking projects.

        a.iii. Septimia Prinn's eyes are no longer fixed upon the human heart but are staring straight ahead, engaging with the gaze of the reader.

           — I specifically recorded that her eyes were fixed on the human heart in her hand and I have verified that there are no other reproductions of her portrait in this edition. Despite my headache, I maintain that her eyes have shifted position.

           — Must research Early Modern optical illusion printing techniques.

    b. While there are no records of an Early Modern printer by the name of Elizabeth Breedlove, there are records of Septimia Prinn.

        b.i. Septimia Prinn was the alleged daughter of Ludwig Prinn, a notorious medieval sorcerer and "doctor" of nature, although he did not practice medicine in the traditional sense. He sought to apply his chemical skills to preparing concoctions in "the manner recommended by Paracelsus." Ludwig Prinn is reported to have lived among the wizards and alchemists of England, Germany and Syria, studying everything from divination and rituals of necromancy to blood rites for "the worm that sought to devour the world." He allegedly recorded this forbidden knowledge in a single blasphemous text, establishing his magico-mystical reputation with *De Vermis Mysteriis* (Mysteries of the Worm).

— There are rumors that Prinn was a shapeshifter, that Ludwig and Septimia are, in fact, the same person. It is postulated that, after *De Vermis Mysteriis* gained popularity, Ludwig's life was endangered by rival cultist factions, so he shifted sexes and identities, and became Septimia, who claimed to be Ludwig's daughter so she could continue to draw upon the influence her previous incarnation had acquired.

— I feel like I'm being watched.

b.ii. As Ludwig before her, Septimia Prinn is said to have lived for hundreds of years, moving around Europe, eventually emigrating to the New World, where she is reputed to have given birth to Abigail Prinn, later executed in Salem for witchcraft.

b.iii. Septimia is responsible for hundreds of occult texts found in arcane libraries across the world, although scholars postulate that cultists assumed the name of Septimia Prinn as part of an initiation rite and published under her name; no such postulations are ascribed to Ludwig's writings.

— Someone just whispered in my ear.

— I have been silent for fifteen minutes, my hands off the keyboard, straining my ears to hear anything that could be construed as whispering, but there have been no more whispers.

b.iv. Could E.B. (Elizabeth Breedlove) and Septimia Prinn be the same person?

— Who is H. Vondrak?

b.v. This text was an economic printing; using octavo format, only a few full pages of vellum are needed to produce a single copy. But the woodcuts would've been extravagantly priced for the period. This was printed during the English Civil War, during the trial and execution of Charles I and exile of Charles II. It stands to reason that it would have been sacrilegious to investigate occultism at this time. The small size of this book also indicates a secretive printing. Did Breedlove adopt the pseudonym of Septimia Prinn to absolve herself of responsibility should her press come under investigation for printing pagan texts?

— Further study into provenance necessary.

Conclusions Regarding *De Deabus Minoribus Exterioris Theomagicae*:

1. I had what I can only call a lucid dream of a tree woman caressing my hair with vines, while a quivering octopoid mass communicated with me by means I do not understand. We spoke, though neither of us used verbal language. I understood that I was being asked to give my consent—for what I do not rightly know. Having suffered from sleep paralysis in dreams past, I know I did not feel frozen, but rather, felt an active symbiosis of worship and supplication as I suckled at the teat of a goat mother and allowed a dream witch to kiss the essence of my soul out through my open lips. I understood I was being coronated and, in so doing, willfully shed my human skin. Underneath, I was a giant worm—although a worm is much too generous a phrase. A maggot is more appropriate, or perhaps a grub, although I was so much more majestic. I was craven with a hunger so sharp and bright that I knew if I were to devour the universe, not even then would I be sated.

a. When I opened my eyes, my limbs felt foreign to me and echoes of chants in unknown languages reverberated in my brain.

b. Took the bus downtown to campus. I lost a couple of fingers along the way. At first, the hum of the bus matched the vibration I felt reverberating from inside my body. I felt so centered spiritually that, when my pinky finger on my left hand fell off and rolled away under a seat, losing it didn't bother me. Even the pungent musk of rot that emanated from its place did not bother me, although it was clear that it bothered the other passengers as they covered their faces and moved closer to the doors.

c. My ring finger fell off sometime between getting off the bus and the library. I only noticed it wasn't there when I lifted my hand to buzz the Special Collections room.

    c.i.   I had this vague notion that this was troublesome, but invocations to the Lesser Outer Goddesses are the only things that truly matter to me now.

d. When Carlo buzzed me into Special Collections, I was suddenly overcome with the sharpest, brightest hunger—so close to the kind of hunger I knew in my dream. Remembering as much, I asked Carlo if he would be so kind as to give me permission to devour him. He said yes. While he offered up his body in humble obsecration, his voice joined the incantations that churned in my mind.

    d.i.   I said I was hungry, but not hungry enough for khakis, so Carlo undressed, revealing an Elder Sign on his chest. It was the sweetest part of him of all.

    d.ii.   I am still so hungry. The deadened husk of my once-arm has fallen off as I type with what remains of my right as a record of my glorious and dreadful evolution.

    d.iii.   In between the breaks in my skin, I can see a bulbous, purple luminescence pulsing inside.

2. I am ready to loose myself from this form, but am I ready to devour the world?

    a. My appetite will serve us well: The suffering for you and yours shall end once and for all, and the festering, protoplasmic ache wracking my grub organs will be satisfied. Conflicts the world over will be quieted as we become one. You will experience the exquisite, sepulchral stillness of oblivion; Humanity united together for the first, and final, time deep within my bowels as the omnipotent waste of the world.

    b. And my hunger will be alleviated.

    c. I will only proceed with your consent. And know that, as punishment for my appetite, the Lesser Outer Goddesses shall suck the soul marrow from what remains of my diabolical folly—and the world shall be made yet again.

    d. If you deny me this indulgence, I will move on to the next world, for there are many. But know that, given a choice, this is the world I would remake; for I am not divorced entirely from my humanity. Although I no longer have need for it in my soon-form, I want to be one with the most fabulous and most profane embodiment of the beautiful chaos of the cosmos.

    e. What say you?

        e.i. May I have your permission to devour the world?

LAVINIA'S WOOD

ANGELA SLATTER

"YOU CAN'T READ, can you?"

The undecayed Whatleys were possessed of an impressive fortune and a strict sense of philanthropy, which was how Lavinia Whatley, either afflicted or blessed—depending upon to whom one spoke—with albinism, came to be invited to the large house located on the correct fork of the junction of the Aylesbury Pike just beyond Dean's Corners.

Despite fine intentions and enthusiastically mouthed better sentiments, all the older members of the Sound branch had, at some point, used phrases such as 'Witch Whatleys,' 'Lesser Whatleys,' and, perhaps worst of all, 'Queer Whatleys.' And they'd used them in their children's hearing; children who stored spite in a more concentrated form, having not been exposed to the world and its doings, to learning things that sometimes diluted the acid of their malice.

Lavinia wasn't hard to look at, although she was different. Bleached of skin and hair, pink of eye, with a weak chin, she'd nevertheless inherited some of her mother's finer features: high cheekbones, pert nose, wide eyes, pouting mouth. At thirty-four, her pallor kept age at bay, and in her tresses no trace of silver or gray showed. She was tall with good posture and a figure designed to draw attention.

With brows and lashes unpigmented, she looked constantly surprised, but she took care with her appearance. The frayed cuffs and hem of her dress were neatly mended and her floss of hair brushed into a thick, tight bun.

What she couldn't help was the smell, though she'd bathed and bathed beneath the pump before setting off. The cloying scent of home never could be washed off, merely made faint, so it didn't matter how she looked, really. Most of the family refrained from nose-wrinkling, but the youngsters, full of their superiority, their advantages and airs, did not bother with the good manners their parents had sought to inculcate in them. In the back parlor, where Aunty Abigail had directed her saying she was too young for the company of *dusty folk*, Lavinia had to deal with cousins Putnam and Wilmot, George and Rist. Sarah and Bealia, Mary and Alice, sat in a corner ignoring her.

"You can't read, can you?" repeated Putnam, louder, as if she were hard of hearing.

Rist shook his handsome head. "Don't, Put."

"I can read." Lavinia gritted her teeth, reminding herself why she'd come. Wilmot and George guffawed, flanking her. Rist stepped closer, trying to pull tow-headed George away, but the beefy youngster shook him off.

"But you didn't go to school," Putnam insisted. "How can you read? Old Wizard Whatley couldn't have taught you. He's mad as a cat in a sack."

Lavinia grabbed a leather-bound book from the nearest shelf and opened it.

"*Wonders of the Invisible World* by Cotton Mather," she read, realizing too late how badly she'd chosen.

The cousins shouted with laughter. "Oh, priceless! Witch Whatley, indeed!"

Pale cheeks burning all the brighter, Lavinia dropped the volume and pushed past Putnam. She tried for the front rooms, where the elders guaranteed safety from teasing, but the youths blocked her path—all but Rist—and herded her to the back door, sitting ajar and leading onto the wide rear porch. Lavinia didn't care. If she could get out, then she could leave.

The bucket balanced above the door tipped as Lavinia pushed through. It was only water, not piss like Wilmot had suggested, but it was cold and drenching, and the pail itself hit her head, so she saw stars. She stumbled, caught in damp-heavy skirts.

"That'll wash the sulphur stink off you!" Putman, George and Wilmot held each other momentarily before collapsing in a heap of snorting, farting hilarity. Rist stood frozen, face twisted; she thought he might cry. Beyond him, crowding around the doorframe were the girls, expressions horrified.

Rist knelt to help her. As soon as she was upright, she shook him off and glared at him, at them all.

"Lavinny," began Rist, mistakenly using the back-country nickname her father did.

She hiked her skirts and ran down the stairs, stopping only to turn and lift one hand, folding the two middle fingers under the thumb, leaving pointer and pinky free. She shook the gesture at them, stopping even Putnam's laughter. Satisfied, she spun away towards the tree line, towards where the woods closed in, brambles and vines grew wild, where animals darted and hid, where she knew her way better than anyone. Surefooted, she bolted, retreating to where the hills shivered and shuddered, and where *whip-poor-wills* perched and sang, waiting for souls to come within reach.

Lavinia wondered if the books might not be better off on shelves.

She thought about how orderly those in the bright, neat Whatley parlor had looked a few days ago. It would make a difference here, though she was not overly given to considerations of housework and such. She could charm Otis Bishop into building a few cases, surely. But then he'd have to be invited in to measure; then he'd go home and tattle to his mother about what he'd seen, heard, smelled. And then Mercy Bishop would blow her stack to learn he'd been near Lavinia, trying to find a way between her legs, which would never happen, though hope of it kept him compliant just as fear of it kept his dam in a simmering stew of rage.

And her father would be equally put out, to discover everything tidied away. He'd never find anything. As things were now, he could locate a particular volume mostly within seconds, pick out which teetering stack it inhabited, in which corner of which room. Their spaces were designated purely by what they called them, rather than by specialized function or furniture. There were chairs and there were books and there were tables everywhere, even in the kitchen. Though she had her own chamber equipped with a bed, said bed was crowded around by more tables and chairs covered with more monographs, octavos, and ledgers. The purpose of the house, Lavinia sometimes thought, was less habitation and more storage. She lived in a library.

She didn't complain, though, because she loved the books, too, maybe even more than her father did; he saw them merely as containers of knowledge. She adored them in their entirety; embraced the dusty, musty covers, the brown-flecked folios, the pages with the ragged edges they'd cut themselves.

And she loved the promises they made.

They whispered to her of a power she might take, of an escape that could be hers. They vowed she could leave, leave home, leave Sentinel Hill, Dunwich and its surrounds. The tarot cards spread in front of her—colors faded, dog-eared, stained with the touch of many hands—told her the same thing: that *he* would make himself known by his actions. That he would reach out and take her from this mundane existence, from her father's howling madness, from the taunts and torments, from the men who thought that, as a Whatley, she was fair game, an easy woods girl.

Lavinia had grown tired of waiting, she admitted. But her faith had been rewarded at last. Freedom was in sight.

She thought about Rist. He'd been kind, the only one to ever be so, to not demand something of her, though she knew he wanted what they all did. But he didn't threaten, didn't pester, didn't press.

She wondered when he would come.

✳

Rist had got himself lost.

It had seemed the simplest thing, to set off from his parents' big house, carrying a basket of food as if visiting a sick relative rather than just a dirt-poor one. He knew the turning to take, too, the one leading into the village of Dunwich, small though neat, respectable in its economic embarrassment. There were some larger homes there, some of stone that weren't strangled by weeds, windows uncovered and shiny bright. Others were borderline hovels if their owners but knew it, though the tiny gardens out front were carefully tended, both flowers and vegetables sprouting.

The loungers were outside Osborne's General Store, nodding suspiciously-but-politely, watching as he passed. They recognized him, yes, and he was grateful he didn't bear any resemblance to Cousin Putnam. That individual never made any effort to get folk to like him—indeed, went out of his way to torment and offend. One day, Putnam Whatley would get his comeuppance and Rist did not wish to be mistaken for him.

You couldn't, he thought, treat people as if they were less than you—even if they were—it just didn't do, wasn't right. Behind him, one of the loafers said something he didn't catch, but the group laughed, so he was glad. He hefted the basket higher, increased his pace, and looked out for the crooked tree he knew would put him on the path to Old Wizard Whatley's house.

To Lavinia.

It was all right for a while. All right after he'd left the village and taken the scrubby dirt track rambling into the hills. Then, somewhere, he went awry, turned left when he should have turned right, or veered right when he should have gone straight. The trees grew closer together, branches reaching to embrace one another, making it harder and harder for Rist to pass between. The ground, covered with briars and creepers, was liberally littered with rocks and stones thrown up by the regular moaning and groaning of the earth; dangerous and unexpected obstacles to a man in his Sunday shoes, the shoes one wore to make an apology to someone.

And if that wasn't enough, the *whip-poor-wills* had started their sweetly-dire chorus. He knew he was being fanciful as he wondered if they were waiting for him. A noise to the left, a clattering then a bleat, drew his attention: a goat perched on a hilly slope, watching him with flat black eyes. Rist thought of the Whatley ancestor, occasionally spoken of in hushed tones, whose perverse tastes led him to keep a magnificent Lamancha as consort for seven years before it killed him with a kick to the head. The billy bolted and Rist shuddered, stumbling to a halt.

He looked back the way he'd come, then forward again. There was little difference except one way sloped up, and the other down. He was lost, utterly, and the birds' looping song seemed to swell the longer he hesitated. His heart beat harder and harder, a double-time thump that threatened to displace his ribs. The air seemed to thicken, the earth rumbled and shook, and the smell of sulphur and shit reached his nostrils.

The avian noise dropped, and another rose to take its place: a humming, a hissing, strangely human, and yet indecently not. Almost a hymn, a cacophony but bizarrely rhythmic. Through the trees, something moved, swiftly, smoothly, around him. Not the goat, nothing brown and hide-bound, nothing on four legs, or at least not consistently. Something pale as snow, pale as bone, pale as milk: the hint of a rounded hip, a nipped-in waist, a breast unfettered. He spun and spun, trying to keep it in sight, almost falling over in the attempt.

Then it was gone, leaving Rist bewildered and unbalanced.

He breathed heavily, turned to resume his trudging, and came face to face with his cousin.

Lavinia's brown dress made her hard to distinguish in the lowering afternoon light, but her hair, in a loose ponytail, stood out like a beacon. She seemed as surprised to see him as he was her. This close, he could make out the fine lines on her high forehead, the crow's-feet, and shallow furrows around her mouth. He did not think they'd come of laughter. He gaped, not managing a sound.

"What yew dewin heer?" Her accent, previously unheard, flowed thick as molasses, and they both startled. She tried again, carefully this time. "What are you doing here?"

"I came . . . " He swallowed, lifted the basket. "I came to apologize. I'm sorry. I didn't know what they were planning."

"Would it have made a difference if you had?" she asked, scorn searing as she pivoted and headed down the incline.

He tripped, almost fell, but followed. "Yes! I'd have stopped them! Lavi—Lavinia, I am so terribly sorry. It was unspeakably cruel. I wouldn't have let them do that. Please believe me."

She didn't say anything, but slowed, allowed him to catch up. They walked in silence for a few minutes, companionably enough. Then she gestured to the basket.

"What's that?"

"Mother sent it, some fresh bread and biscuits, bacon and cheese," he said eagerly, then caught her sharp look.

"Thinks we can't pay our own way?" she asked, pulling a handful of gold coins of ancient design from her pocket. She hid them again before he could ask to examine one.

"Not at all—" he began and she shrugged.

"Matters not a jot—it'll save me from going back to the store, so thank you. You can carry it, though, 'til we reach the path." She looked slyly at him. "Got lost, didn't you?"

He nodded, embarrassed. "And the birds . . . "

"Not scared of those poor little things, are you? Don't believe those silly stories about soul-stealing and such." Lavinia put out a hand and as if by magic, one of the small, brown whip-poor-wills landed there. It did a jig, ducked its head respectfully, then flew off.

Rist had to close his gaping mouth. The woman laughed. "They're quite tame."

Rist asked, "How did you know to . . . ?"

"Loafers outside Osborne's," she said shortly. "I knew you'd go astray, didn't want it to happen in the dark. No one would find you in these parts then, except me."

"You know the land well?" He thought of all the tales he'd heard of Lavinny's traipsing the hills around Dunwich, of the times when her father took to Sentinel Hill to shout at the sky, of Lavinny's mother lost then found, dead by terrible violence and the culprit never located.

"Have you not heard this called Lavinia's Wood?" She thrust her receding chin forward and he knew it for pride. She didn't seem to need an answer.

At the bottom of the slope, where the trees became less impenetrable, she pointed to the trail he recognized as the one he'd started upon hours ago, it seemed. He glanced up whence they'd come and marveled that he'd been able to make it as far as he had.

"There's your way. You'll be safe from here," Lavinia said, and busily claimed the basket with something he thought might be glee.

"Thank you, Cousin Lavinia. I'd have been adrift without you." He gave a smile, which she returned.

"You certainly would."

He hesitated. "May I visit again?"

She raised a straw eyebrow. "Why?"

"To . . . to speak with you. I . . . "

"Come back on May Eve," she said, interrupting before he had to examine his wishes too closely; he even found her scent, much stronger this time, intoxicating. *What had come over him?* He'd be back at Harvard in a few days, back where the world was real and normal and solid, away from this earth where he'd been born, but did not belong. There, he would forget this strange pull towards he knew not what.

Her voice was pitched low and husky when she said, "Come then, Cousin Rist, and I'll show you what the others don't know and don't care to know. Are too afraid to look upon. Come then, cousin, and I'll show you everything you ever desired to see. Don't tell anyone, though, or the deal's off."

And with that, she leaned forward, whispered something in his ear, breath tickling his skin and hair, and raising goosebumps on his flesh, and sending a rush of blood to southern climes.

As she walked away, he watched the slow swing of her hips and wondered what lay beneath. He would, he knew, return.

Lavinia had sat anxiously by the window all afternoon, peering through the thin, antiquated curtains. She'd made a special effort with her dress; it was her mother's wedding gown, starched organdie, yellowed with age. The tiny brown spots on the hem were barely noticeable. Bell-shaped sleeves hung to the elbow. The bodice was cut lower than was strictly necessary, and three rows of once-fine, now-crumbly lace encircled the skirt. Still, she thought, it was pretty and the darkening of its tones meant she didn't look completely washed out. And it was a size too big, giving her some room to wriggle.

She'd braided her hair around the crown of her head, so it looked like a coronet, and threaded crimson beebalm through it, bright as rubies, bright as blood.

He arrived at dusk and she'd had to keep calm, tamp down her relief. Lavinia watched as he hesitated at the edge of the yard, taking in his expression as he examined the lurching gambrel roof of the two-storied house, with its peeling paint and missing roof slates.

Lavinia left him to knock anxiously five or six times, before she stepped onto the porch, and gave him a cool smile and a chaste kiss on the cheek. He blushed, but it barely showed on his smooth, olive skin. He was so young, this cousin of hers, a good decade or more her junior, so well-raised. He'd brought flowers—*What a lamb!*—and not some common bunch either, not wildflowers picked from the roadside or garlands pilfered from the headstones of Dunwich's bone orchard, like some had offered, trying to get into her knickers. No, it was a real bouquet, tied with a ribbon, a *proper* tribute! Lavinia's heart sang in spite of itself.

She put the arrangement just inside the door and when he'd objected, "They need water," she'd covered his mouth with her own to still further protest. When he'd grown quiet and hard, she broke away. Lavinia gathered up the brand she'd prepared earlier, one end wrapped around with hessian and soaked in pitch. She used the flint and steel to strike a spark and the flambeau burst into life.

Rist took the hand she offered and they set off towards Sentinel Hill, the flame dancing in the wind, throwing shapes and shadows before them, flashing in eyes that hid in the undergrowth and bushes on either side as they processed in silence.

※

The path was much easier than the one Rist had tried to blaze a few weeks before. Indeed, it seemed as if the foliage made a point of drawing back so as not to snag Lavinia's ancient finery. He'd been worried sparks from the torch might fall onto her dress, turning her into a Roman candle, but the fire seemed respectful, too.

By the time they surmounted the summit, the flare was dwindling, almost spent, but Rist didn't doubt that his cousin would have been able to negotiate the dark with her confident step and astonishing pink eyes. They entered the circle of standing stones with its table-like rock in the center. Lavinia didn't waste any time, placing the dying brand on the mountain of kindling set closest to where the hill dropped steeply away, but still inside the stone ring.

She turned to face Rist, smiling as the balefire lit and leapt. Lavinia reached up and pulled the dress from her shoulders, sliding it slowly until she stood in a pool of sepia froth. She rolled her shoulders, making her breasts bounce a little.

Rist noticed only that, despite their heaviness, the bosoms still sat high, never having had a child to drag them down. He noticed only the tiny waist, the flaring lower hourglass of her hips, and the bushy white triangle at the junction of her sturdy legs. He was so distracted that he didn't notice the malformations on her flanks, her hips, the myriad tiny eyes embedded there, blinking lashless lids in the flickering orange glow.

✳

She gestured to the table-rock and watched as he disrobed clumsily, quickly, and came to her so she could maneuver him onto her, into her. He was a handsome boy, she thought, though one of the others, one of the shitty ones like Putnam or Wilmot or George, might have served better. Their natures might have been more fit for what was being done here this night. She did not regret having chosen him, though, as her first.

As the young man labored over her—in and out, in and out—the night sky gleamed, lightning tearing across the silvered black, the stars brightening. Nebulae formed and swirled, shot red and blue and purple like pinwheels, and a sort of ebony gold streamed into an enormous shape that was not a shape, that was form without form, with tentacles and eyes like Christmas lights which appeared then faded as fast as blinking. Rist reared up, unable to see what was occurring above and behind him, but sensing it. Though he couldn't stop his rhythmic motion even if he'd wanted to, he tried to turn his head when he felt the cold fire that poured from the crack in the heavens touch his skin and seep in. Lavinia latched one hand to his jaw and held him there with a strength that, in hindsight, shouldn't have surprised him.

"He must move through another," crooned Lavinia. "Don't be afraid, cousin. You're greatly honoured to be his instrument, as I am to be the Lord's vessel."

The cold fire coursed in his veins, chasing Rist, or what was left of him, away; it was as though he fled through the tunnels of his body, until he was trapped in a corner of his own mind. Whatever had invaded him showed no mercy; it rushed in and slammed against the last of Rist just as he slammed into Lavinia, with no fear, only lust, the desire to achieve his end, to find its goal, to spill and soak the fertile soil.

In his last moments, Rist's eyes darkened, took on the color of the stars and sky, the swirling vortexes of the nebulae above, and the being that had taken him showed its face for the first and last time to Lavinia. She felt her blood freeze, her limbs spasm, and, as the boy did his final duty, thought her heart was going to burst. Atop her, Rist disappeared, separated into his component parts, unable to contain any longer the thing that had breached and used him.

Lavinia lay, exhausted, simultaneously emptied and filled.

Her father appeared out of the shadows, old Wizard Whatley whose first name, if ever he'd had one, hadn't never been Christian. Lavinia drew her legs together with difficulty, but remained where she was, breathless, aching.

"Yog-Sothoth might be key an' gate, but he still needs a little he'p with the keyhole," he said and guffawed heartily as he kicked at the young man's pile of discarded clothes. Rist was utterly gone, returned to the dust that floated on this plane and the one beyond. "If this'un dun't take, theys alwus another."

But Lavinia knew there'd be no other, that her seducing days were over and all those suitors she'd turned from her door would not call again; congress with the unseen had its consequences. Her father couldn't see her properly in the firelight. The dancing flames and shadows made it seem as though her face still had mobility, but she knew as surely as breathing that she'd suffered some sort of a stroke. One side of her face was numb and she couldn't make it either smile nor frown, no matter how she tried. The pride she'd always taken in keeping her lips together to combat her weak chin so she didn't look like the worst of the decayed Whatleys—like some inbred halfwit—would no longer be enough. Her left hand was clawed. Her left leg felt like a thick length of wood.

She'd followed the promise of the books, but who knew they'd tell only half-truths? Her days as she'd known them were over. Her hopes of escape were thoroughly dashed. Lavinia Whatley was going nowhere beyond the boundaries of her woods. Her father reached down to help her. She was shorter when she stood, unable to straighten properly. The weight of what had been planted inside her seemed heavy already, though she knew there were a good nine months between her and birth. Lavinia shifted her posture to accommodate it, slouched, slumped.

The *whip-poor-wills* sang a jaunty tune as father and daughter made their way down off Sentinel Hill.

"Cthulhu Reading" by C.L. Lewis

THE ADVENTURER'S WIFE

PREMEE MOHAMED

IT WAS NOT till after the adventurer had been interred that we learned that the man had been married. My editor, Cheltenwick, did not even let the graveyard mud dry decently on his boots before he dispatched me to the widow's house with instructions for a full interview, which I had no doubt he would embellish even more than his wont.

"Delicate sighs, Greene," he said, hurrying me into a cab and pushing a fresh notebook into my hands. "A crystal-like droplet that rolls down her wan face. I want that, and a most particular description of the house, and don't botch it up!"

"Do it your precious self, Wick-Dick!" I wished to shout, but it was too late and my career would be worth less than an apple-fed horsefart if I did botch this article. Henley Dorsett Penhallick had been a living legend for fifty years; any description of a life-imperiling venture or terrifying journey was known as a 'Dorsett tale' in these parts. One never knew of his comings and goings—he was either thousands of miles away, or hunkered in his house ignoring the doorknocker. Every few years, his publisher would release a booklet of his exploits, copied verbatim—at his insistence—complete with the spelling errors and lavish illustrations in his letters. I had seen a few around the newsroom, the long, elegant script tipped exaggeratedly over on its side, as if racing to get to its destination. I was quite sure he had never mentioned a wife. Everyone would have gone quite mad at such a discovery.

Indeed, I expected the house to be mobbed with reporters when I arrived, but the street was empty, thick oaks nodding absently in the heat. Did I have the right address? All I had had to go on was Cheltenwick's scribbled note and a vague memory he had of visiting, once, to deliver a package. *A tall, reserved, gray house,* he had said. *A mass of ivy.*

I could see the white curtains twitch as I came up the steps. I wondered if the widow could stand to stay in the empty house, or if she had gone to stay with family, as ladies often did after a death. My own mother had left us for a fortnight after her brother died and gone to stay with my aunts out west. When she returned, I recalled, nothing more had been said about it; it had been as if no death had occurred.

The widow answered the door herself, petite and slender in her weeds, face hidden behind a veil so thick I doubted she could see, black silk gloves covering small hands. I felt a wellspring of guilt for intruding on her grief, but Cheltenwick's face hovered in my mind's eye for a moment: *Don't botch this up!*

"Mrs. Penhallick," I said, stymied for a moment simply by not having a face to address. "Please, allow me to . . . let me say how very sorry I am for your loss. We all feel it keenly, I assure you. Er, my editor, Mr. Cheltenwick, corresponded occasionally with your husband and . . . I . . . I am so very sorry."

"Thank you," she said, voice muffled by the veil. "Mr. . . . ?"

"Oh!" I fumbled in my pockets for my card case. Finally, I found one, lone dog-eared card in my breast pocket and shamefacedly handed it to her. "Mr. Greene, madame. Of the *Tribune.*"

She studied it, then put her hand back to her side. "Of the *Tribune.*"

The question she hadn't asked, or the invitation she did not wish to extend, hung in the air for a moment and I finally dipped my head and said, "I've . . . been sent to interview you, Mrs. Penhallick, about your husband. May I please come in?"

There was another pause so long and painful that I almost walked down the steps again, but she eventually stepped away from the door and let me in. I scraped my boots so vigorously on the hedgehog that I nearly fell, and then the door was closing behind me and there was a tremendous smell of incense, old wood, and flowers. The parlor was filled with arrangements, hiding the outlines of several bookcases and a grand piano. A few had spilled out into the hallway, red-and-yellow roses and white lilies and chrysanthemums. Ahead of us, the staircase was graced with a wooden statue on each step—an elephant, a jaguar, matched tigers, a woman carrying a jug of water. Paintings and sketches papered the exposed wall above the railing. At the landing, there was an enormous world map covered in little flagged brass pins. It took all my strength not to run up the stairs and note them down; how many dozens, hundreds of places he had been!

The widow apologized as she went, in her curiously fuzzy voice, and explained that we must be inconvenienced to take tea in the kitchen, for the parlor was occupied with flowers, and she had given the house staff a week off, wishing to be alone in the house.

"Oh, madame," I said, reflexively, almost hearing my mother's voice as I spoke. "You should not be alone in the house at a time like this. Do you have family nearby? A mother, sisters?"

"No," she said, after a moment. "No one nearby, Mr. Greene."

I watched her smoothly fill the kettle, bracing her hand with a well-worn pad, and secure pot, cups, saucers, sugar, lemon, and milk. I scribbled that in my notebook, bracing it on my thigh so she could not see what I was writing. The widow is well-versed in the little felicities of a kitchen—unusual, for a lady of good family who would have a lady's maid making her tea. Perhaps she was a servant herself? No one nearby. Where was her family from, then?

She did not speak again until after the tea had been made. I sniffed mine unobtrusively before I sipped—a very strange tea, gray-green pellets, steam redolent of smoke and grass and iron, not your average cup of Darjeeling at all. The widow picked her cup up and adjusted her veil. The house was sweltering. I made another note: *She ceases not her mourning, even in the privacy of her domicile, and now that I have intruded, she wishes to not be seen weeping.*

I thought about Cheltenwick's 'crystal droplet' and cursed him. What would have been the harm, had we waited a month or a year? I already knew his answer, though: Someone else, some other newspaper, a loathed enemy of an editor, would have sent someone out before us and the story would not be exclusive. Damn him, for true. This poor, bereaved, dignified woman, drinking her tea with her veil on—not to mention depriving me of a good look at her face.

I said, "You may be surprised to hear that no one knew your husband was . . . was your husband. Which is to say, we had become quite used to hearing of Mr. Penhallick as an affirmed bachelor."

"No," she said, a tone not quite of surprise but resignation, which I still had to strain to hear through her headgear. "That doesn't surprise me, Mr. Greene. He's . . . he was a private man. To have even friends and family inquire about our marriage, let alone strangers, would have upset him greatly."

She had given me an opening; I dashed through it before it closed. "Oh, I agree, I quite agree; many of us corresponded with your husband and never met him in person. I believe he liked it that way—as you say. When were you married?"

"Two years ago," she said softly, putting her tea back down with shaking hands. "We made no announcement, although it was in the local registry, of course."

"Of course," I said, irritated. How could we have missed that? One of the office toadies did nothing but scan the local and state registries for interesting stories. Man dies in tragic fall into river. Twins born to local industrial magnate. Marriage of world-renowned explorer to mystery . . . beauty? Damn, damn, damn.

Just as I began to speak again, she seemed to come to some kind of decision and with one swift movement, unpinned her hat and removed her veil. I froze to hide my surprise—then, to cover my obvious lack of movement, took a gulp of tea and burned my mouth. For his wife—whom he had legally married, God only knew how or where—was no purse-mouthed old bat from a leading family but a girl with the huge, steady eyes of a deer and burnished young skin as dark and flawless as the carved mahogany jaguar on the third stairstep. Her head was wrapped in a brightly patterned silk scarf, flowers and leaves and birds, underneath the black weeds. She smiled, seeing me so clearly discomfited, and put her hat and veil neatly on the table. "We did not announce it here, Mr. Greene."

"Er . . . I . . . " I swallowed, compounding my rudeness with a rude noise. "I did not mean to stare, madame. I only . . . "

"The story," she said. "That's what you want?"

I nodded, half-holding my breath, as if it might break a spell. She sipped her tea and said, "Then come and look at the house with me."

We returned to the front hall and she led me up the stairs to the big map. She said, "My name is Sima. A name from my land. We met here." She pointed to a place in Africa dense with pins where no borders had been marked. "My home is beautiful," she went on, sitting smoothly and quite naturally on a stair; I moved down a decorous three steps.

"Beautiful, Mr. Greene, and very, very old. I am not sure how old the nation of the white man is, but it was in its infancy when we had been who we were for fifty thousand years. And it was into this culture that my husband first strayed, more than ten years ago. I was young, and was not permitted to go with him and the men from my village as they explored the holy ruins nearby. But every evening when they returned, he would sit by the fire, tell stories . . . he liked to draw pictures while he spoke and he eventually taught a few of us English. You could easily say that several of us became his friends, including myself, as silly as that may sound—a grown man and of his age! But we were friends all, nonetheless.

"All during the dry season, they made trips out to the holy ruins and the priests told him: *You may draw what you see; you may copy the inscriptions, but you must take nothing.* And the men from my village ensured that he did not, though Henley, you know, he's . . . he was a very fiend for collecting things. Everywhere he went, his hands darted out, so, so, like the head of a bird, and he would pick up a little rock, or a fossil, or a feather or a flower or a seed, and put it in his pockets. How we loved to laugh at his pockets!

We had none; everything we valued had a life and a place, and we would never have moved it.

"He filled books and books with this trip—he showed me, later—and he waved goodbye and left, on the funny things we had finally learned to call horses, all alone. And we did not think of him much again for a few years, when he returned once again at the end of the rainy season, with photographic equipment and more blank notebooks, and even hammers and chisels and shovels. The first night, we sat around the fire as always and when he saw me, he cried, 'My friend Sima! How have you been?' and I said, 'I have been well!'

"Oh, my father laughed so loudly at the English we spoke. He said I sounded like our gray local bird, who imitates the things he hears. But I was pleased that he remembered me and I begged him to let me come with them the next day. 'I know the ruins,' I told him. 'Every part of them, I know. We play there so often. Let me come with you!' 'Oh, no, my little parrot,' he said. 'That I shall not allow.'

"Well, Mr. Greene, I was a wild and wilful child, if you will believe it, and when they set off the next dawn, I followed. They swiftly outpaced me, being ahorse, but I knew well where they were going. Our ruins were circular, with a great tower at each of eight points on the circle, though much tumbledown, and one tall structure in the center. We sometimes called them Sun Stones, for the shape, like the sun. Although the walls were so beaten down by wind and rain that a man could walk through at many points if he cut away the vines, there was only one place where anything so big as a horse could pass, a great gate built of neatly cut basalt blocks, and it was for there that they made. As I followed them in, one of the men, Lemba, saw me and cried out for me to leave, but Henley said that I might stay, for I might have some use, perhaps to squeeze in the tight spaces that the grown men could not reach.

"Henley was asking the men about the ruins—who had made them? How long had they been there? Well, the second question we could not answer, none of us. Until the white man came, in fact, we did not realize that we measured time differently than he did. But we could answer the first, so my father's friend Olumbi, who knew many stories, told him it was our own men doing the bidding of the old gods who could not speak. *Who were these gods?* asked Henley.

"Olumbi explained: All the gods of our land speak, and it was they who gave the power of speech to the lion and the jaguar, the buffalo, the eagle and the snake and the elephant. But the old gods had come before, so there had been no opportunity for them to be given this power from the gods who came after. The old gods who could not speak could still command, of course, because they were gods, so they commanded the men who lived there to build these structures, to carve them with holy words, and to bring the stone from far away. Henley had noticed that there was no basalt for many days' walk around our village, which we had not noticed, us in the village, for of course we did not need to work stone. We had clay and wood enough. He taught us the words for basalt and granite, limestone and chalk, while we walked, and he showed us where it seemed as if the stones covering holes in the ground were also basalt, like the gate. I climbed the great tower and took rubbings for him.

"The men who built the ruins did not know just what they were doing, Olumbi explained—only that they must do it. And when it was done, the old gods came through freely, in silence. The men had built a door—as if all the world, Mr. Greene, was a hut, yet it had been built with no way in, and the men had chopped a door into the hut. When the men realized that this had been done, they cried out in regret and tried to destroy what they had made, but the old gods sent forth their servants, called shoggoths, and killed some men, and enslaved some, and went breaking and eating and burning all over the wide world, for the shoggoths could not be seen by man. They were terrible—like things from bad dreams. Then some wise men from a different land made the necessary magicks to hurl the old gods back to their unholy realm, and everyone began to rebuild our world, and soon this door was forgotten. It is a wonderful story.

"Henley was mad for it—what were the old gods? What were these magicks? But Olumbi did not answer him. These were not part of the story that he knew. Near sundown, the guides left the ruins to get wood for torches. Henley pried loose a small stone with a carving on it of a thing with snakes for a face, and slipped it into his bag. He jumped when he saw that I was watching him, for we both knew he had been told to never take anything from the ruins, never, never.

" 'Say nothing, Sima,' he whispered to me. I worried about it, what he had done, but . . . it was one little stone, just the size of his hand and as thick. There were hundreds of the snake-faced creature carvings all over the ruins. *What calamity,* I thought, *could come from just one of so many going missing?* And yet . . . as we walked to the village, I felt a cold wind at our backs, and no birds sang.

"He left a few days later, promising extravagant gifts and tales the next time he returned. But his doom was already upon him. We all saw it. He was pale as the moon; he could not sleep. In the night, he walked and wandered instead, and talked to himself. During the day he seemed his normal self, and laughed and ate with us, and boasted of his adventures. But he was restless. He could not meet the eye. He avoided the fire. It was another three years before he rode back and he was so ill I wondered how he had made the trip. He was half his weight; he looked like a drought-stricken animal about to die. At first, I did not even recognize him. I thought how surprising it was that another white man had come to us. The chief sent for the best healers he knew. Where before, Henley would have waved them away like flies, he lay in the chief's hut without moving except to weep.

"Of myself, he asked for news of the area. *Nothing,* I said. *The hunts are well, our gardens grow. Many babies have been born. There have been dust storms, stripping away the vegetation at Sun Stones. But the old women say there have been storms like that before.* 'There have been no noises? Earthquakes? No cries in the night? No blood on your sand?' '*No, no,*' I promised him.

"He had come at midday. When night fell, I thought he would surely die while we slept, but he did not; in fact, he rose and dressed, and woke me. 'Sima, my only friend,' he whispered. 'Help me. You must. I am cursed; I carried home a curse with me.' I did not know what a curse was, but I knew what 'help' meant and I could not say no. By the time we reached the ruins, I was nearly carrying him. It was so frightening, Mr. Greene—he weighed nothing; it was like carrying a child. We came in through one of the small side gates, moving quickly, for the trees and brush had all been blown down and killed by the wind. He directed me to the center of the ruins—it took hours, as we had not brought light with us and the moonlight was treacherous. Finally, we stopped, and he withdrew from his satchel the ugly carving I had seen him remove all those years before. He put it back in place and looked at it for a long time. I gasped as the ground moved and made a noise, like a lion's roar but under our feet. 'May this end; may this end,' he said to the wall. 'Give me my freedom, though it is not deserved.'

"He did not recover, though he stayed for a long time. When he left, he called together my family to ask if I could come with him. 'If it is her wish,' said my father. 'She has a heart, for which we do not speak.' I had never been so excited in my life, Mr. Greene. I agreed at once; we married in Italy a short while later."

"So, he died from his affliction?" I said, astonished. "We knew him as the heartiest, the most robust of men. What was it? Malaria? Yellow Fever?"

"It did not seem that way," she said, looking up at the map. "He wrote to Miskatonic University and they sent professors to talk to him; he was on the telephone at all hours. He even made a trip up there, carrying his notes from Africa. When he returned, he had copied out great reams from one of their old books—a medical book, I took it to be, not knowing any better—and stayed up late for weeks, reciting from it. I could barely sleep, hearing his voice all night, imagining the house was shaking. But then he did recover. He began to do his exercises again. He began to eat and write letters again. He slept soundly. He even began to speak of the adventures we would have again—all the places we would go together. I felt hunted; I dismissed it. His doom was with us, though. I did not realize what he was doing until it was too late. I did not believe he would do such a thing. I learned the word penance. A word we had no concept of in my language."

"Mrs. Penhallick," I said, when she gave no signs of speaking again, though I dreaded to ask, " . . . how did he die?"

She looked down at me, her great doe eyes suddenly hard and wary. "You'll think me mad."

"No!"

"The old gods who could not speak," she said. "He had struck a devil's deal with them and the cost was his life. They sent a shoggoth for him in the night. To collect payment."

I stared at her. *Yes, quite mad,* I thought. Her head had been filled with these stories. The old man had made it worse, for a young girl from a land far away whose mind eventually snapped from living here, alone in the great house. . . . After a moment, I said, weakly, "I see."

"Don't put that in your article, Mr. Greene."

I was beginning to wonder if I had an article at all now, but shrugged and said, "As you wish."

As she was showing me out, I said, unthinkingly, "What a great pity that the man died without issue; my deepest sympathies for that, in addition to your great loss."

"Why, I believe I said nothing of the sort," she said softly, taking my hat and coat from the stand. "If you must know, part of the deal for my freedom was poor Henley's life . . . but I was well-compensated with a child."

"But . . . "

She stepped aside just as the thing came racing down the stairs, all unseen save for the brass pins torn loose in its wake.

"Necrophagoi" by Liv Rainey-Smith

LOCKBOX

E. CATHERINE TOBLER

IF NOTHING ELSE, remember this: Edgar always knew.[1]

�֍

He found the ruin by mistake, a wrong turn down a street that fizzled out and turned into a rutted dead end choked with undergrowth. Housewarming, helping friends move, whatever the event[2] would have become over the course of a sloppy October night, there was no house Edgar could actually see, until—he said with a dramatic pause—the ground crumbled under his feet and he found himself standing within the shattered remains of what he first called a cathedral. It was, he said, as if an entire abbey had been sunk[3] into the ground and buried over for a hundred thousand years.

---

[1] We may debate exactly *when* Edgar knew at length, but I am not convinced there was ever a single, discernable point one can reference; as the notions herein are circular,[20] I feel so, too, was Edgar's knowledge.

[2] I have often been asked if there was an event at all; I cannot prove the existence of "the event," only that Edgar did leave, around 6pm on a Friday evening, and did not return until 2pm the following Sunday. He told me friends he'd had longer than he'd had me were moving and needed his help, but Edgar's hands never betrayed a lick of work.

[3] *Had been sunk*, he phrased it so, as if some hand had pulled the abbey down with great intention.

Everyone gave him shit—said he was taking our course on Gothic literature a little too literally. *Had he seen any old gentlemen with forty-yard beards?* Thomas wanted to know. Were there women weeping upon the moors—*No moors, you imbecile, and not a single solitary soul, nor any of the others who had been invited,* Edgar said and then his eyes fell to me. The way his mouth slanted up, I knew what he was thinking, that we would go and have each other within that desolate ruin, out where there should have been a house, but there was only a buried ruin that no one could even name.

But I was less careless than he and wanted to know more about this nameless, sunken place before we made to go. I had known Edgar for three years—it was our last year at University, the last year before we were to part ways, unless I followed him to London and I hated London[4] with all my heart, no matter how much I loved Edgar. He was decisive where I was not, disruptive—the kind to run shrieking through a church service, daring those amassed to consider matters outside their quiet circles of contemplation.[5]

Surely, I said to him as he watched me with the infinite patience of a man in love,[6] *the ruin possessed a name.* Everything in the world was named, controlled, precisely defined. We spent afternoons in the library poring over every ancient tome we could lay our hands on, asking the librarians if they had ever heard of such a place and they said no—but I saw it in their eyes. I *heard* the unspoken words clawing at the corners of their closed mouths. I didn't ask more of them, fearing they *could not* say. Edgar and I propped ourselves against the hard walnut shelves in a tangle with books of old, large maps spread across his loose-thighed lap. No matter how close I was,

---

[4] If one cares to look, the reasoning for this can be found in my chapbook, *Terrible London,* Meridian (2012). Everything but the food, dear reader; I found great comfort in warm beer and dry potatoes—No.

[5] Edgar did not possess any religious leanings, which made his discovery of the abbey all the more curious. It wasn't something he would have made up, even to gain favor with me—and being that he already possessed much more than my favor, this only lent credence to the story he told me. It is a terrible thing, to understand the limits of storytelling and be drawn in even so.

[6] Was he? Or was this merely part of the story he was telling?

Edgar drew me closer, long fingers guiding mine over the lines that marked the pages. These were original maps, bound into a book for what had been deemed "safer keeping," and I could feel the difference between smooth ink and rough paper. Coupled with the heat of Edgar's hand atop mine, I thought the maps would smudge beneath our fingers, lost to anyone who came after. When Edgar leaned in to kiss me, I felt the line of the River Tyne on the page beneath my middle finger and drew back from both boy and map.

"Exham,[7]" I breathed.

"Possible," Edgar said and I couldn't tell if his expression of annoyance was over the broken kiss or the accuracy of my guess.

As stories went, Exham Priory had housed the worst of the worst; the most depraved creatures had called those halls home and surely, it could not be that which Edgar had found in the ground. It could *not*—and if it was? Oh, I could not deny the way my heart quickened at the mere idea. If I—If *we* were to discover the ruins of Exham Priory and prove every single thing about the place true—It couldn't be possible and yet, I wanted it very much to be.

"Was it an aunt you had in that region?"

His question to me required no actual answer. Edgar tangled his hand into my necktie and pulled me closer, to forestall all dialogue but that between lip and tongue. The ruin didn't exactly matter then—it *was* an aunt I had near Exham, widowed and alone for more years than anyone wanted to count—and Edgar seemed to put the place out of his mind, until the end of the week when he looked at me over a stack of fresh books we had been perusing and asked if I wanted to go. *Its name didn't matter,* he

---

[7] In my coursework, I had studied the rumors of Exham Priory at length and they were simply not to be believed. There were terrible things in this world, to be certain, but I refused to believe in the numerous atrocities that were said to have taken place at Exham Priory. Inbreeding, people confined within cages, one body sewn to another to create a third thing entirely. Elephantine forms, long in places and bloated in others. Myths and legends, happenings that existed only within the fragments of ballads, ghost stories. Imagination has a way of shaping all things, including culture and politics. Perhaps especially these.

insisted, but he wanted to show me the ruin; he wanted me to see the way the setting sunlight would fill the depression the ruin made in the ground, a pool of gold draining away as the evening descended. We could also call upon my aunt, if I wished, but thoughts of her made me more uneasy. How *that* was possible, given our potential destination, baffled me. Something about women wandering alone, unseen.

He bade me pack my camera and we drove south, until Edinburgh was far behind.[8] Here, the land was untamed, streets turning to dirt before they fizzled out altogether. The idea that a wrong turn had brought him here in the first place seemed unlikely; it had perplexed me, his disappearance over the weekend, the claim of seeing friends into a new house, but when Edgar parked the car and took my hand to draw me out, I said nothing, captivated by what spread before us. It was as he said, like nothing you might imagine when a person explained it. It seemed a whole city submerged, drawn into the guts of the world where it held the last moments of sunlight from the rest of the land.

Within the dry and crumbling earth, walls made themselves known as dwindling sunlight caressed them. I picked out windows and doorways, even the remains of a sloping roof. Edgar grasped my hand and pulled me down a set of crumbling stone steps, into the building itself, and from there watched me was I wandered. The great hall rose around us to frame the twilight sky. I saw each piece of the wreck in turn, through the camera lens as the light faded and faded. Then it was Edgar's mouth lighting up the ruin, against my cheek, my ear, as he held me from behind, buckled my knees, and pressed me into the dirt. Here, the earth smelled like eternity. I watched in some measure of amusement as Edgar caught my camera as it tumbled from my hand. He set it carefully aside, showing less care with my jacket, my trousers. He was insatiable, the ground strangely warm beneath my splayed hands, as if with spilled blood, though it crumbled dry

---

[8] We drove approximately two hours south, though I would be hard-pressed to pinpoint our location beyond this. Indeed, the River Tyne was nearby and we passed through a wood that was surely the Whitelee Moor National Nature Reserve, but I can recollect nothing more specific.

between my fingers when hands turned to fists. When we walked up that long staircase later, as if we were drunk on the world and each other,[9] the moonlight glossing the stone made each step seem whole once more. Each was solid beneath my feet in a way they had not been upon our descent, no crumbling debris but only smooth and worn from centuries of feet moving across them.

I could not put the ruin from my head and wanted to return. Even in sleep, which we took in a small B&B in town proper,[10] the sunken building invited me to wander its halls. I returned to that crumbling staircase and found, not Edgar there but a woman, draped in what seemed shadows, but under my fingers was vintage silk. *Under my fingers*—she stood that close, looking down at me as if she had seen me once upon a time, but now needed a nudge to remember. She did not seem quite real and I presumed her to be my aunt with her silver hair until her lips parted, until she took a breath and drew the world into her lungs.

This, she said in a voice that was not my aunt's, *is not right*.

Her mouth did not move, but I heard the words even so. I could not tell dream from reality, then. I meant to ask her which it was, but it seemed ridiculous as she moved past me, down the stairs—

The night stairs, she said as she passed, the silk of her gown evacuating my grasp as though it were running away. It flowed behind her as a black river down every stone step. I turned to follow, unable to do anything else. My feet would not carry me up and out of the ruin, so down it was.[11]

A sickly yellow-green glow illuminated the underground passages we traversed, as if glowworms congregated somewhere above our heads. No bit of light touched the lady. She seemed cut from the world, only a

---

[9] Reader, forgive my indulgence. I would banish this cliché, were it not true. In trying to keep to the facts at hand, I must include my infatuation for Edgar.

[10] I cannot recollect the name of the town or the B&B, but my memory of each is otherwise intact: small, historical, charming. The woman who claimed ownership of the B&B is one Mrs. Baird, but without a location to search, I have been unable to find her. Baird is often as common a name as Smith.

[11] Given the nature of dreams, perhaps this account should not be present, but to eliminate it also eliminates a truth I feel to this day. I have been unable to forget the feel of that silk between my fingers or that sickly yellow light.

paper silhouette cameo in front of me, the absence of all things. But the longer I looked at her, I began to see shapes within even the shadow of her. The air seemed made of great, dark whorls, as if many-limbed creatures moved *inside* her. No matter how impossible this also was, I went with it. I followed the passage of one such creature down her spine and into what should have been the cradle of her hips. There it curled, as if making a nest, and bared its fangs at me, fangs that gleamed like anthracite. Black on black and blacker still.[12]

Come, now. Women are not made of such things.

She turned down a corridor and vanished from my sight. I gasped at the loss of her—the sensation was terrible, as if I had ceased to breathe, the whole of the world crumbling atop me.— I increased my stride, but around the corner, she was still gone. Screams rose in the near distance.

Margaret![13] I wanted to cry, but the name lodged in my throat.

She was as the ballad said:

Here roams the lady daemon, between childer bound and freeman.
Hair of silver, eye of gilt; soft of foot, through blood she spilt.
—The Lady Daemon (1512)[14]

At the corridor's end stood a door, a sliver of that sickly light visible beneath it. This light shone so clearly upon my shoes that I could see where I had scuffed them the first day I'd met Edgar—I had kicked a stone

---

[12] If need be, I would compare what I saw to something pilots experience: sensory illusions when your eyes grow tired of an unchanging, blank landscape. It was not that I believed myself to be flying, but seeing these spirals made me waver and stumble as if drunk. We had not, however, been drinking.

[13] Lady Margaret Trevor of Cornwall. She married the second son of the fifth Baron Exham. Fourteen-fifteenth century, though I, like so many before, have been unable to establish any firmer dates for her. She refuses to be pinned to any single point, looping through the histories of as many as eleven distinct cultures, but none so firmly held as those along the Welsh border. Children still fear she will take them from their beds, into the priory's cellars where she will bend them, cut them apart, breed them.

[14] Fragment of "The Lady Daemon," a ballad, collected within E. Drake's *Ballads of the Welsh Border (1650).*

unknowingly into his path, putting a similar scar on his own shoe. I pressed my hands to the door and it was like touching ice and fire both. From beyond the door, screams like you would find in your worst nightmares— as if people were being disassembled while they yet lived. There were letters carved into the door, worn by so much time they were mostly illegible[15]. I imagined a knife held in an unsteady hand, each cut into the wood drawing forth a fresh scream from the room beyond. The latch was cold beneath my hands, but would not be freed, no matter how I tried. It was likewise steady beneath the thump of my shoulder, refusing to give.

My fall from the bed woke me, shoulder thumping against floor and not door. I had no good idea where I was until Edgar reached down, fingers stroking my bare shoulder. I cringed at his touch, retreating into the tangle of blankets. My shoulder ached. When I looked, it showed a bruise, which of course could not be. Even Edgar's face betrayed surprise at this and I felt the emotion genuine—there were things he knew and could not yet tell me, but this mark upon my skin surprised him as much as it did me. He touched me again, the bruise warmer than the rest of the arm, angry with blood and injury.[16]

The ruin was different in daylight, less hostile but no more welcoming. I expected to see footprints upon the steps, but while there was evidence of my tussle with Edgar, there was no sign that anyone else had been in the ruin.[17] I pulled Edgar down the hallways I had dreamed and we found the door, the terrible door, and Edgar—

---

[15] Druidic and Roman origins, but nothing so dramatic or simple as HELP or GO BACK carved within the wood. Trying to draw them the following morning led to the strange sensation of having written these words before. Magna Mater—oh, Great Mother.

[16] To this day, the shoulder aches. I have been subject to all manner of medical examinations, each of which shows no injury. Edgar mentioned Frodo Baggins and the ache of the wound sustained on Weathertop. I could not laugh, for yes, it has become that, an injury that draws me into the memory of an occurrence I will not fully explain.

[17] How easily my mind explained *this*, for Margaret's dress had been long and surely, it swept all evidence of her steps away. Childer bound and . . . freeman, the ballad goes. Alone among the horrors, only I walked free. Only I.

Edgar's hands closed over my own, forcing me to hold the doorknob. It burned like ice and fire, as it had in my dream, but opened easily enough under our combined strength. I gasped as the foul stench of the room rolled out to greet us. I could not withdraw, for Edgar nudged me in.[18]

The crypt was vast, vaults lining the walls, rats skittering across the floor. Some were inscribed with names, but most were not. Each was locked tight, flowers turning to dust on the ground before three of the vaults. Edgar left my side to trace the few names he found, as if he would recognize some of the dead.[19]

The floor vibrated with anguish. It was as strong as anything I had ever felt, pulling me across the floor and down another set of stone steps. Into the heart of the priory, the lowest cellars where the worst things lingered. I did not question then what I saw, took it only for what it was, endless torment that Margaret Trevor had a hand in both then and now. How could it be that such things continued long past their points of origin? Or was it that everything was a circle,[20] moving outward before curling under and down to return through the middle and move back out? There was no end to anything begun here.

The worst thing was, despite the horrors around her, Margaret Trevor was something to be worshipped, a glory even in the blood and ruin that streaked her. The stories said that she loved the old cults well, but had taken a passive role beside her husband. But here, in the horrible cellar with its collapsing girders, she was a gold-and-silver goddess while her husband cowered. He held his hands before his face, as if he could not bear

---

[18] We tell ourselves that nothing awful happens in the light of day, true terrors reserved for night and night alone, but daylight hides nothing. People still vanish under the light of a noon sun. Daylight strips the comfort of blackness away and we were not dreaming when we saw what we saw.

[19] When I later asked, Edgar could remember no names. I asked if any of them were De la Poers or Shrewsfields, but he did not know and the more I asked, the more it drove him mad. He had always known and then did not.

[20] Eternal return/recurrence, with its roots in Egypt and India both, further deconstructed by Blanqui (1871), Eddington (1927), Black Elk (1961), Hawking (2010), and certainly, yes, Pizzolatto (2013). Had we been here before? We had, but tell me not.

a magnificence such as she, while she opened the bodies[21] laid on an altar before her to welcome the oldest things anyone in the world might ever know.

What emerged beneath the guidance of her hands was something my memory has forced into a locked box. When I think on it, the world shutters to black and it feels as though iced water runs through my veins.[22] My blood does not exactly stop, nor does my heart cease, but I do not think overlong on the things we saw. I cannot, because the box is locked.

When we emerged, the clouds had broken and thin sunlight dribbled onto our faces. A backward glance[23] showed us nothing whatsoever amiss. Edgar laughed and wrapped an arm around my aching shoulder as we walked back to the car.

"I would have sworn . . . " He trailed off, as if unsure what led us here.

And I frowned, because I almost couldn't remember, either, but then it was night and we slept, and—Only dreamed.

Lady Margaret whispered from Edgar's mouth and I know the heat of the ancient sands parting, as if I, as if *we*, are stretched upon that altar in

---

[21] Bodies. Those they had fashioned in their breeding experiments, made to summon the utterly divine. I—Cannot. Not even here.

[22] Would that it were so easy; a *locked* box and ice water—dramatic, Harry—but of course, I hold the key to this box. Margaret placed it within my skin so I can always find this place, where she calls the deepest horrors of the universe into our very own world. She opened the body as if parting sand, and I felt the warmth of an Egyptian desert. The scarabs whispered as they flowed up Lady Margaret's arms, into her very skin. She turned blue—the way Egyptians had painted the ceilings of their tombs or the Greeks their roofs, bright as the twilight sky. Each and every scarab became a star upon her. She glowed like the heavens and from her body, and the dead before her, vomited new, strange life. Forms I had never seen entered this world, on eight legs and more, and made everyone bow, everyone but Margaret. These strange creatures bowed to *her*. When Edgar did not bow in worship, they seized him, in hands horrible and deformed. I thought they would press him to his knees in the bloody dirt, and perhaps they meant to, but he resisted. His eyes met mine and he knew, he *knew*, and was taken into that hideous maw, consumed whole. Margaret stood as round as Cybele, swollen with the life to come. Edgar, *my* Edgar. When he was spat back out, it was from Margaret's distended mouth, and he was made different, made *knowing* of things others cannot, yet.

[23] Always a mistake, reader. We did not turn to salt and yet, we turned.

offering. She laughs and when I wake, I cannot wholly remember because I have placed that in the box, too.

When Edgar tells me he has to help friends move, I think little of it. He remains friends with people he knew before we even met and some do not know he has a lover. I nod, because I have my studies and there is always a paper in need of writing, so it will be good to have the nights. I think on the week that was and cannot fully place everything we have done, until Edgar returns, pressing a kiss against the corner of my mouth—

(the gleam of fangs
and he's coiled in the cradle of her hips,
waiting to be born,
waiting to be loosed—
unspoken words in the corner of his mouth, his maw.)

He got foolishly lost, he laughs, and there was no house, but there was still a place I needed to see. A place he wanted to take me.

Edgar always knew. And I—

Not yet.[24]

※

There once was a 'ho liked to murder
Adept with both knife & stray girder
She hiked up her skirt
Put the men in the dirt
And nobody talked shit about her.

—The Lady Daemon (1992)[25]

---

[24] Not yet.

[25] Posted by user "daemon-marg" on the Her Story BBS, uk.history.myths. legends.wales (11/1/92)

"Marceline" by Sara Bardi

HAIRWORK

GEMMA FILES

NO PLANT CAN thrive without putting down roots, as nothing comes from nothing; what you feed your garden with matters, always, be it the mulched remains of other plants, or bone, or blood. The seed falls wherever it's dropped and grows, impossible to track, let alone control. There's no help for it.

These are all simple truths, one would think, and yet, they appear to bear infinite repetition. But then, history is re-written in the recording of it, always.

�֎

"Ici, c'est elle," you tell Tully Ferris, the guide you've engaged, putting down a pale sepia photograph printed on pasteboard, its corners foxed with age. "Marceline Bedard, 1909—from before she and Denis de Russy met, when she was still dancing as Tanit-Isis. It's a photographic reference, similar to what Alphonse Mucha developed his commercial art pieces from; I found it in a studio where Frank Marsh used to paint, hidden in the floor. Marsh was Cubist, so his paintings tend to look very deconstructed, barely human, but this is what he began with."

Ferris looks at the *carte,* gives a low whistle. "Redbone," he says. "She a fine gal, that's for sure. Thick, sweet. And look at that hair."

99

" 'Redbone?' I don't know this term."

"Pale, ma'am, like cream, lightish-complected—you know, high yaller? Same as me."

"Oh yes, *une métisse, bien sur.* She was cagey about her background, *la belle Marceline,* liked to preserve mystery. But the rumor was her mother came from New Orleans to Marseilles, then Paris, settling in the same area where Sarah Bernhardt's parents once lived, a Jewish ghetto; when she switched to conducting séances, she took out advertisements claiming her powers came from Zimbabwe and Babylon, darkest Africa and the tribes of Israel, equally. Thus the name: Tanit, after the Berber moon-goddess, and Isis, from ancient Egypt, the mother of all magic."

"She got something, all right. A mystery to me how she even hold her head up, that much weight of braids on top of it."

"Mmm, there was an interesting story told about Marceline's hair— that it wasn't hers at all but a wig. A wig made *from* hair, maybe even some scalp, going back a *long* time, centuries . . . I mean, *c'est folle* to think so, but that was what they said. Perhaps even as far *as* Egypt. Her mother's mother brought it with her, supposedly."

"Mummies got hair like that, though, don't they? Never rots. Good enough you can take DNA off it."

You nod. "And then there's the tradition of Orthodox Jewish women, Observants, Lubavitchers in particular—they cover their hair with a wig, too, a *sheitel,* so no one but their husband gets to see it. Now, Marceline was in no way Observant, but I can see perhaps an added benefit to her *courtesanerie* from allowing no one who was not *un amant,* her intimate, to see her uncovered. The wig's hair might look much the same as her own, only longer; it would save her having to . . . relax it? *Ça ira?*"

"Yeah, back then, they'd've used lye, I guess. Nasty. Burn you, you leave it on too long."

"*Exactement.*"

Tully rocks back a bit on his heels, gives a sigh. "Better start off soon, you lookin' to make Riverside 'fore nightfall—we twenty miles up the road here from where the turn-off'd be, there was one, so we gotta drive cross

Barker's Crick, park by the pass, then hike the rest. Not much left still standin', but I guess you probably know that, right?"

"Mmm. I read testimony from 1930, a man trying for Cape Girardeau who claimed he stayed overnight, spoke to Antoine de Russy. Not possible, of course, given the time—yet he knew many details of the events of 1922, without ever reading or hearing about them, previously. Or so he said."

"The murders, the fire?" You nod. "Yeah, well—takes all sorts, don't it? Ready to go, ma'am?"

"If you are, yes."

"Best get to it, then—be dark sooner'n you think and we sure don't wanna be walkin' 'round in *that.*"

✺

A mourning sampler embroidered in fifteen different De Russy family members' hair once hung upstairs, just outside my husband's childhood bedroom door: such a pretty garden scene, at first glance, soft and gracious, depicting the linden-tree border separating river and dock from well-manicured green lawn and edging flowerbeds—that useless clutter of exotic blooms, completely unsuited to local climate or soil, which routinely drank up half the fresh water diverted from the slave quarter's meager vegetable patch. The lindens also performed a second function, of course, making sure De Russy eyes were never knowingly forced to contemplate what their *negres* called the bone-field, a wet clay sump where slaves' corpses were buried at night and without ceremony, once their squeamish masters were safely asleep. Landscaping as *maquillage,* a false face over rot, the skull skin-hid. But then, we all look the same underneath, no matter our outward shade, *ne c'est pas?*

In 1912, I took Denis's hand at a Paris soiree and knew him immediately for my own blood, from the way the very touch of him made my skin crawl—that oh-so-desirable *peau si-blanche,* olive-inflected like old ivory, light enough to shine under candle-flame. I had my Tanit-wig on that night, coils of it hung down in tiers far as my hips, my thighs, far enough to brush the very backs of my bare knees; I'd been rehearsing most of the day, preparing to chant the old rites in Shona while doing what my posters called a "Roodmas dance" for fools with deep pockets. Frank Marsh was there, too, of course, his fishy eyes hung out on strings—he introduced Denis to me, then pulled me aside and begged me once again to allow him to paint me "as the gods intended," with only my ancestors' hair for modesty. But I laughed in his face and turned back to Denis instead, for here was the touch of true fate at last, culmination of my mother's many prayers and sacrifices. Mine to bend myself to him and bind him fast, make him bring me back to Riverside to do what must be done, just as it'd been Frank's unwitting destiny to make that introduction all along and suffer the consequences.

Antoine De Russy liked to boast he kept Denis unworldly and I must suppose it to be so, for he never saw me with my wig off, my Tanit-locks set by and the not-so-soft fuzz of black which anchored it on display. As he was raised to think himself a gentleman, it would never have occurred to Denis to demand such intimacies. By the time his father pressed him to do so, I had him well-trained: *Something odd about that woman, boy,* I heard him whisper more than once, before they fell out. *Makes my blood run cold to see it. For all she's foreign-born, I'd almost swear I know her face . . .*

Ha! As though the man had no memory, or no mirrors. Yet, I was far too fair for the one, I suspect, and far too . . . different, though in "deceitfully slight proportion"— to quote that Northerner who wrote your vaunted *testimony*—for the other. It being difficult to acknowledge your own features in so alien a mirror, not even when they come echoing back to you over generations of mixed blood, let alone on your only son's arm.

You got in touch with Tully last Tuesday, little seeker, securing his services via Bell's machine—its latest version, any rate—and by yesterday, meanwhile, you'd flown here from Paris already, through the air. Things move so *fast* these days and I don't understand the half of it; it's magic to me, more so than magic itself, that dark, mechanical force I hold so close to my dead heart. But then, this is a problem with where I am now, *how* I am; things come to me unasked-for, under the earth, out of the river. Knowledge just reveals itself to me, simple and secret, the same way soil is disturbed by footfalls or silt rises to meet the ripple: no questions and no answers, likewise. Nothing explained outright, ever.

That's why I don't know your name, or anything else about you, aside from the fact you think in a language I've long discarded and hold an image of me in your mind, forever searching after its twin: that portrait poor Frank did eventually conjure out of me during our last long, hot, wet summer at Riverside, when I led my husband's father to believe I was unfaithful expressly in order to tempt Denis back early from his New York trip . . . so he might discover me in Frank's rooms, naked but for my wig, and kill us both.

Workings have a price, you see, and the single best currency for such transactions is blood, always—my blood, the De Russys' blood, and poor Frank's added in on top as mere afterthought. All of our blood together and a hundred years' more besides, let from ten thousand poor *negres'* veins one at a time by whip or knife, closed fist or open-handed blow, crying out forever from this slavery-tainted ground.

After Denis's grandfather bred my mother's mother 'til she died—before his eyes fell on her in turn—*Maman* ran all the way from Riverside to New Orleans and further, as you've told Tully: crossed the ocean to France's main port, then its capital, an uphill road traveled one set of sheets to the next, equal-paved with vaudeville stages, dance-floors, séance-rooms, and men's beds. Which is why those were the trades she taught me, along with my other, deeper callings. Too white to be black, a lost half-girl, she birthed me into the *demi-monde* several shades lighter still, which allowed me to climb my way back out; perception has its uses, after all, especially to *une sorciére*. From earliest years, however, I knew that nothing I did was for myself—that the only reason I existed at all was to bring about her curse, and her mother's, and her mother's mother's mother's.

There's a woman at Riverside, Marceline, ma mie, my mother told me before I left her that last time, stepping aboard the steam-ship bound for America. *An old one, from Home—who can say how old? She knew my mother and hers; she'll know you on sight, know your works, and help you in them.* And so there was: Kaayakire, whom those fools who bought her named Sophonisba—Aunt Sophy—before setting her to live alone in her bone-yard shack, tending the linden path. It was she who taught me the next part of my duty, how to use my ancestors' power to knit our dead fellow captives' pain together like a braid, a long black snake of justice, fit to choke all De Russys to death at once. To stop this flow of evil blood at last, at its very source.

That I was part De Russy myself, of course, meant I could not be allowed to escape, either, in the end. Yet only blood pays for blood, so the bargain seemed well worth it, at the time.

But I have been down here so long, now—years and years, decades: almost fifty, by your reckoning, with the De Russy line *proper* long-extirpated, myself very much included. Which is more than long enough to begin to change my mind on that particular subject.

※

So, here you come at last, down the track where the road once wound at sunset, led by a man bearing just the barest taint of De Russy blood in his face, his skin, his veins: come down from some child sold away to cover its masters' debts, perhaps, or traded between land-holders like a piece of livestock. One way or the other, it's as easy for me to recognize in Tully Ferris by smell as it'd no doubt be by sight, were I not so long deep-buried and eyeless with mud stopping my mouth and gloving my hands, roots knot-coiled 'round my ankles' bones like chains. I'd know it at first breath, well as I would my own long-gone flesh's reek, my own long-rotten tongue's taste.

Just fate at work again, I suppose, slow as old growth—fate, the spider's phantom skein, thrown out wide, then tightened. But the curse I laid remains almost as strong, shored up with Kaayakire's help: Through its prism, I watch you approach, earth-toned and many-pointed, filtered through a hundred thousand leaves at once like the scales on some dragonfly's eye. I send out my feelers, hear your shared tread echo through the ground below, rebounding off bones and bone-fragments, and an image blooms out of resonance that is brief yet crisp, made and remade with every fresh step: you and Tully stomping through the long grass and the clinging weeds, your rubber boots dirt-spattered, wet coats muddy at the hem and snagged all over with stickers.

Tully raises one arm, makes a sweep, as though inviting the house's stove-in ruin to dance. "Riverside, ma'am—what's left of it, anyhow. See what I meant?"

"Yes, I see. Oh, *pute la merde!*"

Tree-girt and decrepit, Riverside's pile once boasted two stories, a great Ionic portico, the full length and breadth necessary for any plantation centerpiece; they ran upwards of two hundred slaves here before the War cut the De Russys' strength in half. My husband's father loved to hold forth on its architectural value to anyone who'd listen, along with most who didn't. Little of the original is left upright now, however—a mere half-erased sketch of its former glory, all burnt and rotted and sagging amongst the scrub and cockle burrs. Like the deaths of its former occupants, its ruin is an achievement in which I take great pride.

"Said this portrait you come after was upstairs, right?" Tully rummages in his pack for a waterproof torch. "Well, you in luck, gal, sorta . . . upstairs fell in last year, resettled the whole mess of it down into what used to be old Antoine's ballroom. Can't get at it from the front, 'cause those steps is so mouldy they break if you look at 'em the wrong way, but there's a tear in the side take us right through. Hope you took my advice 'bout that hard-hat, though."

You nod, popping your own pack, and slip the article in question on: It even has a head-lamp, bright-white. "*Voila.*"

At this point, with a thunderclap, rain begins to fall like curtains, drenching you both—inconvenient, I'm sure, as you slip and slide 'cross the muddy rubble. But I can take no credit for that, believe it or not; just nature taking its toll, moisture invading everything as slow-mounting damp or coming down in sheets, bursting its banks in cycles along with the tea-brown Mississippi itself.

Ownership works both ways, you see. Which is why, even in its heyday, Riverside was never anything more than just another ship, carrying our ancestors to an unwanted afterlife chained cheek-by-jowl with their oppressors, with no way to escape, even in death. No way for *any* of us to escape our own actions, or from each other.

But when I returned, Kaayakire showed me just how deep those dead slaves had sunk their roots in Riverside's heart: deep enough to strangle, to infiltrate, to poison, all this while lying dormant under a fallow crust. To sow death-seeds in every part of what the De Russys called home, however surface-comfortable, waiting patient for a second chance to flower.

Inside, under a sagging double weight of floor-turned-roof, fifty years' worth of mold spikes up the nose straight into the brain while shadows scatter from your twinned lights, same as silt in dark water. You hear the rain like someone else's pulse, drumming hard, sodden. Tully glances 'round, frowning. "Don't like it," he says. "Been more damage since my last time here: there, and there. Structural collapse."

"The columns will keep it up, though, no? They seem—"

"Saggy like an elephant's butt, that's what they *seem* . . . but hell, your money. Got some idea where best to look?" You shake your head, drawing a sigh. "Well, perfect. Guess we better start with what's eye-level; go from there."

As the two of you search, he asks about *that old business,* the gory details. For certainly, people gossip, here as everywhere else, yet the matter of the De Russys is something most locals flinch from, as though they know it to be somehow—not sacred, perhaps, but *significant,* in its own grotesque way. Tainted and tainting, by turns.

"Denis de Russy brought Marceline home and six months later, Frank Marsh came to visit," you explain. "He had known them both as friends, introduced them, watched them form *un ménage.* Denis considered him an artistic genius but eccentric. To his father, he wrote that Marsh had 'a knowledge of anatomy which borders on the uncanny.' Antoine de Russy heard odd stories about Marsh, his family in Massachusetts, *la ville d'*Innsmouth . . . but he trusted his son, trusted that Denis trusted. So, he opened his doors."

"But Denis goes travelling and Marsh starts in to painting Missus de Russy with no clothes on, maybe more. That part right, or not?"

"That was the rumor, yes. It's not unlikely Marceline and Marsh were intimates, from before; he'd painted her twice already, taken those photos. A simple transaction. But this was . . . different, or so Antoine de Russy claimed."

"How so?"

You shrug. "Marsh said there was something inside her he wanted to make other people see."

"Like what, her soul?"

"*Peut-etre.* Or something real, maybe—hidden. *Comme un,* eh, hmmm . . . " You pause, thinking. "When you swallow eggs or something swims up inside, in Africa, South America: It eats your food, makes you thin, lives inside you. And when doctors suspect, they have to tempt it out—say 'aah,' you know, tease it to show itself, like a . . . snake from a hole . . . "

Tully stops, mouth twitching. "A *tapeworm?* Boy must've been trippin', ma'am. Too much absinthe, for sure."

Another shrug. "Antoine de Russy wrote to Denis, told him to come home before things progressed further, but heard nothing. Days later, he found Marsh and Marceline in Marsh's rooms, hacked with knives, Marceline without her wig, or her, eh—hair—"

"Been scalped? Whoo." Tully shakes his head. "Then Denis kills himself and the old man goes crazy; that's how they tell it 'round here. When they talk about it at all, which ain't much."

"In the testimony I read, de Russy said he hid Marsh and Marceline, buried them in lime. He told Denis to run, but Denis hanged himself instead, in one of the old huts—or something strangled him, a big black snake. And then the house burnt down."

"Aunt Sophy's snake, they call it."

"A snake or a braid, *oui, c'est ca. Le cheveaux de* Marceline." But here you stop, examining something at your feet. "But wait, what is—? Over here, please. I need your light."

Tully steps over, slips, curses; down on one knee in the mud, cap cracking worryingly, his torch rapping on the item in question. "Shit! Look like a . . . box, or something. Here." As he hands it up to you, however, it's now his own turn to squint, scrubbing mud from his eyes— something's caught his notice, there, half-wedged behind a caryatid, extruding from what used to be the wall. He gives it a tug and watches it come slithering out.

"*Qu'est-ce que c'est, la?*"

"Um . . . think this might be what you lookin' for, ma'am. Some of, anyhow."

The wet rag in his hand has seen better days, definitely. Yet, for one who's studied poor Frank Marsh's work—how ridiculous such a thing sounds, even to me!—it must be unmistakable, nevertheless: a warped canvas, neglect-scabrous, all morbid content and perverted geometry done in impossible, liminal colors. The body I barely recognize, splayed out on its altar-throne, one bloated hand offering a cup of strange liquor; looks more the way it might now were there anything still unscattered, not sifted through dirt and water or filtered by a thousand roots, drawn off to feed

Riverside's trees and weeds with hateful power. The face is long-gone, bullet-perforated, just as that skittish Northerner claimed. But the rest, that coiling darkness, it lies (*I lie*) on—

You make a strange noise at the sight, gut-struck: "Oh, *quel dommage!* What a waste, a sinful waste . . . "

"Damn, yeah. Not much to go on, huh?"

"Enough to begin with, *certainment*. I know experts, people who'd pay for the opportunity to restore something so unique, so precious. But why, why—ah, I will never understand. Stupid superstition!"

Which is when the box in your hands jumps, ever so slightly, as though something inside it's woken up. Makes a little hollow rap, like knocking.

⌘

As I've said, little seeker, I don't know you—barely know Tully, for all I might recognize his precedents. Though I suppose what I *do* know might be just enough to feel bad for what must happen to you and him, both, were I any way inclined to.

Frank's painting is ruined, like everything else, but what's inside the box is pristine, inviolable. When my father-in-law disinterred us days after the murders, too drunk to remember whether or not Denis had actually done what he feared, he found it wound 'round Frank's corpse, crushing him in its embrace, and threw burning lamp-oil on it, setting his own house afire. Then fled straight to Kaayakire's shack, calling her slave-name like the madman he'd doubtless become: *Damn you, Sophy, an' that Marse Clooloo o' yours . . . damn you, you hellish ol' nigger-woman! Damn you for knowin' what she was, that Frog whore, an' not warnin' me . . . 'm I your Massa, or ain't I? Ain't I always treated you well . . . ?*

Only to find the same thing waiting for him, longer still and far more many-armed, still smouldering and black as ever—less a snake now than an octopus, a hundred-handed net. The weight of every dead African whose blood went to grow the De Russys' fortunes, falling on him at once.

My cousin's father, my half-uncle, my mother's brother: all of these and none of them, as she and I were nothing to them—to him. Him I killed by letting his son kill me and set me free.

I have let myself be dead far too long since then, however, it occurs to me. Indulged myself, who should've thought only to indulge them, the ancestors whose scalps anchor my skull, grow my crowning glory. Their blood, my blood—Tully Ferris' blood, blood of the De Russys, of owners and owned alike—cries out from the ground. Your blood, too, now.

Inside the box, which you cannot keep yourself from opening, is my Tanit-Isis wig, that awful relic: heavy and sweet-smelling, soft with oils, though kinked at root and tip. You lift it to your head, eyes dazed, and breathe its odor in, deeply; hear Tully cry out, but only faintly, as the hair of every other dead slave buried at Riverside begins to poke its way through floors-made-walls, displace rubble and clutter, twine 'round cracked and half-mashed columnry like ivy, crawl up from the muck like sodden spiders. My wig feels their energies gather and plumps itself accordingly, bristling in every direction at once, even as these subsidiary creatures snare Tully like a rabbit and force their knotted follicles inside his veins, sucking De Russy blood the way the *lamia* once did, the *astriyah,* demons called up not by Solomon, but Sheba. While it runs its own roots down into your scalp and cracks your skull along its fused fontanelles to reach the gray-pink brain within, injecting everything which ever made me *me* like some strange drug, and wiping *you* away like dust.

I *would* feel bad for your sad demise, little seeker, I'm almost sure; Tully's, even, his ancestry aside. But only if I were anyone but who I am.

※

Outside, the rain recedes, letting in daylight: bright morning, blazing gold-green through drooping leaves to call steam up from the sodden ground, raise cicatrice-blisters of moisture from Riverside's walls. The fields glitter like spiderwebs. Emerging into it, I smile for the first time in so very long: lips, teeth, muscles flexing. *Myself* again, for all I wear another's flesh.

Undefeated, *Maman*. Victory. I am your revenge and theirs. No one owns me, not anymore, never again. I am . . . my own.

And so, my contract fulfilled, I walk away: into this fast, new, magical world, the future, trailing a thousand dark locks of history behind.

THE THING ON THE CHEERLEADING SQUAD

MOLLY TANZER

"BIBLE CAMP WAS rad, Natalie! Coming together in God like that . . . at the end, we all made a pledge to live the Gospel after we went back into the world, where temptation and sin are everywhere. And you know what? I'm *really* going to try." Veronica Waite tossed her mane of dark curls, revealing more of her new off-the-shoulder Esprit sweatshirt. "So, what did *you* do all summer?"

"I worked at the daycare at First Methodist," mumbled Natalie, shoving her face into her faded Trapper Keeper. "I . . . wanted to earn some money."

Veronica blushed. She should've remembered; her father had said something about Natalie working at the church.

Natalie's family's finances were often the subject of prayer meetings at First Methodist. Everyone talked about it. It was probably mortifying.

"How did that go?" Veronica asked, trying to sound encouraging. She and Natalie had been friends they were kids. True, they'd grown apart during their first two years of high school, but they'd still seen a lot of one another, both being flyers on the JV cheerleading squad. "I bet it was great, huh?"

Natalie shut her Trapper Keeper with more force than necessary. "The other aids were nice, but the kids were pretty rotten."

" 'Suffer little children, for of such is the kingdom of heaven,' " quoted Veronica piously.

Natalie flushed. "I didn't mean like that," she snapped. "You weren't there, all right? Cleaning up puke, and stopping them from fighting and whatever. It was just babysitting, even if it was in a church."

"Take a chill pill." Veronica rolled her eyes as she toyed with the cross that hung around her neck on a delicate chain of real gold. "What did you need the stupid money for, anyways? Prom's not 'til next year."

"Well, Varsity cheerleaders have to travel and stuff," said Natalie.

"Oh . . . "

"What?" Natalie was getting super worked up; she looked like she might cry. "I'm a reserve, aren't I? I'll be coming to all the practices . . . I might have to sub, if someone gets injured."

"I wasn't thinking about that," said Veronica quickly. Natalie hadn't made Varsity, but Miss Van Helder was too kind to keep her on the JV squad. "You're right."

The bus slowed. Veronica craned her neck; this was her cousin Asenath's stop. The doors opened with a squeal, then shut with another, but in between the two, Asenath didn't get on.

"I hope Aseanth's okay," mused Veronica, grateful to have something to talk about besides cheerleading.

"Shouldn't you know?" From her tone, it seemed Natalie was still sore.

"Daddy and Uncle Ephraim don't talk much," admitted Veronica. "I only see Asenath at school."

"Well, *whatever*. I'm sure she just got a ride. We'll see her at practice."

True—Asenath wouldn't miss cheerleading practice. She didn't just love it; she was the best. She'd been the star of JV since their first week on the squad and would probably be Team Captain next year. And it wasn't just because she was an amazing flyer in spite of her height. She worked hard, and made sure to be friendly and kind to everyone.

Privately, Veronica felt her cousin's aspirations to popularity were a result of the rumors that haunted her family—her mother had left when she was just a girl and her father was a real weirdo. Some said Ephraim Waite was a Satanist; others said he was just a creep. Victoria's daddy wouldn't elaborate on any of it. He just said that Uncle Ephraim had 'chosen his path,' implying strongly it was one that led straight to Hell.

Which, of course, meant Uncle Ephraim wasn't the kind of father who gave his daughter rides to school. Veronica fell into an uneasy silence until they pulled into the Miskatonic High parking lot.

There must really be a first time for everything, thought Veronica, for there was Uncle Ephraim's blue BMW. It was strange, though—peering out the window, Veronica saw a boy and some dirty-looking punk girl with blue hair leaning on the driver's side window, laughing and smoking cigarettes. The boy leaned in for a kiss.

"Oh, *gross,*" she said, disgusted. "Who are those losers? They shouldn't be doing . . . *that.* I'm going to talk to them."

"Suit yourself," said Natalie, joining the throng of students clambering off the bus without a backwards glance. Veronica was surprised—she had no idea what the girl was so upset about.

The fresh air of Miskatonic High's parking lot was a welcome change from the stuffy school bus, but Veronica made a show of coughing and waving her hand in front of her face as she approached the hooligans practically grinding on one another, pressed against Uncle Ephraim's car. The girl had at least seven rings in her left ear and was wearing a plaid skirt obviously from Goodwill. It was pilling and had some prep school's crest close to the hem. The dark-haired guy was wearing a Members Only jacket and Wayfarers. When he finally came up for air, Veronica cleared her throat loudly.

"Do you know whose car that is?" She put as much distain into her voice as she possibly could.

"Yeah, *mine,*" said the boy, lowering his Wayfarers with one long, smooth finger. Then he laughed. "Oh, hey, Veronica."

It couldn't be—and yet, it was! Veronica had no words as she realized the boy was not actually a boy, but her cousin Asenath. Over the summer, she'd cut her hair and bought herself a new wardrobe, but it was definitely her.

Veronica felt heat rising to her cheeks. Asenath looked great. If she'd been a boy, Veronica would have called her a hunk—*dreamy*, even.

But she wasn't a boy. And while the Bible might not be all that specific on this kind of issue, her camp counselors had made it clear there was no uncertainty about the matter whatsoever.

"Asenath, what gives?" asked Veronica, wrinkling her nose. "You look *weird.*"

"And I was just going to say how nicely you'd filled out over the summer."

"Don't be obscene. Were you kissing her?"

"Jealous?" Asenath winked at her as the bell rang. "Better run. Wouldn't want to be late."

"What about you?" Asenath had always been a perfect student.

"You only live once," said Asenath and went back to sucking face.

Veronica was shocked, but the pair were ignoring her, so her only option was to retreat, embarrassed and furious. Who did Asenath think she was? What she was doing, it wasn't right—socially, academically, or spiritually. Veronica felt a brief flash of guilt. Asenath had applied for the Bible Camp scholarship, as her father wouldn't send her, but Veronica had told her father Dougie Smithers was a better fit. But Dougie Smithers had ignored her all summer, and now . . .

Vexed, Veronica threw herself down into a random desk just as the late bell rang, barely paying attention to the teacher, who began calling roll. Her fingers snaked up to the chain around her neck. The cross felt hard and cold under her fingertips.

Her daddy always told her to pray at times of great confusion. Veronica asked Jesus to guide her, but no answer came.

�֍

Asenath was in Gifted, so Veronica hadn't expected to see her during the school day—but it did surprise her when, after school, Ms. Van

Helder came onto the field and told everyone that Asenath had quit the team.

"What? Why?" asked Beth Townsend, the Varsity captain. "Is she okay?"

"She's taking on a different role this year, is all," said Ms. Van Helder. The woman seemed amused by the team's dismay. "Don't worry. She'll still be involved with school spirit. But enough chit-chat. Go warm up. Fifty jumping jacks, then get to stretching. The Warriors are playing Kingsport in a month!"

After its awkward beginning, practice actually went okay. Everyone was eager to get back to drills and to discuss routines during breaks. Beth agreed that Veronica's idea of using "Girls Ain't Nothing but Trouble" would be totally fresh for a halftime performance and Ms. Van Helder said she'd consider it.

Towards the end, Ms. Van Helder had them try some basic stunting. Veronica was one of the more experienced JV flyers, so some of the veteran Varsity bases agreed to try an elevator with her. "One, Two, Three, Up!" they cried, pushing her skyward. As she rose, Veronica tensed her abs and thighs, sweating and trembling; keeping her focus and her balance, she lifted her hands, only to feel the spots wobble.

"Holy crap!" said one. Veronica felt her feet moving apart as the bases lost their concentration.

"Let me down!" she called, not enthusiastic about the prospect of an injury on literally her first day.

That got their attention and Veronica felt her feet touch solid ground without an incident. Once she was on the grass, she saw just what had caused the commotion.

It was Asenath.

Veronica's cousin seemed determined to make a spectacle of herself this year. Instead of wearing Miskatonic's green-and-black Varsity warm-ups, she had donned the school mascot's uniform. Her dark hair was hidden by a Centurion's galea, her chest behind a breastplate. She carried a shield and sword. Greaves glistened on her shins, but her long thighs were exposed—the segmented skirt, intended for a boy, was almost indecently short on her.

"She looks amazing," observed Beth. To Veronica's chagrin, the rest of the team seemed to agree, almost falling all over themselves in their haste to greet her.

"As I said, Asenath will still be promoting school spirit this year," said Ms. Van Helder. "Since Ernie graduated, the position was open, and Asenath's enthusiasm and athletic ability made her application most impressive."

"Thanks!" said Asenath. "Should be fun, everyone. Miz V and I already talked about how it might be cool if I did some stunts in this get-up. What do you think?"

"That would be super!" enthused Amanda Slider.

"Awesome!" agreed Natalie. That bitch needed to shut up. She wasn't even on the Varsity team.

"I don't know," said Veronica, raising her voice a little. The squad quieted down, surprised. "If she's not coming to practice, stunting could be a safety issue."

"Ms. Van Helder thinks it's fine." Asenath's cool tone just further stoked the flames of Veronica's temper.

"Ms. Van Helder won't be lifting you," she snapped.

"What's your deal, Veronica?" asked Asenath.

"What's *your* deal?" she shrieked. "What on earth happened to you over the summer? You've changed—and *not* for the better."

A hideous sound coming from the direction of the bleachers distracted them all. Veronica turned and saw an old man sitting in the stands, doubled over laughing. Though the day was warm, he was dressed in a heavy overcoat and he clutched a Miskatonic High pennant in his withered hand.

"Shit," swore Asenath. "Sorry . . . I told Dad he could come if he kept quiet."

Veronica took a second look, shocked—her uncle was unrecognizable. She'd never have known it was him; he looked as though he'd aged years over just a few months, or as if he'd suffered some terrible illness. "I'd better . . ."

"Do what you need to do," said Ms. Van Helder, glaring at Veronica for some reason. Asenath took off toward the bleachers, her long legs covering the ground within moments. She confronted the old man, then led him away.

"Let's call it a day," said Ms. Van Helder. "Back to work tomorrow. And Veronica?"

"Yes?" Veronica lagged behind the others.

"Try to be patient with Asenath? She's been having . . . family troubles."

In Veronica's opinion, that didn't excuse anything. Asenath had never *not* had family troubles. Just the same, she nodded.

With a heavy heart Veronica changed and went out to wait for her mother by the front doors of Miskatonic High. Asenath was in the parking lot, bundling her uncle into her car, clearly having words with him. She'd changed back into her outfit from that morning; she looked ferocious and intimidating as she shoved the old creep into the passenger's side seat.

"Not unless you can control yourself!" she shouted angrily, slamming the door in his face after he whined something at her that Veronica couldn't hear.

Then Asenath noticed her cousin sitting there as she came around to the driver's side. Veronica, remembering Ms. Van Helder's admonition, timidly raised her hand in a greeting. Asenath laughed, blew her a kiss as she slid into the driver's seat. She pulled away just as Veronica's mother drove up.

"How was your first day?" her mother called out the window.

"Great, Mom," lied Veronica. "Really great."

※

Veronica, mindful of her Bible Camp pledge, tried to forgive Asenath for her antics—she *really* did—but it became increasingly difficult, given how her cousin seemed to want nothing more than to shock the whole school. Every day, she came in wearing a different appalling outfit—tweed blazers and slacks, Hawaiian shirts and brightly-colored shorts, leather jackets and jeans—and with some new girl on her arm, inevitably giggling like it wasn't social and spiritual suicide for her to go out with a woman. Veronica was mortified, and the worst part was, she didn't even have cheering as a respite. Whenever Asenath showed up in her mascot's outfit to practice, the girls went crazy, mobbing her like she was the captain of the football team. Veronica thought that was sick, but she couldn't say anything—Beth, the team captain, had gone out with Asenath a few times. "She's the best-looking boy in school," was her only comment when Veronica remarked on the queerness of it all.

Interestingly enough, for once, the cheerleaders were in the minority in terms of popular opinion; they might coo over Asenath, but the rest of Miskatonic High did not. Girls whispered whenever she walked by; guys shouted epithets. Veronica sensed Asenath was enjoying the attention and would have been more than happy to let Asenath reap what she sowed, just like in Galatians . . . except Asenath's refusal to act normally began to reflect poorly on *her*.

"You a dyke, too, Veronica?" shouted Dougie Smithers. The entire lunchroom heard him, given the laughter this sparkling wit produced. Veronica pushed away her half-finished pack of Handi-Snacks, the yellow cheese and buttery crackers now sawdust in her mouth. "Is it true that this Saturday, you're gonna go cruising for chicks together?"

Veronica refused to acknowledge him, but in her heart, she was seething. It shouldn't be like this. She was certain no other Varsity cheerleader had ever dealt with such scorn from her peers. Pretending to ignore Dougie and the rest, she put on her Walkman and grabbed her notebook. The rhymes of DJ Jazzy Jeff and the Fresh Prince became her world as she scribbled down some ideas for the new Varsity routine. Then, the notes blurred before her eyes when she had a sudden vision of her cousin prancing onto the field in her costume, proudly flaunting the inevitable catcalls and boos to stunt alongside the *real* cheerleaders.

She'd tried to forgive. She'd tried to forget. She'd been cordial to her, offering to let Asenath borrow her more feminine clothes if she needed to, and prayed for her in church, in the hopes that God would touch Asenath's heart and help her return to the fold. But nothing had worked. Something had caused Asenath to give up everything—her popularity, her straight A average, her faith, the cheerleading squad—and Veronica couldn't imagine what it could be.

Dougie slid onto the bench beside her, grabbing a cracker out of her Handi-Snack.

"Hey," he said, grabbing Veronica's headphones. "When you lick it, does it look like this?" And he pantomimed something obscene.

"Beware, ladies—he's clearly no expert." Asenath grabbed the boy by the collar and slung him off the bench. Dougie landed hard on his tailbone on the linoleum floor of the cafeteria with a thump and then a howl. The laughter was more sporadic than before. Veronica did not take part in it. "Sorry if he was bothering you, Veronica, but everyone knows I don't cruise for chicks—they come cruising for *me*."

"You're disgusting." For some reason, Veronica was angrier with Asenath than Dougie. She shoved her notebook into her backpack, snatched her headphones away from the boy still writhing on the ground, and stalked out of the lunchroom.

Once the door slammed behind her, Veronica totally lost it. She slumped against the lockers, tears running down her face. When the school board had announced their decision to integrate sex ed into the health curriculum last year, her daddy had threatened to put her in private school. Veronica had begged and pleaded to remain at Miskatonic because of her friends, because of cheering. Maybe this was her punishment for not being obedient to her father's will.

"Hey."

It was Asenath. Veronica dashed the tears from her eyes.

"What do *you* want?"

"To talk to you." Asenath came closer. Today, she was wearing a button-down men's Oxford tucked into high-waisted Guess jeans that somehow made her long legs look longer. "I'm sorry about what happened back there. Dougie's a real jerk. But—"

"You're sorry?" snarled Veronica. "Oh, great! I'm super-excited that you're *sorry* for ruining my life, Asenath!"

"What?"

"People tease me all the time about . . . about being like *you*." As she said it, Veronica knew how petty she sounded, but that just made her angrier. "And you've ruined cheering, too, prancing around in that stupid costume. They'll shout us off the field the moment they see you!"

Asenath laughed in her face. "That's all it takes to ruin your life?"

"What happened to you, Asenath? You used to be so nice. You used to care about important things, like school and cheering—and what people thought about you." Veronica shook her head. "Now . . . it's like . . . you just can't be bothered."

"What happened to me?" Asenath grinned mirthlessly. "*Life* happened. The real world intruded on the fantastical dream-lie that is high school. Sorry if that's *inconveniencing* you, Veronica. Me? I'm having a great time."

Veronica rolled her eyes. "So, what—you're Laura Palmer now?"

"Maybe Bobby Briggs." Asenath lowered her voice. "I wasn't the one who went looking for darkness. Somebody . . . *showed* it to me." The taller girl leaned in closer, planting her hand on the lockers behind Veronica, bracing herself on them, looming over her cousin. She smelled like cigarette smoke and peppermint gum. "You don't know what's out there, Veronica—the sad thing is, you don't even know what's *here*, in Arkham. You went to Bible Camp, just like your daddy wanted you to . . . sang your little songs, prayed your little prayers. Well, baby-girl, sing and pray all you want, because it doesn't fucking matter."

"What do you mean?"

"I'll tell you what *I* did on my summer vacation." Her cousin's intensity was startling. Her prominent brown eyes were shining like stars as her lips pulled back from her white teeth. Veronica couldn't help but compare her to the mild-mannered, sweet-tempered girl she had once been. "I looked into a well of absolute darkness, a well without a bottom, full to the brim with writhing whispers blacker than the darkness. I looked—and I *listened*."

"What . . . what was in the well?"

"Laughter. It laughed at me. The darkness, I mean. A hole full of nothing, *absolute* nothing, and it *laughed* at me."

"What did you do?"

Asenath stood up, looking around as if to see if anyone had witnessed her losing her cool. "Doesn't matter. But I tell you what . . . after that, I decided to live every day like it was my last, and I advise you to do the same. There's no heaven. There's no hell. There's only you, me and this." She gestured to the hallway. "The things beyond this world don't give a shit what you do—if you pray, if you're good, or if you're bad, according to some outdated notions of propriety."

"You don't sound like yourself," said Veronica.

Asenath shook her head. "I've always been this way. The only thing that's changed is that I know it's not worth hiding it."

The bell rang, and students poured out of the cafeteria. Veronica flinched away from Asenath, instinctively, which made the other girl laugh.

"See you around, *Veronica*," she said.

Veronica barely paid attention to her classes the rest of the day. Asenath's speech had shaken her. What she really needed was a good, hard practice to drive everything from her mind, but of course, Asenath showed up, to everyone's delight but hers.

Asenath seemed full of a savage fury that day. Her jumps were high, her kicks, higher. The term, 'flyer,' had never been so apropos. She seemed to hover above everyone when she was lifted and hang in the air for an unnaturally long time on the dismounts. Ms. Van Helder was so enthusiastic about her prospects toward the end of practice, she suggested Asenath try a scorpion instead of a full liberty after being popped up.

As Asenath executed the move perfectly, Veronica turned away, reminding herself that jealousy was a sin. Uncle Ephraim was sitting on the lowest bleacher. He was always in attendance when Asenath came to practice, gaunt and horrible in his big weird coat, a Miskatonic pennant clutched in his clawlike hands.

After his outburst the first day, he had remained largely silent, hunched into himself and watching them all with unwavering attention, but today, he seemed agitated. He shifted on his seat, twitching. The sight of Asenath in a scorpion further perturbed him. When she fell into the basketed hands of her fellow cheerleaders, he uttered a grotesque, bubbling cry.

Veronica was the only one who heard him, so she was the only one unsurprised when he began to holler and snort as Asenath tried the move a second time. Asenath wobbled and fell; her cohorts caught her, but there was no saving her from the old man's wrath.

"Thief!" he cried, staggering toward her. "Mine! It's *mine!*"

"Asenath," said Ms. Van Helder, as Asenath stood unsteadily, "are you—is he—"

"It's fine," said Asenath, through gritted teeth.

"Thief! Wolf in sheep's clothing!" The old man drew nearer, but Asenath wasn't waiting around—she began to advance on him. "Give it back—it's mine!"

"Shut up!" she snapped, grabbing his arm.

"Mine!" he cried, running his crabbed hand down her smooth arm.

"Maybe it was, but not anymore!" she shouted in his face.

"Asenath, your father's not well," said Ms. Van Helder, putting her hand on the girl's other arm. "You should—"

"Don't touch me!" cried Asenath, wrenching herself free of both their grasps. Her father, unsteady on his feet, fell to the ground with a heart-wrenching yelp.

"Asenath!" Ms. Van Helder was shocked.

"None of you have any idea about anything!" she screamed, and took off running toward the locker room.

A moment passed where they waited to see if Asenath would return. She did not. "Come on, Mr. Waite, let's get you home," said Ms. Van Helder, helping Ephraim to his feet. "I'm sorry. I don't know what's gotten into her."

"She stole it," he mewed. "She's a thief."

"Ms. Van Helder . . . I could take him home." Veronica felt bad for her uncle, the latest victim of Asenath's troubling metamorphosis. Perhaps, if she got him alone, she could talk to him. Maybe he needed help from the Church, or from her father, to deal with his wayward daughter.

"Do you have a car?"

"No, but it's not far. Maybe a mile. I mean, he walked here, didn't he?" Veronica took the man's hand. "Can you walk home with me? Are you strong enough, Uncle Ephraim?"

At first, he shook his head no, then something about his expression changed—brightened, maybe.

"Not far," he whispered, apparently agreeing with her.

The sound of a car peeling out of the parking lot made them all look to see Asenath's dramatic departure. She wasn't heading in the direction of her house.

"Better get him home," said Ms. Van Helder.

Uncle Ephraim nodded his enthusiasm.

❋

Veronica had never been a regular visitor at Asenath's house; not only did her daddy think she should "limit her contact" with her cousin and uncle, the place was just spooky, with its peeling paint and sagging roof. Her father also said the only reason their neighborhood's homeowner's association hadn't served Ephraim a notice was because of his intervention.

Uncle Ephraim had a key hidden somewhere in the deep pockets of his coat. Veronica got the door open and helped him inside.

"Can I get you something to drink?" she said, taking off his coat. It was very warm in the house, and dark; the blinds were all shut and the golden bars of afternoon sunlight that fell over the carpet through the slats didn't so much brighten the room as they showed the dust motes swirling in the air.

He nodded and shuffled toward a chair in the living room that shared his shabby, ill-used appearance. "Please," he mumbled. "Water."

There were no clean cups, so Veronica rinsed out a glass and got him some water with ice. She brought it into the living room and set it beside his elbow on a little tray table.

"I'll leave my number," she said uncertainly, "in case she doesn't—I mean, I'm sure Asenath will be home soon."

"*Asenath* . . ."

"She drove away," said Veronica. "But she was just angry. She'll be back."

"Stay." Uncle Ephraim pointed to the couch. "Please."

Veronica really, really didn't want to stay, but didn't feel like she had much of a choice. "Okay," she said. "Should I . . . turn on the TV?"

"Read to me." The suggestion of a whine in his unsteady voice stopped Veronica's protest in her throat.

"What should I read?"

"Upstairs," he said. "*Secrets*. Under Asenath's mattress."

"I shouldn't . . . "

"I hid it there."

Veronica's skin prickled as she wondered just what in the world Uncle Ephraim had stashed under his daughter's mattress. What if it was a girlie mag, or something even more disgusting? She decided she might as well do as he said. If it was really bad, she'd give it to Asenath and tell her to get rid of it.

The stairs were dark and cramped. Veronica took them two at a time, but she hesitated before grabbing the knob of Asenath's bedroom, unsure what she might find inside.

Like Asenath, the room was . . . different. The antique vanity Veronica had always coveted was still there, but Asenath's beloved Kaboodle full of makeup no longer sat upon it, nor did the shelves hold the toys and dolls she had brought over to Veronica's when they were younger. The strange thing was, nothing had replaced the missing items. It felt bare in there, denuded, stripped of its essence as if it had been bleached.

Veronica shut the door behind her, unsure what she was feeling. Sadness over the loss of a friend, yes, but there was anger, too. They hadn't just grown apart naturally, she and her cousin. Asenath had chosen this path, no matter what she said.

It made her uncomfortable, being in Asenath's private space, so Veronica screwed up her courage and plunged her arm between his mattress and the bedspring. She rooted around until her hands closed on a slender volume.

"*Hieron Aigypton*," she read slowly, running her fingers over the tooled leather of the cover. "By Ana . . . Anacharsis." She'd never heard of it. It looked very old.

She opened it to the first page, curious to see what it was Uncle Ephraim wanted her to read to him. "*Hieron Aigypton, or Egyptian Rites*," she read. "Being an unflinching translation of the dreaded rituals detailed by Anacharsis, who was born a woman, lived as a man, and died neither." She flipped another page. "*Weird.*"

Veronica knew that "rituals" were nothing her daddy would approve of, but just the same, Uncle Ephraim had requested this book. . . . Veronica pursed her lips, but went back downstairs with it.

"Let us rejoice in the true story of one called Narcissus, whose will was stronger than any alchemy," she read aloud, after Uncle Ephraim requested she read from the first chapter. After that first line, it became a story—one she vaguely remembered from school, about a beautiful boy who became a flower and the nymph who loved him until she became only an echo.

"I, Anacharis, went to that glen, where the first narcissus sprouted. There I found Echo, who told me his final words. These were they . . . "

The language was strange to her. As Veronica mumbled her way through the stanzas, her vision began to blur. At first, she thought it was just the warmth of the room—she was sweating through her warmups—but then her eyes focused and saw only blackness.

She was somewhere that was nowhere, standing at the edge of something that was nothing. Inside the nothing was more nothing, but a denser nothing that writhed—and *laughed*.

"Asenath," she whispered, horrified. She couldn't tear her eyes from the abyss. Her cousin hadn't been lying! Did that mean she had read this book? Seen the sights it offered? Horrified, Veronica regretted all the cruel things she had said to Asenath, all the comments she'd made behind her cousin's back. It was no wonder the girl had turned away from God—they said He was all-powerful, but Veronica couldn't believe He had ever been here, at the edge of wherever she was. She wept, knowing He was less than she had believed, if He existed at all.

Asenath said she had turned away, backed away—Veronica needed to find the will to do the same. But try as she might, she could not tear her eyes from the sight. She felt her foot move. It was no longer *her* foot. She took a step forward, not back. The laughter became louder, and when she went over the edge, it consumed her.

✷

When Veronica awoke, she felt sore and nauseated. She groaned, dry-mouthed and cold, and realized she lying was on the floor.

"You're awake." A woman spoke to her. Veronica opened her eyes, hoping Asenath had come home. But it wasn't Asenath.

It was *her*. Veronica Waite was standing there in her black-and-green skirt and Miskatonic warmup jacket, staring at her.

"What?" she mumbled, not in her own voice but Uncle Ephraim's.

"You're weaker than your cousin," she said, or rather, someone said with her voice, as she helped herself up and into a chair. "Asenath resisted all my arts. I couldn't take her body. She wouldn't let me, even though I raised it, fed it, clothed it, for seventeen long years! It was *mine*. The little thief stole it and after she saw what I was about, she made it nearly impossible for me to try again with someone else. But I managed to hide the book, just in case. Good thing *you* came along, my little niece, or I might have been trapped in that awful body for the rest of my days."

"Uncle?" Veronica was so confused; it was so difficult to do anything, even speak. Her jaws were made of lead. "How . . . "

"Don't worry about it. You don't need to know," he said coolly, out of her own lips. "Thank you, Veronica. You always were *such* a sweetheart."

The sound of a key in the lock silenced them. Asenath came through the front door, looking sheepish. The smell of food wafted into the living room.

"Sorry I took off like—oh, hi Veronica," said Asenath. She was carrying takeout from somewhere in her arms. "Ms. V said you took Dad home for me . . . thanks."

"No worries," said Veronica brightly, as Veronica watched in mute horror. "It was the least I could do. I've been *such* a bitch. Can you forgive me?"

"Of course," said Asenath instantly. "Veronica . . . I'm so sorry I've been making trouble for you at school. But you have to understand . . . "

"You don't owe me any explanations," said Veronica warmly. "I'm just glad we're friends again."

"I brought home dinner. Can you stay?"

"No," said Veronica. "Mommy and Daddy want me home, I'm sure. Maybe next week?"

"Sounds good," said Asenath. "Hey—this was really cool of you. Dad and I . . . after his . . . his stroke, he . . . "

"It's okay." Veronica leaned in and hugged Asenath tightly. "See you tomorrow?"

"Yeah," said Asenath. "Tomorrow."

Veronica tossed her hair and strode out of the house, waving once before walking down the street toward her home. Veronica watched her go, barely able to make her mouth move.

"Thief," she muttered, hoping Asenath would understand.

"Shut *up*, Dad," said Asenath, throwing dinner on the table. "You've already lost TV privileges with that little display you put on at practice today. Don't make it worse for yourself." She crossed her arms. "You know damn well what I'm capable of."

"Stolen . . . " Veronica tried to swallow the spit pooling in her mouth, but just dribbled all over herself.

"No more cheer practice for you," said Asenath. "And if you keep *that* up, I'll tell our home care worker you're just too much for a teenage girl to manage—understand? Ugh, stop *crying*." She made a disgusted sound in the back of her throat. "You and I both know you brought this on yourself."

BODY TO BODY TO BODY

SELENA CHAMBERS

I.

I CAN SEE already by the prejudice gleaming in your Puritan eyes that coming here was a mistake. Have you never been to Innsmouth? Have you never seen people who are different from you? Of course you have and you tend to not give them the last word, either. But, given your station in life, Officer, I would wager your people were persecuted, too, during the burning days—for the judges looked down upon all that were disposable: not only those who were different, but those who were poor.

I see I have offended you. Good. Maybe you will better listen to me.

My name is Eunice Babson, and I was a servant to Mr. and Mrs. Edward Pickman Derby of Crowinshield House. Before that, I served Mrs. Derby and her father, Ephraim Waite in Innsmouth. I am aware that I and the Gilmans are under suspicion for blackmail, among other things. On that point, I want to make one thing clear: I was never with the Gilmans but against them. They jailed Mr. Derby in the library, and assisted Ephraim in all of his experiments and exploits. True, I uncovered his crime in the cellar and he paid me a fee for silence. But I neither laughed at him when he withdrew his checkbook from his coat pocket, nor could I be heard swearing revenge. I already had my requital years back, before Derby had ever laid eyes on Asenath's young form.

Every woman's body is a story, you see. This was a rare wisdom bestowed on me by my mother, whose body suffered unwanted attentions and abuse—a sacrificial trade for a notion of comfort and propriety. That was the story of her body and it ended miserably, as everything in the Ephraim Waite household was neither comforting nor appropriate. Each body that stepped foot inside became *his* body. Except mine. But that is not my body's story. My story is of servitude. My body has been nothing but a tool for others to employ. It has served those I've loathed equally as those I've loved, including my sister Asenath.

That's right. It has been one of many well-kept family secrets, but I am Mrs. Derby's half-sister. I was the one who discovered Asenath's body and also the one to save her glow from complete diminishment. However, those two incidents occurred several years apart. To fully comprehend my testimony, I must begin even further back than last Hallowmas past.

I was born in Innsmouth Harbor, in a damp, dry rot shack that was littered with fish scales and fried cod stink. My yard was the sea. In and around it, I discovered as much death as life. My pets were the turtles and crabs I caught while accompanying Mother on her fishmongering up by the pier.

When I grew weary of her haggling, I would wander away from her skirts and walk the shore, watching the fishermen empty their nets on the docks and see how the desperate fish flapped to find the edge back into life. When their struggle stopped, a strange ringing would toll in my ears and an aural soft focus would invade my vision as I found myself staring at the creature, its jaw awry, until it began to gnash and convulse again with a second gulp at life. This happened on several occasions and a town man lurking in the harbor noticed. It was Ephraim Waite, who was fascinated with the wharf and its inhabitants.

He circled me, sinister like a shark, all teeth and menace and rock-hard flesh of an ancient fossil. He spoke through a strained smile, which wavered when he realized I could not comprehend. He picked up my resurrected fish, slapped it against the deck, and shook it at me. Blood splattered my face. Terrified, I cried out and tried to run away, but he grabbed my arm. When Mother came to my rescue, she swiped his arm away from me and lashed him in his own tongue.

They argued back and forth. Sometimes, Mother would slip back into our tongue and I heard the words, "It's in the blood." Every time I heard the phrase, the argument seemed to abate. Next thing I know, I am standing in his library being instructed to call the Harbor Haunt Master by the Gilmans, who would tutor me until I adequately learned Yank. Mother became the cook.

I immediately took to reading and languages. I escaped into books and therefore, stayed out of Master Ephraim's way. Mother, however, became a servant to suffering. She had acted desperately in gaining his employ.

We were but specimens to him. While he was fascinated in uncovering the secrets of our blood, it bothered him to have us roam about in his home. He said we stank up the place with our Harbor essence and would espouse phrenological theories of our features out loud as though we weren't in the room. When aroused into a spiritual fervor by a concoction he'd made in his library, he'd roar about Devil Reef and stupid old Obed Marsh.

"Shipwrecked sailor, my eye! If you want to find your father, child, just grow some gills and go for a swim. I bet you can call on him at Devil Reef anytime, demon!"

When he was at a loss for words, he would beat us. In these instances, Mother would throw herself between us. With his fist in the air and a salacious grin, he would fall upon her and become excited by conquering things weaker than him, and fill the vessel with the only function he felt it and she and we served.

It was in this manner that Asenath was conceived. His interest in my blood-talent waned until he saw the power it had over his only golden child.

Master Ephraim had reluctantly desired access to the Marsh collection at one of the Esoteric churches. Since he now had fathered a child, he saw Asenath as an incidental excuse to take the Order oaths. He married Mother and made her lady of the house. The Gilmans took on all of the household matters, leaving my education in hiatus.

Mother was pleased with her elevated status at first, but after Asenath's delivery, she slowly descended into a catatonic madness. Eventually, she boarded herself up in the attic and affected a black veil. She was going through the Great Change. In accepting that, she entered an extreme zealotry in which she neglected her children to prepare herself for going back to the water. Despite her baby's wails, Mrs. Gilman had to prompt her to feed. Although I was only five years old, I changed her diapers and put bourbon-soaked pacifiers in her mouth when she teethed.

Everyone cooed to Asenath in Yank, but when we were alone, I would teach her the Deep language. It was through me she spoke her first word: "*Fhalma.*" This embarrassed Mother when she was still sane, while Master Ephraim was greatly impressed. He decided to resume my education and gave me free reign of his forbidden library, thinking that everything I absorbed I would squeeze back into Asenath infused with traces of our innate abilities.

Even so, he assumed I only comprehended a third of what was there and I never let on otherwise. I realized that it was better for him to think I was mostly stupid and beneath him, because Asenath's precociousness won all of his affection and his attentions were more horrid than his despise.

II.

As we grew older, my love for my sister evolved from unconditional to concerned. Once she grew out of the sweetness of infancy, she became a little shoggoth, especially after she was told Mother had died.

When you said yes, she shouted no, and would destroy whatever porcelain bauble or glass beaker happened to be in reach. Toilet training was a farce and would begin with her running through the house, diaper flapping, and end in the library, where she'd micturate and defecate on whatever ancient manuscript was open on the table. This is how we lost the *Pnakotic Manuscripts,* a first edition of *Remnants of Lost Empires,* and *Livre d'Eibon* (Comte Saint-Germain's personal copy), while Asenath earned many whippings.

Despite my own rage, I would try to protect her as Mother had protected me. Despite my myriad disfiguring lacerations, she was an ungrateful child. She would thank me by stealing a goldfish—Mother had given me a dozen or so before she left—out of the tank and lay it to dry on Mr. Gilman's secretaire to go unnoticed for hours. After discovering my twelfth fish in this manner, I had had enough.

I found her outside throwing acorns against a tree and I yanked her up to standing by her arm.

"How about I bury you back here? Would you like that?" She twisted under my grip and I only squeezed her wrist tighter. "You are so careless with life; why should anyone let you have your own?"

"But they don't glow. Only humans have it. Father said."

"And he says I and mother aren't human. You think we don't have the glow?" She stopped her sobbing and looked up at me wide-eyed.

"All living things have a glow." I continued. "It's the spark of life. You have it. I have it. The goldfish have it."

"Says who?"

"Says I. Dig them all up. Now!" I pointed at the impressive pet cemetery that had been plotted in the corner of the garden.

She cupped the earth in her hands until all eleven goldfish in their various stages of decomposition were revealed. I made her take the twelfth fish out of my palm and place him with his kin. I hadn't done it since I walked the docks, and I was unsure I could do it still, but I stared at the corpses until I heard the toll in my ears and my vision blurred. One by one, they began to flap until the shallow grave became an earthen sea of hopping fish. Her latest victim moved towards Asenath, each hiccough like an accusation to the child. When its tail-fin brushed her foot, she ran screaming into the house.

I found her in the library, huddled under the globe, sucking her dirty, grave-digging thumb.

"Did you learn your lesson, then?" I asked sweetly and gestured for her to come out of hiding.

"Why didn't you do that for Mother?" she muttered.

We had all been instructed not to tell Asenath the truth. That Mother had died was a white Christian lie like the Easter Bunny and Santa Claus, except this truth was painful. She hopped into my arms and began to cry, repeating over and over, "You could do that for Mother! You could! You could! Why don't you?" At some point, she would have to know and I committed my first of many small defiances against Master Ephraim.

"Because Mother isn't dead." Her sobbing stopped. She wiped her snotty nose and considered me.

"What do you mean?"

"She went to sea. Now she'll never die."

"Can we go see her?"

"No, I am afraid not. But she is in a better place, I am sure."

She thought on this for a while.

"Will you go to sea?" she sniffed.

"Hopefully."

"Will I?"

"I don't know. We aren't as pure blood as she. I more than you. We'll just have to wait and see."

"I think I would like it. The sea, I mean."

III.

After that, Asenath channeled her energy into learning, devouring any story I could tell her about our heritage and about the mysterious histories in the neighboring towns. We had made a great discovery in the library: a locked trunk full of esoteric lore that Asenath picked with a bobby pin and insisted I pursue with her. At the bottom, wrapped in one of Mother's black silk scarves, was a yellowed and worn copy of the *Necronomicon,* in which we found much missing information about the Old Ones and what it was exactly Master Ephraim sought in our race—the subtle art of transformation and transference of the life-glow. This was how I was able to resurrect the fish and we learned it was only the beginning of a great trick, which we immediately practiced all afternoon until Mrs. Gilman rang the dinner bell.

Before we went our separate ways—I to the kitchen to serve and she to be served—I held Asenath back. Every night, he quizzed her on the day's lesson and I knew he would not approve of our new curriculum.

"I don't think you should tell your father about this lesson."

"Why not? It is very clever. He should be proud!"

"No. I think he'll be mad we broke into the trunk. Promise me you won't tell."

"I promise."

When Master Ephraim began his usual interrogation, Asenath ignored him, stabbing at the *lapin à la cocotte* and chasing carrots around her plate. I was in attendance by the sideboard.

"Child, did you hear me?" She nodded.

"'*Fhalma*—" He clicked his teeth. "Er, Eunice taught me about . . ." Dread rumbled in my stomach.

"History."

"History, eh?"

"Em-hmm. The Arkham Sisters."

"I've heard of no such sisters. Witches, I bet." He chewed over this a bit while I refilled his glass with wine. "When did these sisters live? During the Trials?"

"Very recently." She paused and then smirked at me. "Mistresses of transference. People say they've lived for centuries swapping bodies! And people don't speak of it because they are *Deep Ones*." He gestured at me with his forked potato.

"What have I told you about teaching her that drivel? If I wanted her to know about nonsense such as that, I'd throw her into the sea with her mother. See if she'd swim."

This was the first time Master Ephraim had ever spoken the truth about Mother in front of Asenath.

She dropped her utensils and pushed her plate away, muttering under her breath, "It's not nonsense. Eunice and I can perform that which you've only dreamed of performing."

His crooked shark teeth jutted over his lips as he smiled.

"You and . . . that thing there . . . are talented, I admit. But you are weak, not only by your sex, but from your relations." He glared at me. "You are both incapable of ruling over the material world. I expect you to resume the curriculum I designed, Eunice, or I will throw you to the sea, as well."

"Yes, Master Ephraim. I am sorry."

"Excused." I curtseyed and turned to retreat into the kitchen.

"*Fhalma!*"

I looked over my shoulder at Asenath. She widened her eyes and locked me in her gaze. When I blinked, I saw myself standing stiffly against the sideboard. I dropped the gaze with myself and looked down to see Asenath's navy blue cotton dress. I looked up at Master. He looked between me in Asenath's body and Asenath in my body. He narrowed his eyes and considered my body and asked incredulously, "Eunice?"

I answered, but my words rang in Asenath's soprano.

He rolled his eyes to Asenath's body. "*You* are Eunice?" The head I looked out from nodded. "And Asenath is there?" Her giggle trickled out of my smile.

"How is this possible?"

"Silly man," Asenath cackled from my body. "It isn't always a secret, you know; sometimes, it is simply legacy. You knew this when you chose our mother. You knew being merely human wasn't enough. Without us, you are nothing."

"The trunk. You jimmied the trunk! Ungrateful demons, have you no respect!"

He stood up so quickly his chair tumbled under him and in one fell swoop he crossed across the dining room table and struck my body so hard that it knocked Asenath's body out, too, and we both awoke in our own minds and swollen skulls.

He ordered us separated. He would undertake Asenath's education, while I was exiled to the attic, only allowed to leave at night.

IV.

I became a living ghost. I would sleep during the day and live during the night. Sometimes, when I awoke, I'd find a smuggled text from the library *sans* a remorseful message from Asenath. I would strain my eyes reading faded texts about the witches of Arkham, or debates over Mother Hydra's fecundity. When I grew weary of study, I would venture out of the house to go to the Harbor and night-fish.

The waters at Innsmouth are famous for their plentitude, but my expeditions were never very successful. Perhaps there was a certain vibration in my line, a contamination in my lure, that foretold nothing but ill-will would come to whoever was greedy enough to take a bite. Or, perhaps it was because I was impatient and couldn't cast the line far enough, or let it sink deep enough, before it seemed like aeons had passed and I reeled it in. Even so, it was peaceful. My mind could wander while I watched the Devil Reef appear and recede with the tide. Lore had it that fish-people moonbathed on its shores. Sometimes, I would fantasize that I would see Mother there. But all that was a long time ago. The reef was abandoned—perhaps they knew it would be destroyed.

My mind would wonder about the household and what was transpiring while I slept during the day, or remember my mother's transformation during her illness and how, in her sobbing, there was something of a song that I wondered whether I would sing one day, and how she always spoke of taking to the water.

My existence was thus for several years. Then, one April evening, a great struggling awoke me. There was screaming, which at first sounded as if it emitted from Asenath, but, like a dying operatic singer trilling her last scale, it went from soprano to alto to baritone to silence followed by Master's heavy footfalls up the stairs. When the door unlocked, my mother's light frame stood in the doorway. After rubbing my eyes, I realized it was Asenath, now fifteen and completely grown during my years of confinement. I wondered if my body appeared as changed; she was unconcerned with re-acquaintance.

"Eunice," she said. "You can come down now. I got rid of him!" And there was an ironic look that took after her father so much it was unbearable.

"We're rid of his tired, old body. Help me bring it back up here." She eyed me closely to see if there was any trace of euphoria rising within me.

"Well, don't look so glum. Your kind aren't that sentimental." She walked back down the stairs, iron step following iron step, whistling Mother's song. It was mockery! All mockery! This was not the Asenath I'd known. Adolescence and Ephraim's supervision had made her bigoted and cruel.

I followed her down the stairs and into the library. It was in shambles. Books were splayed open on the floor, their ancient spines cracked down the middle. The globe had somehow become dislodged from its axis and had rolled, dented, into the corner. Chairs were upturned and on the long, oak table lay Old Ephraim's crumpled body. Asenath stood before him, her hands on her hips.

"Such a sad sack he was."

"Are you sure he's dead?"

"Not really. I hit him over the head with the globe, so he may just be world-weary." She chuckled now, instead of the trickling cackle she had as a child. "But it's nothing a little arsenic can't fix. Why don't you see to that? I have to get my things together. Next week, I am to start school at Kingsport. Father left it in his will that I am to be the ward of Hall School."

"What about me? The Gilmans?"

"You'll stay here. Keep the house running. Make sure that thing stays dead, for one. This isn't one of your goldfish." She gave me a wink and nodded at the body. "And make an inventory of the library. It appears we've had a little thief purloin some important tomes I will need in Arkham." She leered at me. "I am on the cusp of a great discovery, Eunice. The greatest discovery of my entire life." Speechless, I stared at the body.

"You will see to it, then?"

I looked at Asenath transformed—a young woman with murder on her hands and mayhem in her heart. She had become her father's daughter. Or, more like, just her father.

"Well?"

"Yes, Mistress."

"Mistress. Good, we understand one another," Asenath outstretched her arms and yawned. "Oh, me! I am due for a nap."

After dragging Master Ephraim's body up the stairs and back into the attic, I laid it on my bed and assessed the damage. There was a huge lump on the back of his skull and a few superficial scratches on his face, but there was a faint sieve of breath. I'd seen worse with Mother. I retrieved some smelling salts from the kitchen and waved them under Master's nose. No response. He was catatonic. I sighed and went fishing.

That night, my line seemed magical. At first, I caught several puny smelt. I decided to cut them up with my knife and use them as bait. By dawn, I had thrown back bluefish and perch until I caught a black gill. In the soft, rosy light, I could see its stripes were a *pointillisme* of the periwinkle center of each scale. Rather than throw it back like I'd done its brethren, or bash its head against the dock's edge immediately, I held it up and stared into its flat eyes that flickered with every drowning gulp of air. I could see my body looking back, my harsh, flat face with protruding eyes that now seemed dim and stupid, gulping and hiccoughing and losing its grip. All I sensed was sexlessness, yet a drive to spawn and swim. When I hit against the dock, I was instantly back within myself watching the thrashing fish. That was when Asenath knocked on my skull and I realized what the struggle had really been about.

I strained to block her. While I didn't think she wished me harm, she was that maniac's daughter. In my blood was magic; in her blood was madness. What would she do with my body once she occupied it?

But if I am to survive, she tapped into my skull, *I need a thriving body.*

I muted her with more concentration, but her will had grown stronger over the years.

It's like drowning on air, 'Fhalma. I want to go to sea! Help me, 'Fhalma! Help me go to sea! Help—.

The black gill's flapping replaced Asenath's communications. Inspired, I scooped it into my basket and ran up Washington Street.

V.

Then what happened? Why, it's obvious, isn't it, Officer Shea? My sister is a fish. I trapped her in my body long enough to trap her into the black gill and keep my glow. She swims somewhere deep in Innsmouth Harbor, perhaps around the devastated remnants of Devil Reef. If I am truly romantic, I'd like to think she swims with our mother. For a while, I entertained I could evict Ephraim from her body and return her glow to its rightful place, but on the night that I saw Mr. Derby dragging Asenath's body down into the cellar, I lost hope for that dream. But I was able to bring her body justice against Ephraim, although at Master Derby's sacrifice. The despicable and horrid form that justice took only Mr. Upton can attest, but in Master Ephraim's failure lies the only small success I could aspire to. When a bit of evil is smote from this earth, we're all avenged. At least, the forgotten people.

How do you know I am not Ephraim? You don't, but rest-assured, I have no interest in traveling body to body to body. Perhaps I could glow inside a banker, or a pretty schoolteacher, or even Mr. Upton and build beautiful things, if I were a mind. No. I am content in this body, and I welcome its change and its birthright—for whatever happens to my body, it is happening to me. It's my story.

"Elder Thing" by C.L. Lewis

MAGNA MATER

ARINN DEMBO

IT IS AN ingrained habit of the human species to spin tales about the origin of the universe and to exaggerate the importance of their own place in it. One can collect the evidence of this essential narcissism the world over and find it in any set of cultural folk tales, but in no culture has the practice of self-worship been honed to such perfection as among those of European descent. Europeans call the worship of their own species "Humanism," and have been building great temples dedicated to this peculiar cult and its idolatry for many centuries. Of these, there is none still standing which is greater or more revered than the one that stands on Great Russell Street in the heart of London. They call it "the British Museum."

I walked up to the collection of marble galleries on the afternoon of September 30th, dressed in long skirts and a gray trench coat. I kept my shoulders hunched, my head covered by a gauze snood; the day was too dry and warm, too sunny to use the usual black umbrella to shield my face. After I mounted the front steps and passed through the doors beyond the Ionic columns, a guard stepped up to me.

"Excuse me, Miss." He was moving to block my path. "But you'll have to check that case."

I looked up to catch his gaze and his eyes widened, pupils immediately dilating. He stepped aside for me, getting out of my path—an almost unconscious gesture of deference. Blood flushed his cheeks and his thick neck. For a moment, I saw myself reflected in the mirror of his corneas, seeing what he must see: a woman of his own race, young and fertile, with pale hair and piercing eyes.

The long raincoat with its deep pockets, the leather suitcase I carried in one hand—these were the things that had concerned him moments ago. If he was later questioned by the authorities, he might remember having seen them, but it was likely he would not. He would only remember that I was beautiful. Selective blindness and amnesia—most convenient for this sort of work.

I walked away quickly, releasing him from my gaze, toward the north wing. I was stopped three times on the way to the Library of the Royal Anthropological Institute, twice by guards and once by a well-meaning clerk. I sent them all stumbling away from me confused and blushing, not certain who I was but convinced that I was not subject to their authority, and continued through the echoing halls unmolested.

I had been following my prey for some time, studying his patterns and waiting for the moment to strike. Today was the perfect opportunity. I spotted him immediately as I entered the large reading room, a portly older man in a tweed suit, his head bowed over a recent journal while a stack of similar journals waited on the table at his right elbow. He sat in his favorite leather chair, a lock of long, fine, white hair swept boyishly over the bulging dome of his forehead, a pair of glasses in his hand. The tip of one black plastic earpiece was tucked into the corner of his mouth like a pipe, as he sat idly reading and chewing.

I crossed the room casually, stopping here and there to admire the stacks. There were over two hundred thousand volumes in this collection. Part of me yearned to turn aside and satisfy my own curiosity. I hesitated more than once, thinking of the rare books in the Christy collection and how easily I could spend this day hunting among them. How long would it take to find evidence of my people among those volumes, all written by the first European explorers of Africa, Asia, Oceania? How difficult would it be to pass the guards with one or two of those priceless volumes in my empty case? At minimum, there might be a surviving copy of

Observations on the Several Parts of Africa hidden away somewhere behind glass.

When I was close enough, I took the chair beside the old man. Oblivious, he continued his reading until I spoke.

"Excuse me, sir." He raised his head raised sharply, like a gazelle startled at the watering hole. "But aren't you Louis Beatty?"

He turned toward me, already pleased: There was no sweeter sound than his own name spoken by a young female admirer. He had not yet put his glasses back on and it was obvious he could not see me clearly. I waited for his pupils to dilate, opening for me like black flowers blooming for an invisible sun . . . but he only squinted at me with a grandfatherly smile.

"Yes! Indeed. Guilty as charged, Miss." His voice was bluff, jovial—a voice for funding committees and university deans. "And you are—?"

I sat for a moment, vexed and fumbling for words. Robbed of my powers, I would have to improvise. "A student of your work," I said at last. "I enjoyed your lecture on the Olduvai finds last year."

"Ah, excellent." I could see him begin to dismiss me, his attention already slipping back toward the journal in his hand. His thumb still held his place. "So glad you enjoyed it, dear."

"I was quite interested in your theories," I said quickly. "Particularly the notion of separate pre-Human species in Africa." I cleared my throat nervously. "I am very interested in primatology. Humans are just another primate, after all."

It was a gamble. The old man had invested a great deal of energy in his female protégées over the past decade, sending one brave, determined young woman after another out into the wilds. He had already dispatched three of them over the last decade to study other living apes, two to Africa and one to Borneo.

"You are referring to my arguments regarding *Zinjanthropus bosei* and the other australopithecines of that period?"

Victory! I had earned a second look. The old man shifted toward me in his chair. It was a thoughtless reflex to lift his glasses and put them back on.

He looked into my eyes, blue as the skies above Leng, and then he was mine.

"I was actually referring to your suggested re-classification for *Pan jermynus*." I dropped my voice, pitching it to a conspiratorial murmur. "I've read your memorandum in favor of *Homo jermynus*. I quite approve."

His pupils had expanded like pools of black ink. "But it was secret." It was a weak protest, his voice boyishly high. "That report was only for the Secretary of the Archive . . . "

"Secrets are hard to keep, Doctor Beatty." I bared my teeth in a triumphant smile. "I'd like to go to the examination room, please." I put my hand, still covered in a gray calfskin glove, on his arm. "I need to see her. Now."

�֎

Within twenty minutes, Doctor Beatty and I stood in a brightly-lit basement room in the bowels of the Museum. In the center of the room, there were two dissection tables, one empty and the other with a hinged lid. The lid was closed, and held shut with a chain and a padlock.

"Unlock it," I told him and pushed him, stumbling, ahead of me. I quickly turned and locked the door behind us, uncertain of who might otherwise come into the room. We had passed through several secured doors to reach this lab. Between Doctor Beatty's identification and my own powers of persuasion, it was not terribly difficult. Nonetheless, I had been increasingly nervous as we walked along, forcing him to stop frequently to exchange lingering looks with me in the hall, as if we were young lovers.

By the time we reached the laboratory, my victim was flagging badly, his face gone from the rosy flush of pleasant arousal to a dark red flush of hypnotic ecstasy. His hands trembled and a light sweat had broken out over his face. He would go into shock soon, perhaps even die.

It took him nearly a full minute to fumble the key into the padlock and release the chain. By the time he was finished, I had begun to feel pity for him.

I walked up beside him, feeling an impulse of kindness. "Give me your handkerchief."

He pulled the cotton square from his jacket pocket and gave it to me. I turned him toward me like a child, and gently dabbed his brow and cheeks. "I want you to sit down now, Louis." I put a gloved hand to his cheek and sharpened my voice to issue a command. "You will sit down, close your eyes, and breathe deeply. Do you understand?"

He had already closed his eyes, turning his head to receive my caress like an affectionate pet. "Yes, Miss. I understand."

I accompanied him to the desk in the corner of the room and settled him into the chair. He allowed me to fold his arms on the desk and lay his head across them like a tired schoolboy who has finished his exam. "So beautiful," he murmured to himself quietly. "So beautiful."

I turned away from him. The steel lid of the dissection table shone under the lights. Even from here, I could smell the funeral spices of her body: cassia and cinnamon, natron and myrrh.

I crossed the room and reached for both the handles, blinking back tears, and opened the double lid.

She lay on her left side, chin to her chest, knees bent in a fetal crouch. Her body had been desecrated, of course, for the sake of "Science." The linen bandages were already cut away from her withered face, her right arm, and her right foot. In a specimen box, they had gathered her jewelry, and the amulets incorporated into her wrappings, to ward her in the Lands of the Dead.

Her arms were longer, her legs shorter, than those of a Human. Her hand was delicate, the thumb nearly the same length as the fingers. The robust bones of her face were beautiful and fierce: her powerful jaw, her withered lips pulled back over perfect ivory tusks. Her mane was well-preserved, still golden-blonde over her head, shoulders and neck. Normally, her eyes would have been closed with beeswax, but her Human consort

149

had replaced the long-withered flesh orbs with two polished spheres of blue topaz.

I put my suitcase on the empty table beside her and opened it.

"Wait," the old man said softly. He had risen from his bent position, but could not yet summon the will to rise to his feet. "What are you doing, Miss?"

"I am taking her." I moved briskly, removing a white sheet from the case. I draped it over the mummy and quickly tucked her into the sheet. My strength was more than equal to the task: Centuries after her mummification, her remaining flesh and bones were light and crisp as autumn leaves. I winced as the old wrappings crumbled and flaked away at my touch . . . but there was no time for delicacy.

"You . . . you're taking the Ape Princess?"

I whirled to face him. All of the anxiety I had been holding within me suddenly seemed to burst into rage and grief.

"She is not an APE!" I shrieked the words at him. He cringed away from me, whimpering submission, but I had lost control. I crossed the room again in a single inhuman bound, landing on the desk before him in a half-crouch.

"How DARE you call her an APE!" I lashed out with a fist, smashing a deep dent into the heavy metal file cabinet beside him. He urinated help-lessly in the face of my fury, rank yellow liquid trickling into his shoes and pattering onto the lab floor.

The old man was making little feeble warding gestures of supplication. I caught his wrists in an angry grip and roared wordlessly into his face, the belling cry of a queen's dominance.

"How DARE you touch her!?" I let him go and my fist thudded into the file cabinet again, driving the dent deeper. "How DARE you violate her tomb!?"

"It wasn't me!" he wailed. His crossed his arms over his face protectively. "They only asked me to examine her! Please!" He burst into sobs. "I never meant any harm!"

A male of my own species would have responded with his own

aggression, forcing me to prove my worthiness by crushing him. The swift capitulation of a Human male was like a sedative drug—it quenched my rage instantly, leaving me hollow. Grief filled my chest like rainwater in a blackened crater.

I retreated slowly from the desk, stepping backward onto the floor, resuming my bipedal stance.

"No," I admitted. "It wasn't you. Not you, personally." I turned away from him. "It is the way of your people. You are all grave robbers and thieves. This place is a testament to that, if nothing else."

I bent and gathered up the body of my ancestress, folding her with reverence into the suitcase, and emptied the box of her ornaments onto her shroud—heavy rings, chains and bracelets of electrum, all marked with the hieroglyphic script of Leng.

"Your mistake was to stray outside your own species, Doctor Beatty. Violate the tombs of your own people, rob each other blind, steal each other's corpses and make puppets for all I care! But a woman of my race is no Truganini."

As I locked the case closed, he spoke again. "She isn't Human."

I turned again. He had collected himself, although the storm of terror had left him red and puffy. "I don't know why you're stealing her," he said hoarsely. "But you speak as if you're related to her, somehow." He swallowed, his eyes owlishly wide beneath his spectacles. "That isn't possible, Miss."

I pulled my lips back over my teeth. "She is my thrice-great grandmother. My people live longer lives than yours, Louis Beatty."

"She isn't Human." He spoke more firmly now. In this, if nothing else, he was confident. "Her limbs, her skull, her hands . . . she's a hominid, yes, not *Homo sapiens*."

"No," I agreed. "Our species split apart over three hundred thousand years ago, at the dawn of a great Cold Age. We are still close enough cousins to interbreed, but the results . . . are unpredictable."

He pushed the glasses further up his nose with a palsied hand. "Was she really . . . a surviving *Homo erectus*? In 1755?"

I huffed soft laughter at him, pursing my lips. "Has your own species not changed in the last three hundred thousand years? You can call us *Homo jermynus*, if you like. We do not care. Perhaps the name would comfort poor Arthur, in the Lands of the Dead. Things are always hard for mixed children."

He stubbornly insisted, even though he was still shaking like a leaf. "You cannot be related to her, Miss."

I moved toward him. "You think not? Why is that, Doctor Beatty?" I pulled the lips back over my teeth in a dangerous, aggressive leer. "Because you see a beautiful woman when you look at me?"

He looked up as I loomed over him. "Yes. You are the most beautiful woman I've ever seen."

"Your mind lies so that you can see the truth." I laughed at him again. "Yes, I am beautiful, Louis Beatty. The women of a superior race are always 'beautiful.' You want to mate with me and make strong children. Offspring who will inherit my superior genes and survive the winds of the Great Plateau."

His brow creased in confusion. "I don't understand."

"You will." I caressed his face with a gloved hand. "My people walk the Wastes that span the world, Louis Beatty. Our ancient gates let us venture forth into many lands; the Congo was only one. Wherever we step forth into the world of Man, we are worshipped as gods and take mates as we please. Our children pass on the traits for golden hair, for blue eyes, or stronger bones. Wherever you see those features, you are seeing our descendants among you."

I bent and kissed his tiny mouth in parting, then removed one glove to reveal the pale ivory flesh and golden fur beneath. I looked directly into his eyes and spoke a final command.

"You no longer have my permission to see what you wish to see, Louis Beatty. I command you to see me as I am."

He gave a strangled scream at the sight of my true face, eyes wide in shock, and threw himself away from me with such violence that both he and his chair toppled over onto the hard stone floor.

I left him lying on his side, clutching his chest, as I patiently pulled the gray leather glove back over my strange hand, re-arranged the shawl to cover my mane, and picked up my suitcase.

"Rest easy, Great Mother," I told her, speaking the language of the Plateau. "I am taking you home."

"Keziah and Brown Jenkin" by Karen Hollingsworth

CHOSEN

LYNDSEY HOLDER

"KEZIAH," I WHISPERED and my body vibrated with the thrill of saying her name in the space where she once lived, in the grounds that were still permeated with the thick miasma of her power.

I'd dreamed of her since I was small, though "dream" seems too insignificant a word to describe what we shared. She visited me at least one night a month, she and her strange familiar, always when I was asleep, but our time together wasn't disjointed and vague like the dreams I was used to having. I was scared of her, at first—what child wouldn't be? A haggard crone, and a rat with a monstrous face and menacing teeth, should have no place in the dreams of the innocent, yet here they were in mine.

I was afraid at first, but my fear dissipated quickly and I began to look forward to our visits with excitement. She told me all sorts of stories about gods and dark things and creatures that sounded more terrifying than any monsters I'd read about. I'd never heard of those creatures, or the places they came from, but I believed in them with all my heart.

Ancient, important-looking books covered every available surface of the room we met in and a ghostly, violet light whose source I was never able to determine cast an unearthly glow throughout the space. Everything looked wrong and weird in that light—I wondered, sometimes, if the books scattered around were innocuously pedestrian, and it was only the ethereal glow that made them seem as though they contained instructions for dark rituals. I could easily have looked over at one of the many that lay open and read from it, but doing so seemed as though it would be a horrible breach of etiquette for some reason I couldn't quite explain. I was terrified of upsetting Keziah—initially, because she was such a frightening figure, but later, because I worried that angering her might cause her to stop visiting me.

At first, I was distracted by the strange geometry of the space. I lived with my parents in a rectangular room inside a rectangular apartment inside a rectangular building full of rectangles. I had never seen the kinds of angles and curves and half-walls that outlined the space in which Keziah lived. I made up my mind that I would have a room like hers one day.

It must have made for a bizarre picture: a gnarled old woman in a shapeless brown robe with wispy grey hair; a rat-bodied creature with a distorted face, grizzled beard, and murderously sharp teeth perched on her shoulder; and a dark-haired and bright eyed girl in cheerful, pink pyjamas.

Often, I wondered if she was lonely. Was she spending time with me because she didn't have family, because she didn't have her own daughter to teach these things to? I think I always knew that she was dead, though at that age, I didn't really understand what death meant. I understand it even less now that I'm older.

I drew pictures of her and Brown Jenkin in school, as well as some of the creatures from her stories: the Black Man, Shub-Niggurath, Azathoth. What began as concerned looks grew to worried questions and culminated in a visit to a child psychiatrist. I was, he decided, a lonely child who wanted to feel special, so I had created a world for myself where I was the Chosen One. My parents needed to spend more time with me, he concluded. If they could make me feel important, I wouldn't need to make up stories.

I mulled over what my parents told me of his assessment in the car ride home. At first, I was angry. If I were going to dream up a fairy god-mother, I'd have made her plump and soft, and smelling of cookie dough and brown sugar and full of love and laughter. She'd tell me stories about knights and princesses and happy things. If there were an animal following her around, it would be an energetic puppy.

I hadn't thought of myself as a "chosen one" before he'd said so, but I realized afterwards that it was true. Every child reads stories about how one day, a normal boy or girl finds out that they are different than every other child in the world in the best way possible and every child waits for the day when they, too, find their golden ticket. Most of them are disappointed. Not me. Keziah's presence in my life proved how very important I was. I had a big, amazing story ahead of me.

I stopped drawing pictures of Keziah's stories at school. I realized that it was bothering people because they didn't understand, because I was special and they weren't. I listened to her tales with rapt attention, writing down in a notebook I kept by my bed whatever I could remember upon waking, and reading and re-reading them as I fell asleep at night.

The frequency of her visits decreased dramatically as I grew older. In the ever-growing spaces between our visits, I would spend lonely days seething in silent fury, imagining all of the angry things I would say to her, everything how-could-you and how-dare-you, until my emotions boiled over and I collapsed on my bed, a sobbing, sniffling mess.

I need you, Keziah, I would whisper before sleep claimed me on those nights, as though I could summon her through my desperation. *I need you now more than ever. I want to be your chosen one. I want to be special.*

Every night that Keziah failed to visit me led to another day where I was just another girl. I was an awkward teenager no different from all of the other awkward teenagers. How could she expect me to live like this? Our secret times were everything that made me important. Without them, I was doomed to be another weak and crawling thing like every other human being on this planet: impotent and voiceless, mindlessly shuffling towards my own death, unaware of my own tremendous insignificance. It was worse for me, though, as my eyes had been opened to the possibility of what could be, whereas the other unchosen were comfortable in their beds at night, believing that their pitiful existence was how things were supposed to be.

The instant I saw Keziah, however, my rage was forgotten. I had so much to learn and such little time with her that spending any of it on being angry seemed a terrible waste. Anyway, she wasn't part of this world in the way I was—maybe time was different for her. Maybe what were weeks for me were hours for her.

On the night after my seventeenth birthday, Keziah came to me for the last time. I knew it was the last time even before she said anything. Brown Jenkin was agitated, running circles around me, climbing up my back and crawling down into my lap, staring at me with his beady black eyes. I reached out to him tentatively and he nuzzled my hand, stirring a strange kind of love in my heart.

There were no stories that night. Instead, Keziah instructed me on how to get to the Witch House, the building in Arkham where she'd once lived. The original building was gone, she said, but something else was there now, though she wasn't certain what. The building had changed ownership more than a few times since she'd left this world and it was difficult for her to keep track of our timeline. I'd need to get into the attic there, she said. I'd need to bring someone with me—a child, preferably no more than three years of age—to use in the ritual.

I never thought I'd miss Brown Jenkin's hideous form, but I cried when I woke up and the warmth of his small body was absent. Arkham was a fair distance from my home in Vancouver. I'd need a passport and money for traveling. These weren't things I could acquire quickly.

The next four years were easier than the months I'd spent waiting for Keziah to visit me. I had a mission, a purpose, and I was moving towards it as fast as I could go. I found a job, and saved up as much money as I could. Keziah's Witch House had become The Witch House Brewery and Pub, who, as luck would have it, were looking for a new server.

It wasn't hard to get access to the attic after closing time. I thought it would take them longer to trust me to be there alone, but on my third shift, I was given the keys and asked to close up.

I had a difficult time maintaining my composure until everyone else had left. Once the pub was empty, I ran up the stairs to the attic and squeezed myself in amongst the boxes of supplies. I closed my eyes and called to her.

Brown Jenkin came to me first. Tiny claws pierced my shirt, scraping flesh underneath, as he scaled my back and settled on my shoulder, chattering gleefully.

"Where is the child?" Keziah's raspy voice came from behind me.

I turned around and opened my eyes. Brown Jenkin jumped down from my shoulder and returned to his mistress.

"Can't," I breathed, "can't it just be me?"

Keziah arched a thin eyebrow. "You realize what it is you are offering."

It wasn't a question. Her eyes, sharp like a crow's, stared into me, through and through. I closed mine, terrified that she would find me unsatisfactory and I would see it written in her face. This way, she could just disappear back into the shadows if she didn't want me, an easier letdown.

"Please," I whispered in a voice that was barely audible even to my own ears.

"Come with me, then."

She walked into the darkness of a corner that should have been solid, and then through it. I followed, but carefully, unsure of how to proceed. As strange as visits from a haggard crone and her monstrous familiar had been, I had gotten used to it. Walking through walls, though, wasn't something I had ever done—or even considered possible—before now. I couldn't let on, though. Keziah had put her trust in me, I realized, and I needed to act like the kind of person who deserved such a precious thing.

Keziah led me down a spiral staircase that seemed to be floating. No handrails, no walls, just infinite blackness and stone steps that hung in the air. I was scared of falling off, but I was more scared Keziah would change her mind if I protested, turning me back out to live the rest of my days in the world of dullards, so I feigned bravery and followed her down.

The stairs ended at a small space that was lit with the same violet glow I had seen in Keziah's room. There were no walls: The edges of the room were marked by the same empty abyss that bordered the stairs, A stone table sat in the middle of the floor.

I knew my role as if I'd done it a thousand times before. Perhaps that's part of being the Chosen One. I climbed up onto the table and lay down upon it. Brown Jenkin scurried up after me, holding a metal bowl with strange inscriptions on it. He brushed his rough cheek against mine then hurried off.

As Brown Jenkin began a strange, tittering chant, I felt my body relax into the hard, stone surface of the table. This was my fate. This was my gift.

Keziah produced a long, wickedly sharp knife from within her robes. It gleamed in the soft light.

I had never known it was possible to be so happy. I was being carried off by a tidal wave of ecstasy. A smile blossomed on my face and I shone like a beacon, radiating joy throughout the tiny room. This was what I was made for. I wasn't one of the sheep, one of the stupid cows. I was different. I was chosen.

Keziah raised her arm, aiming the knife at my heart.

"Thank you," I said. "Thank you for choosing me."

BITTER PERFUME

LAURA BLACKWELL

I KISSED MY great-grandmother on the top of her dusty black wig and asked what she would like for her birthday. I had already sewn her a jewelry roll and mixed her a new skin-softening oil — the best I could afford to do since I had lost my job — but you don't turn a hundred and twenty-five every day.

Abuelita turned her milky eyes to me and lifted a trembling, withered hand from her rosary to beckon me closer. "*Quiero morir,*" she whispered in my ear. *I want to die.*

I shivered, not from the cold of the windowless room, but from recognition. "*Yo también,*" I told her in a voice just loud enough for her to hear. "*Espera, por favor. Espera.*"

Me, too. Please wait.

Grandpa Estéban eyed us suspiciously from his recliner. "What are you talking about, Melissa?"

I straightened up and forced a smile, raising my voice a bit more to carry over the hum of the compressors. "I promised her some birthday cake. Would you like some? It'll be good. Sara made it."

He grunted. Sara's spice cake was a rare treat and he wasn't too far gone to know it. "Just a spoonful of frosting."

"Can do." I stopped at the controls in the hall on my way out and added some oxygen to their sitting room. The hall door closed behind me, its rubber seals gasping as it shut.

In the kitchen, my grown daughter and my elderly uncle were finishing up their boring-but-healthy dinner of vegetables and rice. No meat, hardly any fat, no sugar. Sara said it would extend our lives; I didn't see the point of life without flavor.

"Time for cake and presents," I said, unzipping my coat. It was cool in here, but not outright cold, and the sight of the long prairie sunset through the window made me feel toasty. "Might as well leave the dishes. There'll be more soon."

"Okay," said Sara, rising from her place to spoon leftovers into an old yogurt container. "How many plates?"

"Five plates, three forks, and two spoons."

"They're both eating the cake? I'm flattered."

"Just the frosting. You might want to sprinkle a little extra cloves on it so they can smell it."

"You bet."

They started putting on their coats and gloves. I nabbed the jewelry bag from my room, but I left the skin oil. I would mix her a fresh batch and change up the ingredients a little.

While Sara pulled the cake out from the fridge, Tío Gaspar picked up the small pile of presents. We didn't usually make a big deal out of birthdays, especially Abuelita's and Grandpa Estéban's, since they'd had so many. We certainly never invited anyone from outside the family, since we were the only ones who knew Abuelita was still alive.

If that was what she really was.

"I guess we should leave the candles off," said Sara.

She meant because of the heat. I didn't mind, seeing as Abuelita had already made her wish.

※

Grandpa Estéban and Tío Gaspar always had the Herrero name. I took it back after my ex left and changed Sara's along with mine. She was just little, then. Everybody in North Dakota called us "the Herreros," pronouncing the H like a harsh gust of wind.

Sometimes, they called us "the Mexican family," although none of us has ever even been to Mexico. Abuelita was from Barcelona originally, but the rest of us were born in the U.S.

We liked North Dakota okay, though. The air was clean, the food hearty, and people kept pretty much to themselves.

I was born in Omaha, which I remember not so much as a place as the time Abuelita could still get around. I should have called her Bisabuelita—she was Grandpa Estéban's mother—but she preferred to have everyone but her son call her Abuelita. I was seven when the white old-lady hairs on her chin fell out and never grew back.

After that, we moved to St. Paul, where Grandpa Estéban did refrigerator installation and maintenance for restaurants. It was where I met and married my ex, where Sara was born. My parents both died in a car accident there; Tío Gaspar came home and cried after identifying them. My soft Tía Rosa, who wore loose clothing and sloshed when she walked, was buried there, too. Sara remembers them all, but barely. My brother still lives there, doing radio voiceovers and murder mystery dinner theatre.

Grandpa Estéban was born in New York City, but out of respect for Abuelita, he never talked about it.

❈

I ate Abuelita's birthday cake for breakfast every day until it was gone. Then I stopped eating desserts after dinner, gave up snacks altogether.

"You're eating so much better," said Sara approvingly.

That was what I got for sending her to medical school. Even though she's an anesthesiologist, she still knows more about nutrition than Man was meant to know.

I made Abuelita a new batch of skin oil. I mixed in the powdered remains of the green paint we'd found under the wallpaper of this farm-house when we moved in. Abuelita liked the house; there was a chance that it was older than she was. She didn't have that experience often in the Midwest.

Although the arsenic and the lead shouldn't have much scent, I added a few drops of myrrh oil. It made it smell smoky and thick.

In our family, we know a lot of things that people aren't supposed to know.

✸

When Sara started kindergarten, I got a good job at the regional hospital. Doctors dictated; I transcribed. There wasn't enough of anything in particular to specialize, so I heard a bit of everything. Most of it went in one ear and out the other, but sometimes, I slowed down a little so I could listen.

My turnaround on toxicology reports was never as good as on other things. Autopsies, either.

✸

"*Me siento extraña,*" complained Abuelita as I rubbed the oil into her skin with my gloved hands. "*Y huelo mal.*"

I fished around for the words to ask, "Is the bad feeling tingly? Are you losing sensation?" But my Spanish isn't all that good, so I just said, "*Es el regalo, abuelita. Lo que pidió.*" *The gift you asked for.*

"Ah." Her blind eyes lit up. "*Muerte.*"

166

�֎

It was during our first winter in North Dakota that things started to go wrong for the Herreros.

Grandpa Estéban was excited about the cold. No urban heat island, no tall buildings to break the fierce prairie winds. Dirty, gray snowdrifts buried the shelter-belt trees up to their lowest branches.

He knew we'd get frostbite if we stayed out in the snow unprotected. But what if Abuelita stayed out on the back porch of this farmhouse? Someone had put up screens against mosquitos at some point. They would hold out most of the snow.

"Think of how it could slow the deterioration," he said, eyes wide as a child's.

"I don't like it," I told him. "Abuelita won't, either."

But Sara was too little to know what was going on and Tío Gaspar never said a word against Grandpa Estéban. Grandpa and Abuelita sat out there one night, over her bitter complaints.

When they tried to come in the next morning, Abuelita's left leg, frozen and brittle, broke clean through. Grandpa Estéban developed a cough that didn't go away until there was nothing left in his lungs.

The next time he shaved, his whiskers didn't grow back.

✖

The month before Abuelita's birthday, one of the two HR reps caught me on the way back from lunch. The door of the office next to hers was closed, so I knew what was coming when she sat me down.

"I'm sorry to tell you that your position has been eliminated," she said. "The doctors are going to start using dictation software, instead." She pushed a folder across the desk to me. "You're not being singled out."

The folder included a list of positions and ages of the newly unemployed. There were no names on it, but a glance showed that it was the whole department. The hit list went from the recent college grad up to my manager and me, the only ones in our fifties.

"I know you'll do well, Melissa. You have great skills. Excellent skills. And this is an excellent severance package."

I read the whole folder's worth right there at her desk, taking my time. Somebody told me once that I "wintered well," and although they might have meant "plump," I liked to think it meant I could wait anything out. The HR rep sat there with an expectant, apologetic smile.

The severance was better-than-decent. I signed the papers and walked out of her office without saying another word.

My manager, Debbie, was leaving the other HR office. "I guess they took us in order of seniority," she said. "At least they didn't make me lay anybody off." She laughed mirthlessly. "I'd feel like a murderer."

"Oh, I don't know," I said, walking toward anesthesiology in no kind of hurry. "I don't think you would."

Sometimes, Grandpa Estéban talked about moving further west.

"It's getting too settled here," he said one Sunday. All of us had gathered in the so-called living room, the living standing in our coats and the dead sitting down, to listen to Mass on Internet radio. "I keep reading that the state's population is climbing."

"That's out west," Gaspar told him. "It's the crude. There's no fracking here and we'd have to drive through all that activity to get anywhere quieter."

"Nobody would care about us passing through. And who says we should go somewhere quiet? We can get lost in a city."

Sara perked up at that. She hadn't lived in a city since she went to medical school in St. Louis. "Portland, you mean? Or Seattle?"

"Maybe. The best place would be Alaska, but that's a hard journey."

He looked at Abuelita, hunched in her wheelchair. She was stroking the velvet and the lace on the jewelry roll I'd made her, although she kept it empty. She held it almost as often as her rosary, these days.

With Abuelita's broken leg that could never heal, it took two of us to even move her from bed to wheelchair and back. Alaska was out of the question.

✳

I took turns with Tío Gaspar in the garden that summer, stinking of mosquito repellent and raising the healthy vegetables I didn't much like. They soaked up the long summer sun and got big. Huge.

My hands grew callused and clumsy. My arms and legs grew strong. I ate the big vegetables, and the plain rice, and the boring barley soup. I shed the soft layers of myself.

I did not want another winter.

✳

One day in September, I went to town to pick up a shipment of our supplies. We have a little lab at home, and Sara's very handy, but you can't make everything from scratch. Luckily, you can get almost anything over the Internet.

I was standing in line at the post office when Debbie spotted me. "Melissa! Oh my gosh, I didn't recognize you!"

She was doing okay, she said, working in a doctor's office as an office manager. Bit of a pay cut, but when you added in the severance, not too bad a year.

"And you look great, Melissa! You lost so much weight! What are you doing?"

"Oh, you know. Lot of gardening," I said.

"You working?" She eyed the slip in my hand, maybe hoping the carrier couldn't drop off packages because I had a new job. Truth was, we just didn't answer the door.

"No, I'm on unemployment. Good until almost Thanksgiving, as long as I keep looking."

I did look, but there wasn't much for middle-aged women with excellent skills in medical transcription, skin care, and poisons.

Autumn was a brief, brown season. Years ago, when we still went to Mass in town on Sundays, we used to drive a special route in the fall. There were blocks and blocks lined with birch trees, their white trunks striped with black and their branches arcing pale-gold overhead. It was like driving through a cathedral. I was always sorry that Abuelita didn't get to see it.

Bronze birch borers took all the trees a while back. By then, we weren't going to Mass anymore, so it took us a few years to notice.

"Abuelita's not doing good," said Tío Gaspar to me over lunch one day of that last October.

Sara was at work, and Abuelita would be at her rosary. We could hear the compressors chugging along through one of the last warm lunchtimes in a season tinged with cold at the edges of the day. Grandpa Estéban would not come out into the unchilled part of the house in this heat.

"You mean the way she's slowing down?" I said cautiously.

"Uh-huh. It's been a long time coming and I think she's ready." He locked eyes with me. "You know, she never wanted to live the way we do. She thinks it's a sin."

After me, Abuelita spent more time with Tío Gaspar than anybody. And his Spanish was better. I nodded and spooned up some more potato soup.

"I think it'll be a relief for her. I'm more worried about Sara," he said.

"She's still young. She has better things to do with her life than take care of old people and living corpses."

"I don't plan to be a living corpse any time soon," I told him firmly.

Tío Gaspar gave me a sweet, almost chummy, smile. "Me, neither."

※

Once, years ago, I had gotten Grandpa Estéban to tell me about New York. Sara was thinking about medical school at Columbia and he wanted me to tell her she couldn't go.

"I can't talk her out of it if you don't tell me why you're asking."

"It's not a good place for us."

"You haven't lived there in must-be eighty years. Everybody who knew you and Abuelita will be dead."

"Eighty-five. And they won't remember me, but Mamá and I remember New York." His forehead furrowed. "You know my father died when I was young."

"Abuelita said you were eight years old. The flu, she said."

"They called it the *Spanish* Influenza. That made it even worse for a young widow and her son. There was no more school for me after that." Although he didn't need to breathe, Grandpa Estéban still sighed when he wanted to. He drew a breath then just to let it out.

"But Mamá was strong. She and I were the only ones in the family who survived. And she worked hard. We had an old house and she let rooms in it. Mostly to other Spaniards, who knew we hadn't brought the influenza. One was a doctor. Doctor Muñoz."

His usual raspy whisper dropped to a softer, more affectionate sound. "I brought him his meals and whatever he needed delivered . . . supplies, medicines, some of the same things we use today. He was kind to me, like a new father. But Mamá . . . " His mouth twisted in disgust. "Mamá said his work was unholy. After a while, she wouldn't let me visit him, anymore. No one ever took good care of him again. He passed too soon to learn one of the chants we sing to this day, one that might have prolonged his life.

"When Doctor Muñoz passed, I stole some of his notes. Some of his books. His work is the foundation of this family, of our life everlasting."

I worked my numb fingers inside my mittens. I had never heard this story before. "That still doesn't tell me why Sara shouldn't go to Columbia if she wants to."

"Your *bisabuelita* was fluent in English."

"What?"

"She had a heavy accent, but she was fluent. But the day Doctor Muñoz passed from our home, she stopped speaking it completely. The shock."

He gripped my hand in his, bone-cold even with a mitten between us. "She's the reason we'll never go back to New York. It would kill her."

I told Sara I would mail her application to Columbia, but I threw it in the trash, instead. I have since come to regret that, not just because of the betrayal, but because of the reason behind it.

✹

The unemployment payments on my ReliaCard ran dry in November and sure enough, I didn't have another job. I'll be fair: I was picky. I didn't want to work someplace chatty and I didn't want to work far from home. Abuelita was slurring her words and having trouble following conversations. She ran her fingers over the velvet of the jewelry roll until she dropped it from weak fingers.

It was hard to be sure, since she'd been blind and bald for years, but I think it was the lead in the paint that was doing the trick.

I added frankincense to Abuelita's skin oil to welcome the season and sweeten the scent. She rubbed it into her skin carefully, reverently. I helped apply it to her legs and feet, since she couldn't bend to reach them.

She still knew the touch of my hand, even through gloves. Abuelita and I were always close in a way that Grandpa Estéban and I never were. Whatever it was that made him want to live forever, we didn't have it.

"*Tu regalo*," she whispered. *Your gift.*

With unemployment over and years to go before I was eligible for retirement, it seemed like all I had to give anyone.

❋

I ran into Debbie at the post office again just after Thanksgiving. Always the over-achiever, she was mailing out Christmas packages. She turned as if she were going to say something, then closed her mouth and looked away. She couldn't tell me I looked great, because I didn't. I was gaunt and graying.

I didn't mind. It was a relief, one more connection severed from the world.

❋

Abuelita died on December 23rd. I tiptoed in to check on her in her tiny, cold room and took off a glove so I could hold her hand as she passed. She didn't breathe, and her hand was already cold, but it went slack—more limp than it did in sleep—and a foul smell crept in under the scent of frankincense and myrrh.

I was sorry she didn't get another Christmas Eve. Although she hadn't been to Mass in decades, she always listened to Midnight Mass on the radio. She loved the hymns.

"*Vaya con dios*," I whispered. For the first time in years, I dared to kiss her on the cheek. It was tissue-soft and very, very cold.

❋

Immediately after Abuelita's passing, I trudged through the blowing snow out to the old barn. We used it for storage, mostly, but it was also our garage for the RV and the truck. I started the truck in the dark and let it warm up, keeping an eye out for lights in the house. No one stirred.

Careful in the snow, I drove the truck further out into the country, out to the property of a self-described gentleman farmer who spent his winters in Phoenix. I ran the truck into a ditch. Then I made sure the windows were secure, turned up the heat, and peacefully breathed in the fumes as the snow gradually covered the windshield.

I woke to the smells of frankincense and myrrh and old woman.

Abuelita was gone and I was in her bed. The jewelry roll was sitting on the dresser, all rolled up as if it actually had jewelry in it. Sara was sitting in my old place, the chair beside the bed.

"Welcome back, Mom," she said. She looked exhausted. "You're just in time for the New Year."

I tried to speak, but it came out in a whisper. "What . . . "

"You really did a number on yourself." Sara gave me a sharp look through her tears. "Mom, couldn't you have told me? I could have mixed something for you. Something safer. They kept you in a locker at the morgue for a day. I was afraid they'd do an autopsy on you, just like on Tía Rosa, and you'd never be right again."

"Where's Abuelita?"

"She died. You knew that, didn't you? You wouldn't leave her." Tears spilled down Sara's face. "We took you home and said we'd bury you, and we buried her in the grave Gaspar made in the barn a while back. We're hoping nobody ever exhumes it, but if they do, maybe they'll think it's you."

"I wanted to die," I murmured. "Really die."

"I won't let you, Mom," said Sara. She took my hand. I felt the pressure, but not the warmth. "I'm an Herrero at heart and we always take care of our mothers."

✻

We loaded everything we needed into the RV and the truck over the next five days. They packed me into a chest freezer for the journey.

"Are you comfortable?" Tío Gaspar asked. "I could get you a blanket for padding. You're not giving off heat."

"I'm fine," I told him. "I don't really feel anything." It was just barely nightfall and the temperature was already dropping. I was outside after dark without a parka, without gloves, for the first time in months.

Tío Gaspar nodded. He looked back at the house, where Sara was fussing with the last things to pack. Grandpa Estéban was testing the vapor-absorption systems for the freezer and the RV. I could smell ammonia.

Gaspar leaned in. "I know why you did it," he whispered. "I would do it, too, if Papá died, or if he wanted to. But you know how he is."

Grandpa Estéban started singing to himself. His voice was cracked and tiny, but I could make out "We Three Kings of Orient Are."

"You have relatives in other places," I whispered back. "Omaha. St. Paul. Maybe even New York, for all I know. Or you could go somewhere new."

He shook his head. "I'm going to Portland with you. It's what Papá wants and where he goes, I go."

"Westward leading, still proceeding . . . " sang Grandpa Estéban.

"I don't have to agree," said Gaspar. "I'll always stay with my family, no matter what we are."

He closed the freezer lid gently. I heard some stumbling as he helped Grandpa Estéban in. The whole RV would be cold. Since Grandpa Estéban had never gotten a death certificate, he could have the run of the cabin.

"No matter what we are," I repeated in my forceless murmur.

"King and God and Sacrifice," sang Grandpa Estéban, barely audible through the freezer walls.

I heard the RV's motor start, smelled the ammonia anew. I buried my face in my hands. Without breathing, I took in the scents of frankincense and myrrh: the oils I had blended, the scent of our stone-cold tomb.

EIGHT SECONDS

PANDORA HOPE

EVER PLAYED A hand of poker with the Devil, knowing that if you could keep the game going for eight seconds, just eight seconds, you'd beat the bastard and then you'd get to be a god for a day?

That's how it is for me with rough riding.

Before she left me, Lula said that only a person with a sickness in the head would want to sit a thousand-kilo bucking bronco and stay on for eight seconds. She said a lot of other things, too, wound after wound, but I hung on, not saying a word. I'd learnt in the ring that you just had to hold on until you were beyond feeling the pain. Beyond feeling anything.

I remember Lula at the door of the motel room, screaming that I had no right to be a mother, that she knew I was going to get hurt every time I rode. The only question was, *How bad?* Maybe a bruised leg—maybe a broken neck. Lula saying she couldn't live like that anymore, that she wished I would just die out there, on the sand, and get it over with. I couldn't explain about the Devil, shuffling those cards. I couldn't explain that life was just a matter of hanging on, hanging on for those eight seconds when the world threw everything it had at you and you survived. Or not.

I always made a point of being honest with her, so in the end, I said, "Yeah, you're right, Lula. I never should have been a mother."

Lula was an accident in a motel room in Mount Isa where the toilet didn't work properly and the sheets had a thin layer of red dust on them. I had beat the Devil that day. The prize money was $650—even back then,

Mount Isa had the best-paying rodeo in Australia—and the event had never been won by a woman before. There was this pretty-boy tourist up from Melbourne, doing a backpacker jaunt through Outback Queensland. Well, when you beat the Devil, you get the crazies, like the whole world is chanting your name, so I took that pale-skinned kid to the motel and nine months later, Lula was born.

Lula took off when she was sixteen. It hurt more than I thought it would, but I always said people should lead the lives they want, no questions asked, and if Lula didn't want to stay with me, well, that was her business. She never wrote or rang and I never knew where she went. Laurie, who was a rodeo clown and likely my only friend, said I shouldn't have told her about not wanting to be a mother. He said that would break a kid. But I believe in telling it how it is and what does a clown know about kids, anyway? Except how to make them laugh.

So, now, I looked at the flimsy, photocopied leaflet I'd found shoved under my door and I said to Laurie, "Looks like Lula's found a new mother."

We were sitting on the barrier surrounding the Noonamah arena. I'd fallen badly that day. I was starting to wonder whether I was just getting too old for the game and that pretty soon, I'd be lying in the sand for the last time, just like Lula wanted. Laurie's clown makeup was streaked down his face so he looked like a painting that got itself rained on. He'd worked hard at the show, pulling the riders from under the broncos, bulls and steers.

He looked at the leaflet in my hand. It said, "Temple of the Great Mother," above a blurred photo of goats, grazing in an idyllic green pasture with the ruin of a castle in the background. No place like that in the Northern Territory, that's for sure, and probably not in the whole of Australia.

"What d'ya mean, new mother?" he said.

I showed him the penciled scrawl on the back on the leaflet. A single word written so rapidly you could barely make it out: "Mum."

"Shite," said Laurie. "Shite. Are you sure it's from her?"

I shrugged. "Who else? Found it slipped under my motel room door."

Laurie took a filthy rag out of his striped clown pants. Instead of wiping the grease-paint off his face, he just stared at it, creasing his face like he was thinking real hard.

"You know, Sam, there's that cult down by the canyon that go by that name. Been there for a long time. A lot of folks reckon they're Satanists or something like that. A couple of tourists hiking up that way disappeared, oh, just last year. These cult people come into town sometimes, handing out leaflets, trying to get people to join."

"Look like a pack of goat herders to me," I said. I hate it when people don't get to the point. It's a waste of time. Because I could tell by his nervy expression he was going to wander in circles like a sick dingo and waste more words, I said, "Okay. You reckon Lula's in some kind of trouble. Well, she's a big girl and if goats are her thing, that's her business."

Laurie shook his head like a sheep dog that couldn't understand why its bone had been taken away. He was soft and that was a bad thing to be in the Northern Territory, especially if you followed the rodeo circuit.

"That canyon—the aboriginals call it a Sick Place," he said. "It's not just the cult. There's some poison that comes out of the caves thereabouts. It was in the local paper. Radioactive gas or something. There's uranium there—enough for a thousand bombs, they reckon. You could get real sick, living out there. Stupid place to raise livestock. Stupid place for people, too."

"That cult is a pack of idiots, then," I said.

"Maybe they don't tell their followers about the danger, Sam. They're a weird mob. I've seen them hanging around after the show, talking to the tourists. They look, well . . . kinda unnatural. I'm guessing a lot of inbreeding goes on down there. Or maybe it's the radiation. They just don't look like normal folks."

I grunted. "So, instead of leaving the cult, Lula puts recruitment papers in my room. That makes a lot of sense."

"Maybe it's not the sort of cult that lets you leave," Laurie said and I knew he'd been waiting all along to say that.

"Maybe," I said. I hopped off the barricade. People have a right to live their lives like they want to, good or bad. I hate people who fence things in worse than the wild broncos hate them.

Laurie scrambled after me. "You can't just leave her there, Sam! What if she wants to go and they won't let her? You want your own daughter to get radiation poisoning, or maybe . . . hell, I don't know. Get sacrificed to the Devil or something . . . ?"

I couldn't help laughing at that. Laurie had been trying to get me off the circuit and playing happy families with Lula for years, but this one took the cake. I looked back at him. "Sacrificed to the Devil? That's the best one you've come up with, yet."

"So, what are you going to do, Sam? What are you going to do?" He had that whiney sound in his voice that really irritated me. Pressed buttons I just didn't want pressed.

"Exactly what you want me to," I muttered and I flung back over my shoulder. "I'm going to get this dirt off me, go to the pub, and have a few beers. Then maybe I'll go and check out some goats."

It was an hour on horseback to Bunyip waterhole, where the tourist road ended. Nothing worth seeing beyond that but salt bush, tiger snakes, and red dirt. The canyon was another two hours beyond the waterhole, but both locals and tourists were discouraged from going further into the Outback. Though it wasn't exactly sacred ground to the Aboriginals, there was an unspoken agreement that the canyon was off-limits to whites. It wasn't the first time I'd heard it called the Sick Place. The tribal elders had probably known for centuries that whatever was in those stones caused illness and deformity. There was something evil there—call it a spirit or call it uranium, the name didn't matter.

Laurie was riding Blimp, who was older than God, so we had to take it easy. Shade wanted to gallop; I could feel his muscles quiver under my thighs, and he'd turn his head and nip at Blimp if Laurie got too close.

Blimp was so slow and broad-backed that Laurie rode him like an armchair, letting the reins hang slack while he squinted at the cult's leaflet. He was whistling like he'd won the lottery, which pissed me off. I knew what he was thinking—dreaming of a mother-and-daughter reunion, with me cooking pancakes for breakfast and wearing skirts, Lula skipping off to college and coming home to cooked dinners. He never told me straight out I was getting too old for the rodeo, but I saw the scared look in his eyes whenever I climbed into the pen.

Pretty soon, we were making our way down a gorge, steep slopes of sandstone boulders on either side blocking out everything but a strip of blue sky above. It was that fake, cartoon-blue sky you get out here in the desert. Looks pretty in the tourist brochures, but hurts like hell to look at. The track was just wide enough for a small truck—I could make out wobbly wheel tracks in the sandstone grit. Probably how the cult made their way into town to pick up supplies and hand out their leaflets.

"Get this, Sam," Laurie was saying. "This leaflet here reckons a race of cosmic aliens are gonna take over the earth and the only way to be saved is to worship the Great Mother. She's like a shepherdess of the flock. Shub . . . er, Shub-Niggurath, that's her name."

I snorted. "Sounds like Lula found the mother she was looking for."

Laurie made a disapproving noise. "You are too hard on that girl. She left because she thought *you* wanted her to go. Because you thought she was weak. Not everyone can ride a bronco—hell, Sam, most people don't want to."

"Maybe that's why we have clowns," I said, knowing it would hurt him, but saying it, anyway. "The world's hard. You got to be harder to survive. It's just the way things are."

"So, what are we doing here?"

I didn't bother replying. Not that he expected me to. He knew me pretty well after twenty years on the rodeo circuit. I wasn't great on answering *Why are we here?*-type questions. He'd got what he wanted. I just wished he'd shut up about it.

We rode in silence for a bit, then Laurie began to whistle tunelessly and edged Blimp closer. "You know we're being watched," he said softly.

"Yep. For the last three kilometres. A blind dog couldn't miss them."

I nudged Shade into a trot towards one of the sandstone boulders and a figure dressed in a grubby, white gown scrambled for cover behind another of the massive stones. I caught a glimpse of a shaved head, the crown unnaturally flat, and a protruding forehead like a stone ledge. I guess he had eyes, but I couldn't make them out. I'd seen pictures of victims of nuclear disasters, so I knew exposure to radiation could do weird things to a person, cause deformities. There was something different about this man, though, an unnatural quality that made the hairs on the back of the neck rise up. And I could tell Shade sensed something was off. He was skittish, his eyes rolling, and he danced away from the boulders. I guessed there were at least twenty of them, maybe more, hiding on both sides of the ravine.

"Maybe they think we're coming to join up," Laurie said hopefully. He waved the leaflet in the air like it was a flag of surrender.

"I'm not seeing green pastures and goats!" I said in a loud voice. The word, "goats," echoed down the ravine like a bad rap song. "Hey! We're here to see the Great Mother!"

Okay, maybe my tone wasn't the most respectful, but for people who were so keen on recruiting, they sure weren't eager to come out and say hello.

"I think your whip is making them nervous," Laurie hissed.

"You think so?" I slipped the coiled leather from the saddle and sent it lashing against a nearby boulder.

The walls of the canyon came alive with the scuttling figures of the white-robed watchers, all of them clambering for higher ground. They were as agile as monkeys and just as scared.

"Come out, come out, wherever you are!" I called out, lashing out with the whip again.

"Sam!" Laurie squealed, "Don't provoke—"

The track turned sharply to the left and widened suddenly into a circular cul-de-sac. Massive sandstone walls reared up about thirty metres, dotted with hundreds of holes. The caves . . .

The place reminded me of a beehive, a human beehive. People sat at the lip of those caves in complete silence, staring down at us with a kind of hungry patience. Hundreds of them. They all wore identical white robes. While most of them had normal features, some had the flattened skull and protruding forehead of the one I'd disturbed behind the boulder. There was something eerie about the unnatural passivity of these people, the feverish tension hidden behind unblinking eyes.

"Well, will you look at that," Laurie breathed. "It's like an . . . like an arena. An arena of bones. And up there are the box seats."

I sucked in a breath. Shade was fighting the reins like he wanted to bolt. I didn't blame him. The ground was littered with sun-bleached bones, thousands of them. Most were unrecognizable, but I could make out skulls, goat mainly, but there was a fair number of human skulls, too. Shade balked as the bones crunched under his hooves and only the soothing murmur of my voice kept him moving.

"Mum!"

I hadn't noticed the beat-up old truck parked in the shade cast by the walls. Hadn't noticed it until Lula's voice swung my glance that way. There she stood, dressed in the white robes, just like all the others. She was holding a rope tied around the neck of the scrawniest goat I'd ever seen, trying to pull it out the back of the truck.

"Hi, kiddo!" I called out to her, as if I'd just seen her on a street in Darwin. "How's things? Thought I'd come and check out the stock. Buy a goat or two, maybe."

She laughed at that, a horrible, shrill sound.

Laurie was kicking Blimp, trying to get the horse closer to follow Shade. But Blimp wasn't planning on moving, not unless it was in reverse.

"You okay, Lula?" he said. "We've come to get you, if you want. No need to stay here with these people. Who's in charge here, anyway? Where's the Great Mother . . . ?"

Laurie was babbling and I wished he'd just shut up. Bad move, bringing him with me. You could feel the panic coming off him in waves. I knew that whatever lived in this place would feed off that.

"The Aboriginals call these caves the Sick Place for a reason, Lula!" Laurie was shouting across the cul-de-sac. "There's radiation in those caves and it can hurt you bad. You need to come back with us before you get sick."

Lula shook her head as if she didn't want to hear what he was saying and tugged again on the rope. "I got a job to do here," she threw back at him. "The Great Mother loves me. She gave me a job. I'm the Mother's goat girl. Somebody's got to look after the goats." Then she gulped and made a funny noise. I wasn't sure if she was laughing or crying.

"Well, the Great Mother can get herself another goat girl." I dug my heels into Shade's flanks, forcing him towards Lula. He was a big, strong animal and could carry the two of us back to Noonamah easily. But he trembled, fighting the reins.

As if Shade's terror was some sort of trigger, the people in the caves started chanting. A hundred booming voices, bouncing around that cul-de-sac until you thought you'd go crazy at the sound. "*Iä! Shub-Niggurath, Iä! Shub-Niggurath, Iä! Shub-Niggurath.*"

Lula had started to cry. It couldn't hear it over the chanting, but I saw her contorted face, the uncontrolled shaking of her body.

I kicked Shade harder than I'd ever kicked him, or any other horse, and he leapt forward as if wasp-stung. In seconds, we were at the truck. I bent and grabbed Lula by the arm, dragging her across the saddle like she was a calf.

"Shub-Niggurath is my mother!" Lula was sobbing hysterically now. "She won't let me go. Not unless you pay the price. She won't let me go. You're a bad mother. And Shub-Niggurath won't give me back, not unless you pay. She's good to me. She's a good mother and I'm her goat girl."

"Bullshit," I snarled, yanking on the reins and turning Shade towards the exit of the cul-de-sac.

That's when I saw it. I guess it was human. Everyone has heard of people being born with two heads, so why not this? *Radiation poisoning,* I kept telling myself. *That's all it is.* A mutation caused by the uranium. The cult had lived here for decades, bred here for decades. Who knew what kind of monster could come from that?

"*Iä! Shub-Niggurath! Iä! Shub-Niggurath!*" There was a sound of rapture in the chanting now. As if a signal had been given, the cultists began to sway from side to side in their beehive caves.

The creature they called Shub-Niggurath was standing over Laurie, who lay sprawled in the dirt like a broken doll. Unconscious or dead, I wasn't sure. He wasn't moving, though, and the angle of his neck made me feel sick. I'd seen rider's heads twisted like that more than once in rodeo arenas.

Shub-Niggurath's left arm was curled around Blimp's neck, crushing it. That's how big it was. Freakish big and freakish strong. Blimp's struggles were about as useful as a kitten's.

People are born with two heads. Extra arms and legs. So, why not this? *Sure!* my mind screamed. *Anything is possible.*

It stood upright, about two metres tall. While the upper half of its body was a woman's, below the waist, it had the haunches and legs of an enormous goat. And its head . . . yellow, slit-pupiled eyes stared out of a goat's head the size of a bull's skull. There was a brutal intelligence in those eyes—savage glee, an hysterical sort of amusement. It made sure it had caught my eye and slowly it tightened its arm around Blimp's neck.

I turned away, burying my head into Lula sweaty hair. I heard Blimp's squeal become something else, something impossible to listen to and ever forget. I never heard a worse sound, I swear it, than the shrill scream of that poor horse as Shub-Niggurath's grip tightened. I heard the snap of bones— Blimp's neck, breaking as easily as a chicken's. Then a terrible quiet. Maybe the chanting had stopped, or that hideous scream, severed so abruptly, had swallowed all sound. I whispered into Lula's hair. "What's the price, Lula? What does Shub-Niggurath want?"

Lula was crying quietly, her hands knotted in Shade's mane, the knuckles white.

"The Great Mother only asks for what you love most. Eight seconds,

Mum. Those precious eight seconds you live for, the most important thing in your life. That's what she wants. That's her price." Then Lula twisted her head and looked at me, and there was something smoldering in her eyes, something that made my guts churn. Maybe it was hatred, all mixed up with resentment and confusion and despair. Maybe I saw love there, too, or maybe I just needed to.

I slid off Shade like I had a thousand times before, grabbing the coiled whip on the pommel, and forced the reins into Lula's limp hands.

You can't let yourself think, *This is the last time I will do this, or see this, or touch this.* You can't think like that when you're a rough rider, climbing on the Devil's back, when you feel the heat of his fury rising up through your leathers. There's only one thing you say to yourself: *Eight seconds.* That's all it takes. Stay on for eight seconds and you win.

"You go, girl. Shade knows the way." I spoke calmly, as if everything was going to be just fine, and I stroked Shade's silky mane. It felt as beautiful as life under my fingers.

"Mum?" Suddenly, her voice was thin, a little girl's voice, a little girl waking from a bad dream.

"Go, girl. Get out of here. I just—I just want you to know . . . I couldn't change what I was." I guess it was an explanation of sorts, or maybe an apology, if a person could apologize for being born what they were.

I whacked Shade on the rump before Lula could reply and he shot across that arena like a bullet. I didn't look at Lula. Lula—my *daughter.* The word had a strange feel in my mouth, like the taste of a life I would never know. Maybe I was getting soft, easier to break on the inside. I knew I wouldn't be able to look at her and then have the courage to walk across the arena to the monster waiting for me.

As Shade galloped towards the path out of the cul-de-sac, Shub-Niggurath threw back her head and wailed. Inhuman as the sound was, I recognized in it the anguish of loss. For a terrified moment, I sensed the creature was poised to leap after Lula, so I unfurled the whip and sent it snapping outwards with a crack like the sound of thunder. It was a challenge that couldn't be ignored.

Shub-Niggurath turned back to face me with promised violence in every line of her hideous form and the chanting of her worshippers became frenzied, thick as blood—a victory chant.

I hope I walked across that arena like I owned it. I know I managed not to look away from the creature's goat eyes, though it was like staring into a furnace. You don't crawl whimpering to your death, not when you're a rough rider.

Ever played a hand of poker with the Devil, knowing that if you could keep the game going for eight seconds, just eight seconds, you'd beat the bastard and then you'd get to be a god for a day?

I have. Not a lot of people can say that. But the day comes, sooner or later, when the Devil has the winning hand. There's a legend that says a rough rider can tell when his time is up by looking into the eye of the beast. You hit the dust and you know you won't be getting up again. Today was my day. I saw my end in Shub-Niggurath's eyes.

But eight seconds is enough time to get out of Hell, for a girl on a good horse. And that's good enough for me.

THE EYE OF JUNO

EUGENIE MORA

SEALED WITH WAX and scribbled in spidery script, the General's letter commanded us to *come swiftly, before I kill her.*

In the exaggerated language of the Roman elites, I understood this to mean, *My wife will not do as I ask*, but my master insisted on heeding the summons.

Thick, icy rains greeted our journey. In the Doctor's sneeze, I heard the indignation he would keep silent until he could expend it in violence, presumably upon my back.

"You said this was the road," he accused.

The cadences of his Roman brogue were as familiar to me as the perfume of rain-soaked Caledonia. "It is. Do you not see the fort?"

The Doctor made a shelf of his hand and squinted into the bleak night. "Don't see anything."

I pointed. "Where the oaks are. See how the tree line slants?"

A hundred miles south, stone pillars rose out of the dirt like mountains. Lit torches burned nightly beneath wooden roofs, a beacon and a warning both. There was no such gleam here. Emperor Severus had lent his name to the sod wall that girdled Rome's influence far into the Briton north, but there was little of glory in these ramparts.

We approached the fort in silence. Engatius did not enjoy being shown up by anyone, let alone a slave girl. He nudged his horse to a trot as soon as he glimpsed the first man-made structure—a row of wooden hovels leaning drunkenly upon each other—and pranced on ahead. Saddlebags weighted with wine and food slapped against the flanks of his white mount.

A garrison had been dispatched here in the warm summer months, when days were long and game plentiful. It was spring now and as best I could tell, the legionnaires had not finished erecting the *vicus*, nor bounded the stables with more than a few rickety planks. The granary was a squat stone enclosure, waist-high, lacking a roof.

I would have thought my understanding of our destination wrong, were it not for the two watchtowers overlooking the sod wall, or the *praetorium* between them.

Engatius dismounted into a puddle. In Calleva, where Engatius had purchased me, roads were paved and awnings shaded the doorways of the poorest homes. We would have been hard-pressed to skulk to the door of a villa without some servant to intercept us.

Here, the Doctor rapped his knuckles against the wooden door three times before there was the slightest inkling of human life.

"Who're you?" A soldier's silhouette filled the gap. His uniform had seen better days. Dark patches pocked the bronze plate and his woolen tunic was torn at the sleeve. Although he towered over Engatius, the grip he held on the hilt of his sword was that of a frightened recruit.

I wondered which of the North's many dangers could instil such dread in a grown man.

"Marcus Engatius, physician and friend to your general. Is . . . he not here?"

One of the horses whinnied.

The soldier's gaze locked onto mine. Contempt was the prevailing Roman sentiment for my people, but I saw surprise in the legionnaire's eyes, as though he could not fathom what might bring a plainly Pictish woman back to her ancestral home.

"May we come in?" Engatius entreated, shivering at our host. "We've been riding with the rain for days."

That broke the soldier's fascination with me. He welcomed the Doctor inside and directed me to the stables.

As soon as the door swung shut, I led the horses around the villa and freed them of their saddlebags behind a small shed. A wooden plank kept the worst of the rain from their heads. Damp scrub grass would do to feed them.

I wanted the animals near. Something about this thick, oppressive night made me both anxious and excited. This was the closest I'd come to the Highlands since I was a girl. I could all but smell the pine and heather.

Inside the villa, a different scent pervaded—that of corruption and death.

Calleva had accustomed me to scores of slaves bustling in and out of kitchens, baths and bedchambers. Their absence spiked my pulse. I took stock of the foursome of soldiers in the atrium and felt their eyes creep down my body with equal circumspection.

Just as I gathered my courage to ask where I might find my master, Engatius' voice echoed through the silent villa.

"Seonag, I need you!"

Relief washed over me. I tracked the Doctor's inimitable timbre through the *tablinum* with its carved writing tables and padded stools. The courtyard beyond it was striated with the shadow of sandstone colonnades, yet the fish ponds reflected only darkness, a faint flicker of movement trapped in the shimmering pools.

Weighted down with our saddlebags, I shambled awkwardly across the tile floor, momentum carrying me past the bedchamber door before I could ask permission.

"Stop right there," a stern voice reprimanded.

The brutal slam of a wide palm to my ribcage halted me in my tracks. Its owner glared with brown eyes set in a scarred, indubitably Roman face.

"Let her through, General," Engatius urged. "She has my potions. Your wife needs smelling salts. Has she been ill long?"

"Every night since . . . " The Roman caught himself. "Yes, a while. The trance takes her at midnight."

At once forgotten, I skirted around the General to bring my master his medicaments.

The bedchamber was a small room with a wide entrance and a vaulted ceiling. A bedroll in the entryway told me a slave had been assigned to the General's wife. There was no trace of her now. The mistress of the house lay on the bed, her eyes moving rapidly behind closed lids.

"Spirit of Hartshorn," the Doctor told me sharply.

I rummaged through the bags, my fingers combing through powdered lemon plant, rose petals soaked in wine, dried laurel, poppy seeds, aniseed to treat the bite of a scorpion—and yes, finally, the blue vial of liquid Hartshorn.

Marcus snatched it from my hand and uncorked the concoction. He was comparatively tender with the General's wife, holding her head up so she might inhale.

Her nostrils flared.

The General cleared his throat. "They tell me sometimes, she wakes in a cold sweat. Sometimes, not at all."

" 'They?' " I repeated, before I could quell the impulse.

The furrow between the General's brows deepened. "The slaves."

"Have they abandoned you?"

He crossed his arms across a barrel chest. "Is this relevant?"

"I think she's coming around," announced Engatius, in a tremulous voice.

Indeed, the General's wife blinked her eyes open with some effort. Her sinister kohl-black gaze found mine first, then her husband's.

"I'm a doctor, my lady," said Engatius. "General Antonius sent for me."

"Have you told them?"

The General huffed out a breath. "That you talk nonsense? No, of course not. The doctor will give you something for the road. We leave by first light."

Astride a horse? I thought. *Again?* Fatigue slumped my shoulders, but I knew better than to protest. We had ridden far to tend a woman who seemed in fair health—if slightly cross with her husband.

I had been wrong to trust old prophecy. The spirits in these woods did not take kindly to tainted blood.

My master sighed and nodded. "Can you tell me what ails you, sweet lady?"

"My name," said the general's wife, "is Iunia Gratiana." She pushed herself upright, folding pale legs beneath the hem of a sheer-white shift. "And *I* do not wish to leave this place."

"Iuno Sospita!" The General strode forward, his jaw clenched. "Whatever daemon you hold inside you, the doctor will pry out."

With limp, sweat-soaked black hair sticking out at odd angles and bags drooping beneath her eyes, Gratiana thrust out her chin as defiant as a queen. "And if he cannot?"

"Then I will do it myself!"

I flinched, all-too-familiar with the Roman appetite for threats.

The unyielding tension between husband and wife was quelled by the sudden blare of a horn.

Engatius looked up from where he was rifling for some miracle cure. "What's that?"

"Barbarians," spat the General. "Have her ready for the road!" Fury twisted at his mouth as he whirled around and left us.

"My husband speaks to you as a friend," Gratiana observed.

"We, ah, had the good fortune to study under the same tutor in Calleva." Engatius shot a wary glance to the door. He'd never been in a battle, let alone so far from Hadrian's Wall. Naked fear shone on his wrinkled face.

Gratiana slid back to the sleeping couch with a huff of laughter. "Fortune! This place has not known any in a year."

"You've suffered many attacks?"

"The tribes harass us. They steal cattle and horses."

Engatius bid me upend a vial of tonic into a cup of wine. "I see the people have fled. No one is left but for you and the garrison—"

"Yes, five souls and my indomitable husband."

Gratiana turned her head on the cushion. I had the uncanny feeling that she was following me with her gaze, a yellow flicker in her eyes.

When I chanced a look, I discovered her peering at the ceiling.

"My husband led a skirmish into the oak wood, you see. Two hundred perished, but he returned. *I* saved him . . . and this is how he repays me." She rose up onto her elbows. "He turned my son away when he was born. Such a small, fragile parcel of life. I laid him at his feet and he said, *The eyes aren't mine.* Now our son sleeps with the spirits of the forest and my husband wages war, *and I do not wish to leave!*"

I shivered, though the elaborate brazier in the room tinged the air with a warm glow.

Engatius blew into a clump of burnt rosemary to dim the embers. The pungent scent filled the room like incense. "For purification," he explained.

He wasn't truly listening to the General's wife, but I was. Curiosity got the better of me.

"How did you save him?"

Gratiana met my gaze. "A pact with the wood. My husband's life for our eternal gratitude . . . as though that might slake its hunger!" She laughed hoarsely. "*You* believe in daemons, don't you?"

"She is a simple girl," scoffed my master. "She is seduced by simple superstition."

"Is it superstition if I say you may not see morning, *Doctore*?"

Marcus nearly dropped the rosemary. "Surely, the barbarians cannot penetrate these walls . . . " This villa was Rome and Rome was eternal.

"It is not barbarians you should fear," Gratiana informed us. With a careless hand, she snatched the goblet from my grasp and downed its contents in a single swig.

Crimson dregs spilled onto her shift as she collapsed, as though even this small effort had exhausted her. The bed gave a small, disconsolate groan.

I hunted for my customary scorn and found none. The blare of the horn had given way to the sounds of battle, which ricocheted from the walls of the villa like stray arrows.

"That was no tonic," I murmured, wounded.

Engatius gave a careless wave. "A soporific to clear her mind. She will be restored when next she wakes." He had roused the General's wife from her strange torpor only to medicate her into another unnatural sleep.

Gratiana had struck me as perfectly lucid, but the Doctor's judgment was the only one that mattered. I left him to his task, creeping out of the bedchamber on cat-quiet feet.

Rain spattered the ground, but the rattle of the downpour was not enough to disguise the beastlike howl of warriors. My heart swelled.

I remembered their cries. The music of their battle. I was home.

Fishhooks snagged in my flesh with the sudden urge to find the nearest door and run, to join them and disappear into the oak wood with the daemons. I took my first step to the baths.

Something tumbled from the roof of the villa. A soldier, my addled mind supplied. His skull shattered upon impact with the tile walkway at my feet, helmet rolling into the azaleas.

I stumbled, yearning curdling in my gut. Before I made it more than a pace, my shoulder was seized.

"How dare you disrespect me so before the General? I should whip you . . . " The Doctor's gaze ticked down, past me, to the body in the garden. "Gods above . . . "

"Above is Rome," intoned a fearsome voice. The General's shoulders stooped as he stepped into the light, a bull bracing for a fight.

Were it not for the breathless heave of his plated chest, I might not have guessed he'd been in a battle at all.

"And that man was a coward."

"He fell," I protested.

"He *jumped*. The North acquaints men with their fear."

Marcus shook himself. "But—what of the battle?"

"Won."

"So soon?"

The smile on General Antonius' mouth was cruel. "Vermin dare not approach this house. Hallowed ground, my wife calls it. Speaking of whom . . . "

"Sh-she will be well enough to travel by morning. The potion I administered will help." When he spoke, the Doctor's voice shook badly. He had yet to look away from the corpse.

Noticing this, the General gestured to two of his men to tend to their fallen brother.

"Good. Then you will take the adjoining bedchamber and rest. We leave at first light."

I waited for my master to ask how many of my own people had died, how many lay wounded in the fields outside the settlement, but he did not.

He seemed so eager to leave that I wondered if we should have come at all.

That night, Engatius snored blissfully on the sleeping couch, impervious to our eerie surroundings.

The steady rise and fall of his chest filled me with aggravation. While the Doctor drifted off into the arms of Morpheus, I was charged with keeping watch. There was no telling my master that I was ill-suited to the task, or that I jumped at every shadow.

Once, a crow alighted on the lip of the ornate fountain at the heart of the *peristylium* and I slammed my head against the wall in fright.

I rubbed the tender spot, keeping the pain alive, and strained my ears.

Gratiana's words rang in my skull like the echo of a howl in a cave. Did I believe her? Yellow-eyed daemons suited the legends of my childhood and I could not shake the feeling that more than foul weather and barbarian skirmishes were at play here.

A rustle of movement pricked my ears. I dug my knuckles into the bedroll and shifted my weight. I was uneasy around soldiers, but with only a handful left, I doubted they'd venture far from their post to seek me out.

The shadow of a man drew itself sharp onto the tiled floors, putting paid to my hopes.

I flattened my back to the wall, blood pulsing in my temples, and fumbled for my short dagger, the only weapon Engatius permitted me when we were away from home.

An hour or an instant passed as I waited to be attacked or ravished,

Roman impunity sure to prevail on my innocence. It took what little courage I had left to chance another glance into the courtyard.

My gaze found the figure at once. It was shambling away, gliding more than walking, a sword held aloft.

The guardsman in the atrium must have sensed the same frisson I had. He squinted into the shadows between the colonnades, features smoothing into a mask of recognition when he made out the source of the disturbance.

"Oh, it's you—"

The shade drew back its *gladius* and swung it in a clean, decisive arc.

I buried a shriek into my palm.

Swords killed. That much I knew from the day my village was attacked. But it had been years since I'd witnessed their prowess. I could not look away. Blood spurted from the soldier's throat, spattering painted tile and staining his uniform. He was beyond caring, a nearly headless amalgamation of raw meat and split skin, bone protruding glaringly from his jaw.

The figure stood over him a moment, naked hunger in its gaze. Though my vision was unimpeded, I could hardly make out its features. It was not human. It could not be. Yet, as I watched, it crouched down with a creak of human knees and reached a long-fingered hand into the soldier's face.

My gut churned.

The jelly-white of human eyes gleamed in the moonlight, lustrous like marbles. Gratiana's opium-addled blather slammed into me with startling clarity.

He said the eyes aren't mine.

As I looked on, the swordsman brought first one eye and then the other to his mouth, and bit down as though into a grape. Then, satisfied, he rose and turned his steps to the front of the house.

I was paralyzed with fright, but knew I had to move—now and quickly, before the creature returned. I stood on shaking knees, half-stumbling and half-bolting the short distance to the Doctor's bed.

"Master. *Master*, wake up . . . "

He mumbled something indistinct and batted at my shaking hands.

I knew I would regret my impudence tomorrow, but in that moment it seemed desperately more important to rouse him. With trembling fingers, I pinched his nostrils together, the way my mother would do to my siblings and I when we were small.

His eyes fluttered open. "What . . . "

"We must go," I gritted out. "Now. The General—"

Before another word could pass my lips, the villa erupted with a shrill and sudden bellow. It was a cry of anguish. *Another guard dead,* I thought, reaching for the Doctor's arm.

He shook me off. "What—are we under attack?"

"No, no . . . it's the daemon." I hadn't allowed myself to think it before, but deep in my heart, I knew.

The creature that fed on the soldier's eyes was not of this world. Gratiana had tried to warn us. I spared a thought for the General's wife as I grabbed for the Doctor's satchels, loading myself with his surgical equipment and herbal potions. Once we escaped, we would not be returning to the villa, for Gratiana or anyone else.

I knew the stories too well.

"That's not—there are no such things as daemons," Engatius insisted.

A second cry rippled through the villa. I flung a desperate, searching glance at my master. How could a man of such learning be so obtuse?

"I saw it with my own eyes!"

"Then we must find the General." He was up in a heartbeat, moving with swiftness that belied his age.

"There is no time!"

"He's a friend," the Doctor shot back. He shook off my grip when I seized hold of his sleeve, rounding on me with a snarl and a raised hand.

The slap snapped my head to the side. Heat spread down my neck and collarbone, sunk its claws deep into the cage of my ribs.

"He's a dead man!" I gritted out.

But it was too late. The Doctor turned for the door that led into Gratiana's *cubiculum,* the beaded curtain that separated our bedchamber from the *procoeton* jangling like a wind chime.

My master and I had little in common beyond a mutual hatred, but without his Roman protection, I would be another runaway Pictish slave and Rome's reach could be long in these parts.

I swore and followed him through the stooped doorway.

"This is madness," I snarled, a complaint that fell on deaf ears.

Just three feet into the General's bedchamber, Engatius stood unmoving. Between his old friend and him lay Gratiana's ornate sleeping couch. The woman herself was held at sword point.

"General," Engatius began haltingly. "Antonius, what—"

"*She* killed them! Every single one. All the soldiers, all the villagers . . ." The General's forearm bulged with the effort of holding a blade to his wife's throat. His knuckles whitened around the hilt. "She made a pact with the *di inferi!* She is Discordia-made-flesh!"

"She is your wife."

"Husband . . . " Tears beaded on Gratiana's spidery lashes.

I squeezed my fist around my dagger. Small as it was, it was our only hope.

"Silence!" The General's fury sparked like a flint. "Your poison tongue has taken two hundred lives! All my nightmares, all those unanswered questions—it was your doing! I should have slit your throat when you brought that *thing* into the world! Mothers of good Roman legionnaires rejoice! The gods themselves would welcome me into Elysium!"

Engatius inched forward. "Antonius, are—are you injured?"

"What?"

"Your hands. You—is that *blood*?"

The General blinked at him, bemused. His hold on Gratiana slackened. "It . . . it happened again." He grimaced, shaking as if in the throes of a seizure, and abruptly doubled over.

As a doctor's servant, I had witnessed patients expel the contents of their stomach before, but never had their bile contained human eyes, half-digested, yet still distinct on white linen.

"Antonius!"

My master started forward with arms outstretched, heedless of the offal on the bed. He blocked my view of the General but not of his sword.

The *gladius* did not stave him off, though it sank deep into his gut and emerged through the slats of his spine like a needle perforating cloth. A red flower bloomed in its wake.

Engatius buckled, his unbelted tunic catching on the blade. He folded gently.

The General's face floated above him, blood around the mouth and eyes wide.

I did not think. I hefted my dagger and lobbed it with as much force as I could muster.

Had he worn his plate, the short blade would not have made a dent. Had he woken from his nightmares and come for me rather than the Roman guards standing watch, I would not have been here, now, to pierce his chest. But he had not.

The General crumpled like a puppet, his frown giving way to astonishment. He was not so invincible, after all, if a mere slave—a woman, at that—could fell him with a single blow.

Gratiana crawled away from her husband's body and dragged herself up with both hands upon the soiled bed. She seemed no more eager to approach his body than I was to check if the Doctor was still breathing.

"It's over," I said, swallowing past the lump in my throat.

"Yes."

"Can you ride? We should . . ." *Leave this place. Flee whatever darkness hangs upon this house.* The General was gone, but the forces that had animated his mortal coil still hovered in the air around us. I could hear their whispers. I sensed their bodies rustling in the shadows.

My fear was Roman, but something inside me was awed by such horrific power.

I thought that the General's wife might refuse. She'd said before she did not wish to leave this house. But Gratiana nodded, her lips curling in distaste as she took in the sprawl of our two masters—Roman, proud and very much dead.

"Yes," she said again and only briefly hesitated before taking my arm. She seemed stricken, but not out of her mind with grief, as I helped her astride Engatius' white charger. "Where will we go, Seonag? What are we to do?"

"South."

Hadrian's Wall would be our destination for the time being and then, who could say? Calleva? Londinium? As for what to do—I cast one last glance over the lugubrious villa, its walls stooped and dark against the shuddering oak wood.

Something had been awakened in this forest, born of Gratiana's sacrifice and hatred, an ancient power that stole through the General and turned Rome's sharpest weapon against itself.

"Does it still hunger?" I asked, scratching my hand into the steed's snowy hair.

Iunia Gratiana offered a thin smile.

"South," I repeated. South to Rome itself, to the stretch of a prosperous empire reclining upon stolen land, full of men whose dreams were ripe for plucking like eyes from a human skull.

"Cthulhu" by Lisa A. Grabenstetter

CTHULHU OF THE DEAD SEA

INKERI KONTRO

"THEN TO MY conclusions." Anna wishes her voice would stop shaking. She has done this a hundred times and the nervousness only gets worse with age. One would assume it would get easier, but her hands are shaking more than ever and she has had to do quick, furious circles with the laser pointer to hide how jumpy she is. The ugly truth is that she is running on a fragmented five-hour sleep and she knows it is showing.

"Due to its high salt content, the Dead Sea was previously thought to be a virtually uninhabitable place for even microorganisms, which are present in quite low amounts. The average salt content of the Dead Sea is increasing due to current climate conditions." Don't say climate change. Anna has seen one scientific presentation which turned into a proverbial slaughter when some older gentleman took issue with a PhD student's choice of words. The moderator should have cut the fight short because the old fart was clearly out of line and off-topic, but sometimes, moderators are a bit old-farty themselves. Anna is not taking that chance.

"However, we have discovered a new type of Archaea, belonging to the class *Halobacteria*, which appears to be thriving. The organism appears unrelated to previously discovered species, therefore we named it *Halofractal cthulhu*."

The name felt like an excellent idea when she came up with it. Most of the lab sided with her immediately. The professor actually is a huge horror fan, and was completely overjoyed over being able to name something *Cthulhu*. The thing did look a lot like a Little Old One, though, to be fair, it resembled a mash-up of Cthulhu and a Pac-Man ghost more, with its short and thick tentacles. You just can't name a new species Pac-Man; that would be completely unprofessional.

The genus was the difficult part. Little *cthulhu* did not seem to fit in any existing slot, so the laboratory decided to name it according to the surface structure. Anna was not really familiar with the concept of fractals, but the more mathematically inclined scientists were overjoyed with the creature's tendency to pack into clusters that imitated the shape of a single critter. Also, the electron microscope images showed that the "tentacles" were covered in little bumps, which also seemed to have a tentacle-like structure going on, so salt-loving fractal god it was. *Halofractal cthulhu.*

"The species thrives in very high salt concentrations. In our laboratory, we have observed it surviving and even reproducing in salt concentrations exceeding fifty-two percent, which is markedly higher than previously reported for any *halophile.* We hope studying this species will shed more light into the fascinating range of conditions in which life can survive on Earth." A quick round of acknowledgements means the majority of the presentation is cleared. Only the worst remains.

"I am happy to answer any questions."

The moderator stands up. The applause doesn't even have time to die out before hands are shooting in the air. Damn it. The compulsory hammer guy goes first. Every conference has one: a scientist so blinded by the excellence of his own technique that he asks a question about it— regardless of how out of place it is. Anna has seen enough presentations at this conference to know that the small-angle X-ray scattering guy is a typical hammer scientist. SAXS is his tool and when you have a hammer, everything looks like a nail. Also, if someone dares tell you they actually have a screw, you can still bludgeon the person into submission with your hammer.

"No, we have not done SAXS," Anna replies with a polite smile. Someday, she will have to find out what that is, but ultimately, it is not of importance. Hammer guys come in all flavors. "I am personally not familiar with the technique, but we shall certainly consider it."

An urgent hand is raised from the other side of the room, but the moderator ignores it in favor of the waiting ones. Anna clears the rest of the questions with enough grace and the moderator cuts the discussion when the merciful clock reaches the end of the session. The angry hand is left without a turn.

The owner of the angry hand comes up to Anna during the coffee break. She is a woman in her mid-forties, dressed in a well-fitting blazer and little black dress, with a whimsical necklace with plastic cut-outs draped around her neck. If it weren't for the neon-pink tights drawing attention to her legs, which end in yellow boots, she would look like a business-woman out of place at the science conference. Now she just looks out of place.

Most women at the conference dress in a fairly casual, masculine manner. The few exceptions mostly aren't program participants; a few elderly ladies clearly accompanying equally elderly professors, dressed in pastels accented with pearl necklaces, golden rings and the most sensible high heels you can find for money.

"Professor Jacobsen," the woman introduces herself. "I really enjoyed your speech. I just wanted to let you know that you should not care about Max. SAXS is a complete waste of time."

Before Anna has a chance to reply, Max the SAXS guy materializes from thin air. His affect is chilly and he neither introduces himself nor waits for Anna to. He clearly knows Professor Jacobsen from before and the argument is on with full force. Anna nods politely, though she hardly understands a word. When a third scientist comes to congratulate her on the presentation, she gratefully bows out of the conversation.

The coffee break is almost over when professor Jacobsen finds Anna anew. She apologizes and tells Anna she would love to have her visit her laboratory. Anna thanks her and brushes it off as ordinary politeness. She is genuinely shocked, a week later, when the renewed invitation appears in her inbox.

Anna feels out of place at Lise Kjær Jacobsen's laboratory. Most people speak Danish to each other and though they always switch to English when they feel she should be included, she finds herself often hanging on the outskirts of the group, guessing whether it would be rude of her to remind them she is present.

When they do remember her, though, they are warm and welcoming. They ask her to join them for after-work beers, make sure she has something to do on the first weekend, and offer to take her sight-seeing. They seem genuinely invested in making her enjoy her few weeks in Copenhagen. Especially the young post-doc, Bianca, wants to spend time with Anna.

Bianca is a bubbly personality, but her English skills are obscured by her thick French accent, which makes parsing the sentences hard work. She carries around a bag of crisps and eats them everywhere except in the wetlab. "Ee like ze salt. Like *cthul'u*." she laughs. She is also fascinated with Anna's samples, and goes on and on about her love for supernatural things. Anna nods politely.

Anna feels slightly bad whenever she is irritated at Bianca's accent. She knows her own English makes it very clear her native language neither uses intonation nor manages to teach it well to schoolchildren.

Professor Jacobsen is as cheerful and as oddly dressed as at the conference. She has tons of ideas that she flings in rapid meetings, expecting her underlings to catch them all, weed out the impossible ones and do the rest within a day. Anna works long days in the wetlab, testing the growth of little *cthulhu* in different environments.

Max the SAXS guy turns out to be a close colleague of Professor Jacobsen. He always remembers to switch the conversation to English, which is only one of the qualities that make him a highly likeable guy despite his hammer-like qualities. When he asks for samples, A'nna sees no reason to say no. "What would Professor Jacobsen say?" she asks jokingly.

"Lise has many good qualities," Max answers with a wink, "but understanding my technique is not one of them. How I waste my time is not her business."

✳

Anna feels unnerved by the Archaea. They seem to be thriving in all sorts of conditions, as long as lethal amounts of salt are present, and looking in the microscope is puzzling every time. The edge of the biofilm looks the same regardless of the magnification, with the nested patterns present in all size scales.

When the critters are thriving, they easily grow into colonies that cover the whole petri dish. The edges of the colony are frayed, but one end (the top, Anna calls it, even though it makes little sense in the context of the edge of a horizontal pattern) being smooth and the bottom growing in tail-like appendages.

If Anna puts a sample in the microscope and zooms in, the edge has little tentacles. Zoom into the edge of a tentacle, and it is covered in smaller tentacles. She repeats this until the microscope runs out of resolving power. Electron microscopy shows the same. It is unsettling having to check the size bar of images to know what the scale is.

"How do they do that?" she asks Max rhetorically.

"How do they do this?" Max asks back, showing her graphs that make little sense. Max explains that the fractal structure goes down as far as he can see, down to nanometers.

"We could see that from electron microscopy," Professor Jacobsen points out sharply.

"Can you quantify it from your precious microscopy? Can you get out a number? Standard deviation?" retorts Max, but no one is interested in the fractal dimension he has so meticulously calculated. No one except Max seems to even know what a fractal dimension is—except Bianca, who exhausts Anna with a discussion Anna has little to say in, seeing as she neither understands the underlying mathematics nor the crucial words due to Bianca's pronunciation.

When Anna disrupts the centimeter-sized, ghost-shaped colonies and scoops parts of the gel to new petri dishes, they regenerate their shape. No matter which way she slices the thing, it repairs itself to a new ghostly image. "Zey know which way zey are growing," Bianca says. Max comments that perhaps the shape of the Archeon favors packing in a certain direction. There is talk of an article in the air.

"It is going to sound like a joke paper," says Anna. " '*H. cthulhu* grows in its own image'—who would publish that?"

"Who *wouldn't* want to publish that? We just have to figure out why this happens. Have some faith. Don't be so depressing." Max smiles.

"I'm Finnish," Anna retorts. "We don't do optimism." Everyone laughs.

�֎

The stay in Copenhagen takes its toll. Anna sleeps badly and often startles awake in the middle of the night, damp with cold sweat. She doesn't remember her dreams, but the unnerved feeling she wakes up to stays with her until early afternoon.

The time difference to Helsinki is negligible, although she blamed her tiredness on that for the first few nights—she had to take the morning flight out and wake up at five o'clock Finnish time. During her second week, the viability of the excuse has run out.

Every morning, she is met by a chipper Bianca in the wetlab. Anna frankly doesn't know why Bianca spends so much time there—she would have supposed a postdoc would have left the tedious, repetitive experiments to Masters students or lab technicians. Bianca's chatter is a non-stop mix of hard science, interesting TV programs, and her own worldview, which is a collection of oddly science-based New Age beliefs. She has perfected the art of changing conversations from genetics to the power of thoughts to shape the reality and back again without a blink. Anna notes that Bianca, too, seems more and more tired, but the growing dark shadows under her eyes do not seem to affect her mood.

"So, how do you like Bianca?" Max asks on one coffee break, when Bianca has just abruptly left to check the temperature of her culture. Bianca's exit leaves unfinished her long-winded story about people who have spent a lot of time together hearing each other's thoughts due to quantum coupling.

"She's nice," Anna says noncommittally. "Very perky."

"She's under a lot of pressure, but she is a good scientist, you know," Max says. "Just not a physicist. You have to let the force fields and twisted quantum telepathy go in one ear and out the other. What she does in biology is close to magic. In a good and scientific way."

"So, you can be a good scientist without being a physicist?" teases Anna. Max smiles.

"It is rare," he admits with a wink, "but you can be a good scientist even if you are not a physicist. Not knowing about SAXS, though, that's another matter."

Anna laughs.

"How do you feel about going home?" Max asks.

"Fine, I guess. I haven't slept so well here. I guess I'm in need of a long holiday," Anna answers truthfully. "Frankly, I miss my cat. My parents are taking care of it."

On her last Saturday in Copenhagen, Anna fails to sleep at all. She cannot pinpoint the reason for the nervousness that makes her hands shake. She falls into a restless slumber, only to jolt back to consciousness mere minutes later, drenched with sweat and shaking from the cold. She is sure she has seen nightmares, but cannot remember. The feeling of dread lingers.

Anna finally gives up and takes a long, warm shower to wash off the sour-smelling night sweat. Not knowing what else to do sleepless in a strange city, she decides to go into work. Riding the noisy bus only strengthens her resolve. She cannot handle crowds in this state of tiredness—it is best to exhaust herself with work and maybe take the beginning of the next week off for some last-minute sightseeing.

The lab is almost as dark and empty as one would expect, but Anna notices a cone of light through the open door to the wetlab. Curious, she turns towards it and steps in a puddle of water.

"*Perkele,*" Anna swears, then looks around to see whether anyone heard her. The laboratory, which until that point was quiet, bursts into a high-pitched hum, drowning out the rest of her surprised, Finnish curses.

The water level is higher closer to the laboratory. There are waves going around in the liquid. Anna dials the campus security and tells them there is, at a minimum, a plumbing problem in the microbiology laboratory.

"Do you know what happened?" asks the bored-sounding person on duty. "Can you go and check? Perhaps this could wait until Monday."

"I'm ankle-deep in water," Anna retorts. "I don't know what happened, but I'm certain it cannot wait."

The phone operator promises to stay on the phone with Anna while she goes to check. Anna sighs. Her shoes and trousers are already wet to the knee, so there's nothing to be gained by refusing. The light from the wetlab flickers and the piercing hum drowns out every thought in her mind.

She imagines burst pipes, wet laboratory books, and ruined experiments when she walks towards the laboratory. Nothing could prepare her for what she sees. The phone falls from her limp hand—the water has risen above knee-level and the foaming wave tops brush Anna's fingertips when her hands fall meekly to her sides.

The laboratory is covered in water. Bianca stands a few meters in front of Anna, her face turned towards the middle of the room and her hands raised in a salute. Laboratory benches have fallen. There is a vortex in the middle of the room and from that vortex rises a familiar shape. It is green and yellow, and smells disconcertingly of salt and biofilms under the stench of rotten guts and sulphur.

Anna tries to look at the ghost-like shape of the *cthulhu* and her eyes are drawn to its short, thick, strong tentacles. The edges of them are lined with villi, each one a perfect miniature of the creature standing in front of her. The creature's edges are dissolved into a fuzz. Anna suddenly realizes it is because every tentacle is lined with perfect little *cthulhu* shapes, which have perfect little tentacles, which have perfect little *chulthu* shapes . . .

Bianca turns to face Anna. Her eyes are wide and bloodshot, her mouth frozen in a scream, but Anna cannot hear it. She does not know whether it is because Bianca is not making a sound or because the buzz of the creature fills her ears.

Anna tries to grab Bianca's arm. "Come! Run!" Her tongue feels thick in her mouth, but she manages to spit the syllables out. Bianca looks at Anna without a sign of recognition. Waves of darkness emanate from the Ancient One and the dread almost brings Anna to her knees. The vortex spins faster—the water is almost up to Bianca's neck.

Anna reaches out again and manages to get a hold of Bianca's forearm. Bianca looks startled, and Anna tries to pull her away from the horror. Away from the vortex, away from the impossibly rising water.

Bianca loses her balance and Anna manages to pull her, floating, towards the doorway.

"*Apua!*" Anna pants, all the words in the English language gone from her mind. "Run! Help!"

Bianca struggles to regain her balance. For a moment, she looks at Anna and there is a sad smile on her face. Then it is gone and she emits a manic laughter. She grabs Anna's hand in a death grip and pulls her towards the center of the room.

"Stop!" Anna screams. Bianca's fingers are like steel and she pulls on Anna with a determination Anna can barely match. She grabs onto whatever she can, but the wall is sleek and there is nothing to hold onto.

Suddenly everything stops. The buzz and hum dies out. Bianca stops pulling and the terror in the middle of the room raises its front tentacles. Even the vortex stops.

The *cthulhu* slams down its tentacles and time starts again. The vortex changes direction and Bianca is not prepared. She is slammed into Anna, who makes a final, desperate grab and gets one arm around a thick, round pipe. When it starts to give away, she realizes it is not a pipe.

The safety chain of the nitrogen bottle gives away and the bottle starts to fall. It goes into a slow, wobbly spin, almost regaining its balance before finally toppling over. The top hits the wall, the nozzle breaks, and the explosion sends the bottle bottom-first towards the center of darkness. The light flickers once more and goes out.

Anna struggles to get her head above water, but she doesn't know which way to go for. She is thrown around by the vortex. Her legs are cramping and her sides sting from fighting the reflex to breathe.

Then there is only darkness.

Anna wakes up in the hospital hooked up to what feels like dozens of monitors and IV lines. The nurses are kind and speak good English, but Anna struggles with putting together the simplest sentence. Her lungs are on fire, her skin dry and brittle, her lips chapped.

"Water," she rasps. Then, "Bianca?"

The nurses bring her water.

✼

Later, Anna hears that campus security reached the lab a few minutes after the explosion. The nitrogen-bottle projectile had gone through the room and through the opposite wall. No one mentions the horror it slammed through on its way there. No one speaks of a vortex. Maybe no one saw it, save Anna and Bianca.

Bianca was not saved. The broken-off nozzle hit her squarely in the stomach. The guards did what they could, but she succumbed to her internal injuries in the hospital.

Anna had swallowed and breathed in a quantity of salt water. The security officers had found her unconscious and throwing up in a puddle, and saved her life by preventing her from choking on her own vomit. The hospital has tried to keep her hydrated to fight off the salt poisoning and she prevails.

Professor Jacobsen and Max visit her in the hospital. Max looks the same as always, but Professor Jacobsen has black tights under her skirt and no jewellery. They have a gift from the lab members: The laboratory has pooled their money to pay for a new cell phone for her. Anna feels uncomfortable taking it. It is far too expensive, from people she knows far too little. The phone is dripping with guilt. From police questions and now Professor Jacobsen's explanations, she learns that everyone believes Bianca had a mental breakdown, destroyed the laboratory, and tried to drown Anna in a bucket of salt-water. Buckets and buckets of salt-water. There was also a pipeline break. Anna cannot understand how the story makes sense to anyone. Perhaps it doesn't.

Professor Jacobsen is clearly distraught. "Maybe I pushed her too hard," she says. Anna rasps in response that it was not anyone's fault. There is nothing else she can say. How can you grant absolution when you don't think you deserve it yourself?

Max the SAXS guy looks old and sad. "Poor Bianca," he says. "Poor you. Take care of yourself." He tells Anna that all of the *cthulhu* experiments were ruined by the flood in the laboratory. Little ghost-like patches of the cultures were found here and there, rapidly dying due to drying. Now the lab reeks of chlorine and cleaning agents, and will be rebuilt later. Anna wonders what happened to the rest of the creature— maybe the rest of it went down the drain in little pieces. Her eyes dart towards the bathroom. The door is slightly open. She has difficulty concentrating on her visitors.

Professor Jacobsen reassures Anna that they still have a complete data set and a publication can still be written. Anna feels sick to her stomach. Professor Jacobsen goes on and on—she seems oblivious to Anna's discomfort. Max tries to interrupt her several times politely. He finally puts a light hand on her forearm and scowls. "Stop. Just stop. Not the time, not the place." Anna looks at the pair of them and wonders when the hammer scientist turned into the lesser tool.

After they leave, Anna forces her aching legs to take the few steps to the bathroom. She grabs a towel, closes the door, and puts the tightly rolled towel in front of the doorstep. It is not watertight by any means, and it will be difficult to explain to nurses, but it still feels better than nothing.

The thought of the little *cthulhus* being washed into the drain, into the water treatment plant, finally out into the sea, fills her with dread. She tries to tell herself *H. cthulhu* should not thrive in the dirty sewage water where salt concentration is rapidly dwindling, nor in the low salt of the Baltic Sea. Not even in the moderately salty Kattegatt, should they float in that direction.

Anna doesn't know how she can go back home. How she can ever step into a laboratory again. She thinks all samples of funny, harmless *Halophile cthulhu* should be burned to ash.

It doesn't thrive in sewage, she tells herself time and time again. Nor in brackish water, nor sea water.

Then she thinks of the vast Dead Sea.

NOTES FOUND IN A DECOMMISSIONED ASYLUM, DECEMBER 1961

SHARON MOCK

THE MAN IN the blue suit says this is a hospital, but I know better.

They give me a room to myself. It is large, but all it has is a bed. No headboard, no footboard, no table, no chair. Fluorescent tubes that switch on and off through no will of my own. One small window, glass and chicken wire, so high up all I can see is the sky. If I need to use the bathroom, I will have to pound on the door and hope the guard notices.

This is all for my protection, the man in the blue suit assures me. I have experienced a trauma. I must be held for observation. So many large words, as though syllables will hide the truth.

They brought me here in the back of a delivery van. Across from me slept the man who had tried to kill me. Until he woke up. Until he opened his eyes and opened his mouth and cursed my name and blasphemed my blasphemous salvation.

They told me I was safe. They pointed out that his arms and body were firmly restrained, bound to the van's steel walls.

Problem was, so were mine.

✳

The walls, thick gray stone, swallow sound. But when I shut my eyes, I hear everything. There is a woman who laughs immoderately and demands cigarettes from the orderlies. There are men whose minds race, men whose thoughts are a plate of scrambled eggs spilled on the floor. There is a boy who throws blocks and dreams of fire.

Below all this, I hear Bill's voice. Muffled and slurred, as though from very far away. He calls out in his drugged and frenzied slumber, repeating those same foolish words he cried out as he tried to kill me.

He calls out to you, I think in an unguarded moment. *Will you go to him?*

I tell myself the laughter in my head is my own. Isn't it true now, either way?

There is a procession in my head, where dreams used to go. A mummer's dance, full of black gloss and fairy lights and lurid color. When I try to see more clearly, it evaporates, twists into the faces of angry men.

I am too young, too new to this. I don't understand what you're trying to say. Forgive me.

Near dawn, Bill's voice roars loud in my head, then suddenly stops. I jam my fist in my mouth to keep from crying, in case anybody is watching. I know what has happened. The drugs have worn off and Bill has taken his life.

I don't want to know how, but I'm sure the man in the blue suit will tell me.

✳

You is such a useful word. It can apply to anything. Male, female, singular, plural: any, all, or none of these. It implies nothing, save the familiarity of direct address.

It would be nice if there were a third-person pronoun like that. So useful. Maybe there's something in another language that will serve. I resolve to research the matter more fully when I get free from this place.

�֍

"He tore out his carotid with his own fingernails," the man in the blue suit says. "His throat. The veins in his throat. Do you understand?"

He has a name, not just a suit. He gave it to me the night before, when the rescuers brought us in. I refuse to remember it.

"I didn't need to know that." I'd just reminded him that Bill was not just my fellow student, not just my companion. He was my fiancé.

"You don't seem that upset."

How am I supposed to respond to that? I make the mistake of closing my eyes to collect my thoughts and my head fills with everybody's thoughts but my own.

I open my eyes and tell the truth. "It's all . . . overwhelming," I say. "And I'd rather not cry on your shoulder right now."

The man scribbles nonsense on a yellow notepad. "Very self-collected." He sounds proud of himself. "Why don't you tell me again what happened the night of the fourteenth?"

I tell him the same thing I did the previous afternoon. The same thing, more or less, I told the responders, though I was not much for talking at the time.

We drove up from Boston that morning on short notice to investigate an archeological site that Bill's advisor had learned about from sources he didn't discuss. Because of the short notice the team was just Bill and myself, borrowed from the sociology department. I sat in the back and got carsick while Bill and Dr. Davis discussed matters in voices pitched too low for me to hear over the rumbling engine.

We arrived on the island in the afternoon, made camp in a farmer's field at the edge of some woods. I wondered why we didn't stay at the motor lodge down the road, but didn't ask. I didn't want to cause a fuss. While Bill and I set up the tents, Dr. Davis went to scout out the site.

It was starting to get dark and the Professor still wasn't back, so we went looking for him—

"Both of you? And your colleague agreed to this?" the man in the suit asks, as though he's caught me in something. All I say is Yes. In fact, we'd argued about it, but he doesn't need to know that.

We found a hole in the woods. A tunnel, sloping, down under the base of the slate cliffs. Bill went first. He wouldn't let me come along. I watched him for a long time, until I couldn't see him in the darkness, only the light of his lantern.

He shouted. He wasn't making any sense. He said Dr. Davis was dead. He started to say something else. Then he screamed.

Then the gibberish started.

He rushed out of the tunnel with his camp knife in his hand. He'd dropped the lantern behind him. He was a shadow, a shadow with a knife, shouting things that made no sense. You heard him. Same things.

I ran. I hid. I hid behind a rock and Bill didn't find me. What am I supposed to tell you? I was afraid. He was bigger than me. He had a knife. Somebody must have heard all the ruckus. There were houses not that far away. I was hiding when he found you. I was hiding when you made him quiet, when you called out and said that I would be okay.

I will be okay. Right?

"I don't think you're telling me everything," he answers.

"I'm telling you everything I can remember." Everything I have words for. Everything I care to say.

Everything he can understand.

Other things, I leave out. Because I know the man in the blue suit would find them unimportant, or important in the wrong way.

Like, when I agreed to come along on the expedition, I thought they needed my expertise, my experience. An extra set of hands and eyes, at least. By the time I realized my sole purpose was to be a secretary, we were already underway. And Bill wouldn't even look at me. And Dr. Davis just turned up the radio when I asked him why he couldn't have pulled an undergraduate out of class.

(I understand now. He didn't want to have to answer to somebody's rich parents. We were both on scholarship. Our parents didn't matter. If he knew what we were going to find, why did he think he was going to survive it?)

Or that I can't even remember now why I'd agreed to marry Bill, except that he was the only man who asked me. That I have always suspected the feeling—or lack of feeling—was mutual.

Even so, he didn't deserve what happened. If only he'd been able to see. To accept.

Or that when I say I feel like I've dodged a bullet, I mean it in more ways than one.

They let a psychiatrist talk to me. At least, I think she's a psychiatrist. She doesn't introduce herself as Doctor. Maybe she is like me: somebody's girlfriend, a convenient secretary.

She asks me why I'm here. I tell her the same story I tell the man in the blue suit. The only difference is, this time, I feel guilty about the omissions. Maybe this is why they sent her in. Maybe the man in the blue suit thinks I'll say more interesting things to a woman.

When I'm done, she says, "Bill—you were engaged to be married, yes?"

No ring, no date set. But, "Yes."

"I'm so sorry."

There is some ghost feeling inside me that thinks it might feel good to cry, but it won't come to the surface. Hiding behind rocks, terrified. "Thank you," I say and wonder if she can tell that I mean it.

"Do you want to tell me about him?"

Yes. But even as I explain how he was different from the rest of the doctoral candidates, he was a veteran, he'd served in Korea, always treated me a little differently, a little more respect, like we were both not quite fitting in—I cannot shake the sense that I am saying all the wrong things, until the words slow, stumble, stop altogether. "I feel like I should be crying or something."

"You've been through a shock." She looks down at her yellow pad. It's empty. "A terrible thing. Don't worry about how you should be reacting." Then she glances at the door and I know she is thinking of the man in the blue suit. "With me, at least."

I cannot fully trust her. Not with my story, not with my dreams. Talking to her makes me feel better, nonetheless.

There's a pattern to my days. Mornings with the suit, afternoons with the maybe-psychiatrist, the rest of the time alone in my room. They do not want me talking to the other patient-inmates. It might not be good for them.

On the third afternoon, they relent. After my session with the psychiatrist, they let me work in the little farmyard they keep for occupational therapy.

As soon as I close the gate, the goats crowd around, nibbling politely at my uniform, staring up with yellow, alien eyes.

Above, from a high window, the man in the blue suit watches. He thinks I do not know he is there.

I choose to feed the chickens.

❊

The next morning, the maybe-psychiatrist and the man in the blue suit argue in the hallway, as though I cannot hear them. She says there is nothing wrong with me other than the trauma I have so recently endured. He wonders how she can be so sure. He asks whether I don't seem . . . unnaturally collected. Just like that, with that meaningful pause.

She asks what happened to Bill, why I'm here, what happened in those woods. He doesn't tell her. He tells her to just do her job, stop being hysterical.

She storms off in anger. I'm glad I'm not the only one to feel that way.

❊

I think I'd tell her, if I could. Despite the danger. How before Bill came out of the tunnel, there was something else. How before the spill of lantern-light, there was shadow.

And this is why I can't tell her. Because there are no words in this language to describe what advanced toward me. Everything was contained in those shadows: male, female, both, neither, irrelevant. They filled the world, bent it with the weight of their production. I say 'they,' but even that is wrong. Imagine a singular being but an infinite expression—

On the other hand, don't. That's what broke Bill. Trying to define.

I didn't define. I let the presence wash over me, pull me out to sea like a riptide. Never fight a riptide.

I was in awe.

The shadows filled me and they smiled.

And my feet were still on shore.

That was when Bill came rushing out of the tunnel, knife in hand, screaming the name for something he could not understand.

I held up my hand. On my face was a smile that felt cruel and not my own.

"You shame her," my voice said. "She will not answer you."

I said *she* only because I knew that was all Bill would recognize.

His knife came down on air. I was already behind the rocks, hiding, shivering. Thinking I should go to him, help him, save him, even though he would probably kill me. Even though I had already run.

You know better.

Why, yes, my lord, my lady. I do. But it hurt so much to leave him. Hurt me then; hurts me now.

Yes. Tender. Cruel.

Necessary.

Even now, the shadow is a whisper in my soul.

❋

I think I can turn out the lights in my room if I concentrate hard enough.

The lights go out.

Light has its uses, but I prefer the dark.

In the darkness, lights are dancing, ghostlights in the shape of women and of men. They dance together, men with men, women with women, in ways I do not recognize, in ways that would shame me if I still cared about shame.

I do not understand, but then I see. This is the future, a ghost future, a future that still may not be.

My savior is lonely, trapped here in this well-defined world. She misses her children. He longs for his throne.

Tonight, the voice inside me says and I understand.

✳

That afternoon, the psychiatrist does not come. It is the man in the blue suit instead, as though I cannot tell the difference.

"Under what grounds are you keeping me here?" I ask.

"You're under observation," he says.

"And what have you observed?"

"I'm still trying to figure that out."

"Nothing. You've seen nothing."

"You'd like me to believe that."

"My parents will be looking for me."

"Your parents," he says, not bothering to hide his smirk, "are distraught. You wandered away from your campus with little more than a note. It is thought that your paramour persuaded his advisor to join him in a search for you, a search which seems to have gone tragically awry. It is suspected that the pressures of your studies proved too much." He leans forward. "They fear your body will never be found."

I lean back. "Thank you. Now I know where I stand. How long do you intend to keep me here?"

"As long as it takes for you to show your true colors."

"You think I killed him."

"No. We know what killed your companions. What we don't know—what we seek to understand—is why she decided to let you live."

I told you. All they understand is *she*.

"I have no idea what you're talking about."

He stands. "Then we'll just have to wait until you do."

And he leaves me in that room without another word, without looking back, leaves me there until an orderly looks inside and notices me and decides to bring me back to my room.

This world is changing, my savior wants me to know. Like a fruit at the end of summer, it is about to split open and disperse what has been hidden in its heart. Tonight, when I close my eyes, I see a naked woman covered in blood singing in a cathedral and all the men in all their suits are afraid. Is this real? It comes from so very far away.

Life and creation take infinite forms, give birth to infinite young. Some people this breaks, this terrifies. Like my lover, like the professor. For me, it is only awe.

I hope you find this, Doctor (I hope you are a Doctor). I hope you find this and walk away, tell the man in the blue suit to go to hell. There is a child who dreams of fire and the whole world is about to burn.

The doors are unlocked. Soon, I will walk through these sleeping corridors and out the front door. Soon, I will change my name, my being. I will indeed be, as my captor claimed, a body never found. The man in the blue suit will ask people if someone passed this way, but nobody will be sure if what they saw was a man or a woman, a boy or a girl.

In time, I will let my parents know that I am okay. By then, it will be too late for him and his kind, even if he does not know it.

I'll be honest: I don't know what to think of this world my savior is showing me. It is full of blood and fire and death and suffering. It is full of people who have no interest in being the children of an inconceivable god. They do not deserve this. They deserve better.

But maybe there is nothing better to be had.

I want to think that we will meet again, Doctor. I want to believe that when I lose my footing in this world, I will sit in front of you again. You will be tasked with putting me in a category, and I will laugh and tell you that categories are useless.

Will you listen? Will you believe me? I want to believe you will.

I want to believe you'll see this letter.
But there's only one way to find out.
It's time to go.

WHEN SHE QUICKENS

MARY A. TURZILLO

AYAHUASCA FELT COLD stone under her head, back and legs, smelled lilies and corruption, heard bird song, human stirring and animal cries, as if it were dawn. She tried to remember who she was this time. It was always the same in some ways, different in others. Her body this recent time was a woman of thirty years, destroyed by a disease of stomach pain and evil dreams. Her soul, and her formal name, were unchanging: Ayahuasca, Empress of the known world, eternal thread of the world necklace.

This must be death, then. She dimly remembered other deaths and she knew she would live again, and reign again, in a new body. But horrid truths came to her. She began to mourn the life and the body she had just left. And what of her subjects and her friends? Their deaths were more permanent than hers. Even Yaje, her favorite, who wept and swore to follow her to the death house, would be ashes and dust, or the food of worms, all too soon.

She would have cried aloud at the biting cold of the stone, but her throat was paralyzed in death. Her eyes, the eyes of this body, were shut forever and the room in which she lay—the chamber of passing—was so dimly lit she could not see even faint red light through the blood in her lids.

The only warmth she could feel were the two other beings whom she had loved almost as much as Yaje: her yellow hound Burrow and her small gray cat Dark. She tried to stretch her neck to nuzzle Burrow, her toes to

231

feel the silk warmth of Dark, but she could not move. She was, after all, dead.

But she could hear purring and the dog's soft whimpers. They must certainly realize something awful had happened. Both had stayed faithfully beside her through her illness, through the belly-pains and the evil dreams. And they had followed her, maybe secretly stealing in after the shaman's acolytes had arranged her on the slab, to keep vigil. Would they recognize her when her soul transmuted? That child was still a baby, though she'd indicated its identity.

She herself had no bodily issue. At least she would be spared seeing her own children grow old when she herself lived in a new body, and in the body after that, and a series of such bodies, each chosen carefully before transfer, unto the end of time. For the scriptures taught the hard truth: When the Empress died a true and permanent death, then the empire itself would fall and all would be mortality and dust.

She waited. Soon, the shaman would start the ceremony to transmute her soul into the chosen unborn girl. She felt cold and sadness but no fear. She had prepared for this passage. She did not remember previous passages as personal experiences but as stories so vivid they brought both tears and the heat of joy.

Flowers: She could smell the flowers and the incense. From memory, she knew the slab on which her swathed body lay was lapis lazuli, the sacred stone. She could feel the presence of her little cat and dog. But were the mourners asleep? She lay unconscious for a length of time, then awoke to a voice she knew and then another voice.

Yaje. Her favorite. She remembered ecstasies, the warm pressure of his kisses on her lips, her belly, her feet. Yaje was speaking. She yearned for him, yearned for the moment she would reveal herself to him in her new body, though that could not be for years, not until the new vessel was grown to be a woman.

Voices. Yaje and the Nai'uchi, the head priest.

"Whom did she choose as her vessel?" Yaje said. "We have to appear to obey her directives."

Ayahuasca's love-longing turned to bewilderment. *Appear* to obey? Was this her Yaje, who covered her feet with kisses? Who swore he would go into the shadow world with her to await transplantation to a new body?

"You atheist!" said Nai'uchi. "Ignore her instructions? Then, when she's transplanted again into a new vessel, she'll destroy us."

"Oh, you pretend belief, you old hypocrite. But your eyes lit up like the full moon when we talked of gold and riches coming your way. Come on, you're already in your vestments. Burn the herbs, say the words, create appearances."

Nai'uchi said, "I took your offering, but there is no bribe that can make me forget my duties. I won't taint the transmigration ritual."

"I can outwait your stubbornness."

"But the people will not. Listen! They press against the gate, awaiting her resurrection. They scream to know what vessel will hold their ruler. Even in the zoological gardens, there are signs: The snow leopard paces, refusing its meat. The baboons gibber. The snakes are striking at the bars, bloodying their jaws."

Bribe? Ayahuasca didn't understand. She had made her will and chosen an infant to contain her soul. The baby had been born two years past, in the month of the scorpion, a child of the water-dragon house. Ayahuasca's testament should lead them to the ordained little girl, marked with a strawberry mole like a third eye upon her brow.

"If you refuse, Priest, I'll expose you. Witnesses saw our transactions. Lady Natema—"

"Your concubine—"

Concubine? Ayahuasca's soul trembled like flame. Yaje dared touch another woman while First Consort in her court?

"My tool, yes. Don't tax me with her; you've had alley-lovers enough. Just do the ritual. Say that Empress Ayahuasca's soul goes into Lady Natema's unborn child."

Ayahuasca's fury glowed molten. But her body was cold and unmoving, and her incorporeal soul could touch nothing.

"Unbeliever!" The shaman rolled his eyes to heaven in fake piety.

"Gold and spices and slaves may buy my actions but never my conscience." Then his voice softened. "Yet, I must send the Empress' soul somewhere—shall it be to your bastard child?"

Yaje's voice was crafty. "You sly old fool, did I say the child is mine? What if it is? But on the off chance that the soul exchange is real, let's not risk Ayahuasca's strong character invading that baby. Send our bitch-queen's soul elsewhere. The child shall be all mine. I'll send Natema abroad—no, better, Lady Natema won't survive the birth. Under my protection, the new Empress will teach her subjects respect—and they'll double and triple their tributes."

Ayahuasca's fury exploded like green wood in fire. She had ruled fairly, demanding only modest tribute. Under her, the country had prospered, no child hungry and no foreign power threatening the people. She wanted to scream and tear her hair. Yaje was a parasite! He'd been false all along! Death had come to her too young, her last days filled with evil dreams and agony in her belly. And why had she never conceived, either by the now-dead Emperor, or by her consorts? Perhaps he'd even conspired to poison her.

Nai'uchi insisted. "I need some vessel for the Empress's soul. I can't perform the ritual without a target, even if I lie and say the soul lives in your bastard."

Yaje's voice went flat, as if he had already dismissed the issue. "Send it to the puppy or the cat, then."

Nai'uchi burned sweet herbs; arousing Ayahuasca's spirit. Chanted words set her spirit heart beating. The shaman spoke the high language only royalty and shamans understood. His words meant: *Go unto the cat, great Empress. Infuse the cat and return to living land.* The chant went on, entreating her to live, creep into the pet's body.

Entreating. She had a choice: Return to the poisoned world of pretended love, pretended loyalty. And in the cat's body, in this house of traitors, how long would she survive?

She had a choice. As incense floated around her, her soul flowed like blood from a chalice.

Her eyes opened. The colors of the trees filled her vision. She felt blood in her veins, the hair on her back rise. The smell of manure from the baboon cage flooded her senses. She flexed her great claws, and muscle and fur rippled on her flanks. Her screams brought the keeper.

The keeper looked at her with terror. She bore down on him, broke the gate latch and bounded down the boulevard, out of the zoological gardens. Toward the shaman house.

THE CYPRESS GOD

RODOPI SISAMIS

ROSA COMES BACK from the hospital and takes a bat to Jimmy's wind-shield. I miss the entire thing because I'm working in my mom's bodega on a Saturday morning. I'm pricing bottles of Head and Shoulders with a permanent marker when the air around me turns into an electric current. I hear the muted screaming and car alarms seconds later. I throw down the bottles and marker, running to the front of the store, before I hear my mom telling me to get away and get back to work. I miss the whole thing. I'll always remember that Rosa came back from the hospital and destroyed Jimmy's windshield with a bat, but I'll never remember the look on her face, the rage on Jimmy's, or the way his windshield went from solid to gummy as it sagged into the driver's seat.

    I curse not being able to enjoy my weekends the way my friends do. I could rebel more. I could put my foot down and demand to be allowed to have a social life. Even though I'm an only child, I have somehow disappointed my parents so deeply that nothing I do is right. If I can't be what my parents want me to be, the least I can do is be obedient. Even my looks seem to offend them. My hair radiates from my scalp like a froth of brown curls, some days simply reaching for madness. My front teeth have a gap and instead of lateral incisors, I have short, chubby fangs. For all these reasons, I don't really get away with anything. I don't even try. When my mom wakes me up to go work in the bodega with her, I go. I stay there all day, even though I want to be anywhere else. I envy the customers who walk in to buy things, then head happily into the sunny, warm afternoons, the rest of their days filled with unknown possibility. When I bring this up to my mother, she mentions that I enjoy food and shelter, and this is what it means to work.

"But don't people who work get paid and have days off?" I ask, a limp rag hanging from my hand. I have been cleaning coagulated soda from the bottom of a refrigerator. She gives me a dangerous look then goes back to the mail she's beens sorting through.

"La nevera con los galones de leche necesita limpieza."

I hate cleaning the milk fridge. There's always some weird, slimy, black stuff that covers the gallons of milk when they're delivered that makes me wonder if they're stored in some kind of factory filled with rats that like to shit on the plastic gallons. I wipe them down, anyway. I organize them by expiration dates, The fresh gallons of milk in the back of the fridge and the older ones in the front.

I look at the clock and calculate another eight hours to go before we close. Even then, I'll have to go home and do nothing. My entire life feels like a prison sentence. The next morning, my mom stands over my bed as I'm sleeping and asks me if I'm going to church with her. Whether I say yes or no makes no difference: Either way, I have to go with her. I sit up in bed and, without waiting for an answer, she makes her way to the kitchen to make my father breakfast.

As we head out, my mother frowns at my hair and starts muttering under her breath, so I walk ahead, waiting for her in the apartment building's hallway until she's ready. The entire walk is a litany of criticisms. I'm relieved when we make it to the church. The large sandstone cathedral has two bell towers and a center tower with a rose-stained glass window in its center. The towers spiral toward the sky like daggers, overlooking the neighborhood, standing in judgment over its people. The cathedral has stood for as long as I've been alive and stood before I was even conceived. It's one of the most successful dioceses in the city, in part because of its flexibility and its acknowledgment of its changing flock. As the people who lived in the neighborhood changed, so did the faces of the gods and goddesses.

The singing from inside is soft, growing louder as we walk up the marble front steps. As I step through the first set of double doors, awe and humility rise inside of me almost immediately. I buy a thin, white candle and light it at the feet of the Mother as she rises in the dark foyer, sucking all the light to her body, her lily-white arms extended, her face peaceful, smiling, as she steps on the head of a man who is in the process of turning into a snake.

"Save us from the patriarchy," a woman nearby whispers in prayer.

I look at the face of the man: battered, bruised, his face twisted in humiliation. I don't feel sorry for him. My grandmother told me about those men. The things they did, the violence and the horror that they spread upon the world.

"They thought they would get away with it forever. And for a little while, they did. A long time, they buried our mothers, our daughters, our sons, and husbands. But we bided our time. We bided our time and we came back."

She puffed on her cigar and closed her eyes, her face smooth.

We enter through the heavy, wooden double doors. The floor stretches in front of us, a green, marble lake flecked with spots of white and black. The pillars are giant gods of marble, leading the eyes to the ceiling, which is filled with frescoes of the rich history of our faith. Saints at writing desks; angels leaning over their shoulders, whispering secrets. Saints in long, red robes, radiant suns around their heads, their lips crimson smiles, eyes cast upward.

My mother's auburn hair shines in the soft light as she leads the way down the rows of pews. The fourth pew from the front is our place. We slide in and I pick out the program for the weekly mass from the hymn book rack. We both kneel and pray quietly. I ease off the kneeler and sit back in the pew, the program in my lap. The altar is being quietly set up by all the volunteers.

I recognize some of the girls from school and see Erica Francis among them. She volunteers in the church and is the head of the youth group. She also participates in school council and is the captain of the cheerleading team.

My stomach does flips when I see that Brother Jonah is going to be delivering the mass' sermon. Erica moves over to Jonah, touching him lightly on the shoulder. My stomach lurches to my feet and my eyes sting. When Mass is over, I wait until almost everyone has filed out before I head towards the side of the church, which is made up of small, stone shrines that are architectural miracles in themselves. Each shrine houses a god, and enough space for penitents to light candles and leave offerings.

I can feel the waves of energy pulsating through the floor as I make my way to Marchosias' shrine. She's standing in the center of a low-set stone altar. All the candles around her have gone out. The small, stone cave is quiet and I work automatically, knowing by heart where all of the incense and fresh supplies are. I empty the censer with the resin-fused incense blocks. Pour fresh water into the chalice at her feet, sprinkling sweet-smelling spices into the water. A few drops of the oil I blended myself. I carry the charcoal between thumb and forefinger as I hold a lit match beneath it. When it begins to sizzle, flame moving like a tiny red worm around the diameter, I place it in the center of the censer, dropping the chopped resin in.

The smoke undulates, thick as hair in the dark. Fire comes last. I bring out fresh candles, knowing that no one visits this small stone grove except for me. I feel around for the glass bottles of candles and place them tentatively at her feet. I light them, my eyes adjusting to the flare of light, as the glow begins to slowly grow all around her, around me. She's carved entirely out of red wood. The clear glaze around her body gives her the appearance of being covered in fresh blood. Her hands are extended on either side of her, one hand extended towards me, palm open.

I reach out and touch her fingers with mine. I take the biscuits from the ziploc bag in my purse, placing them in an empty silver dish at her feet. They look dark and cracked in the candlelight, but I know she will be pleased. I light one last candle, a dark maroon taper. I kneel on the cushion at her feet and cross my arms on my chest.

When I'm done, I dip my fingers in the lukewarm water, press them to her bare feet, then to my forehead and heart. I pull the golden bangle from my wrist and slide it on to hers. The necklaces that I have brought her throughout the years glitter around her neck and torso like chain mail in the flickering light. Her wolf eyes glow yellow. At the sound from the entrance, her snout furls and her eyes shift to the doorway. I am putting the supplies back in their place when Erica enters. My anger at her intrusion in my place of worship bubbles like a sulfur swamp.

"Hey, Sorha." My name is chewed through her mouth, mispronounced, sounding sloppy and glib.

"It's pronounced Sor-hah." My voice comes out quieter than I'd like it to.

"You know, they're thinking about opening up more space for more traditional saints."

Her voice is saccharine, her perfume floral and too heavy. I shrug my shoulders with my back to her, placing the fresh carnations in the vase. They are pink, fluffy and baby-soft. I gently pass my fingertips over them, feeling the slight warmth that they emanate. A pity that they'll be dried up and dead soon enough, but that is the nature of sacrifice.

"They might take her out of here. Empty out this entire shrine; put her in the dark storeroom."

I unwillingly shiver at the thought of Marchosias being placed in a cold, dank basement, forgotten. I can tell that Erica has noticed and that it's what she's been hoping for.

"Kind of like you. Figures this would be your god of choice."

I turn to her, the silver vase in my hand. "You shouldn't say things like that."

Erica sneers and rolls her eyes, tossing her hair behind one shoulder.

"You're the only one who believes any of this is real." she extends one hand towards Marchosias. I instinctively tighten my grip on the silver vase. "Aside from the old people, I mean. No one believes in any of this in a non-metaphorical or non-ironic manner."

Her smile is full of teeth and I find that I want to smash her face in.

"Welcome to reality."

She turns on her heel and walks out, leaving me shaking with anger and hurt. I try to dispel the idea that one day, Marchosias won't be here, that my tending to her shrine is a temporary thing. I place the vase with the carnations at her feet take one last look at her now-peaceful face before I walk out. My mother is waiting for me outside the gate and we walk home in stony silence. The sky has turned gray. The wind smells like leaves and overturned earth.

"What are you thinking about?" she asks.

I don't know how to tell her that I am thinking about Jonah, the way his slender fingers hold the heavy book with the engraved, tentacled sea monster, that I saw him running at the park without a shirt on, that he has a tattoo on the inside of his well-formed bicep of a trident with two snakes coiled around the staff.

Our priesthoods are compatible. His dedication is recognized by the church but I still have to pass the tests, and finish my volunteer hours. When I become dedicated, our gods and priesthoods would be compatible, it would be one thing we would never have to argue about, if we were together, if we ever had children . . . I shake my head to dispel the dreams that cut me like sharp little knives when I'm alone. I can't tell her that everything inside of me feels like white fire when he comes near me, or that I hate Erica Francis for taking away from me everything that I want for myself. I shrug. She doesn't insist and we talk about the sermon instead.

"I'm very impressed with the new young priest. Jonah, is it? It's a very intelligent choice on the part of the Council to add him to the roster."

"How so?"

I never considered that there was anything strategic about the priests that were chosen for sermons.

"He's going to draw more people to church, obviously. He's young, good-looking. You should have seen all of the women that were flirting with him on the way out. Even married ones!"

She's scandalized.

It makes sense, I suppose. If the women were filling up the church, then their children would follow. I remember Erica Francis' words and a violent shiver moves up my spine.

Monday is a gray day with a white sky and nothing but crows move in the trees. I can smell the rain that's coming. I put on a thick, white Rogue t-shirt underneath my school uniform's sky-blue blouse. I pick my silver necklace from my own statue of Marchosias. It's coiled around her neck and draped over her wings. She sits on her haunches and peers ahead, as if suspicious of what the future could bring. I uncoil the silver from around her and clasp it around my neck.

The pendants are a gold wishbone, a wolf's head, and a heavy locket with a crescent moon on it. I let it hang outside of my blouse and slip gold bangles on my wrists.

School itself is a blur. I sit with my friends Katie and Salazal during lunch. I don't discuss Marchosias with them. Instead, I nod and smile at the stories they tell about their boyfriends, concerns over exams, things that in all fairness, I should be concerned about, as well. Whatever the cost, I know: Marchosias has to stay.

My blood runs cold, and then boiling hot, as I see Brother Jonah walk in through the cafeteria's double doors. He's wearing blue jeans and a dark burgundy polo shirt. I stare at him helplessly as he walks in with Brothers Peter and Saul at his side. They're laughing about something and I feel that he's detected my gaze. I duck my head when he turns to look in my direction.

I count to ten before I look up again and my stomach drops in horror. He's looking straight at me, unsmiling. I look away first, my ears burning. I feel his gaze on me until well after I've left the cafeteria, finished eighth period, and am making my way to the rectory office to look at the schedule.

Marchosias' shrine is on the list in need of cleaning. I sigh in relief. It means there have been a number of offerings made, which bodes well for her and her popularity. I sign my name next to Marchosias' slot as care-taker, giving Susan the secretary an exhausted smile. I walk down to the basement where the lockers are. St. Magdalena's is more open than other churches to keeping its doors open after hours, sometimes well into the night, allowing us volunteers free rein of the grounds while we work. I slam the locker door, tying my apron on. It has a tag with the word 'Volunteer' and my name on it.

I walk down the silent and dark hallway, hands in my pockets, challenging myself to not fear the dark. The church is transformed after hours. It's all dark except for the candles flickering from the altars, a few wall lamps that are lit so we can see. Outside of those spheres of light, the darkness swarms heavy, and this place of worship and safety suddenly seems sinister. I grab the metal pail at the head of the stairs and make my way over the sea of silent marble to Marchosias' shrine.

I can smell the blood biscuits going stale, some meat that's beginning to go bad. I light the match and touch its flame to the wall torque, lowering the stained glass covering the torque so the light is dimmed to a purplish, pinkish glow.

It settles around the shrine and around her body. Her belly is rounded beneath her flowing robe, her hands settled around the soft mound. Her wolf grin is pleasant in the glow of the shrine. Her penitents this week are putting me to work tonight; her offerings are raw steaks, already beginning to turn black, some breads and pastries.

The goblet is filled with milk, some of it sloshed out of the cup and onto the stone beneath. I dump the food into the pail, using a piece of biscuit to clean off each plate. It makes a wet sound that slightly disgusts me when it hits the rest of the food in the pail. I pull my rubber gloves out of my apron, making my way with a full pail back into the basement, this time turning left where I turned right previously to go to the lockers.

The dark hallway leads to several doors, but the one I'm looking for is to my right. The courtyard is dark and silent. I bite the handle of my flashlight between my teeth directing the light towards the compost pile. Flower beds rise and fall on every side of me. I pull open the gate and it creaks, leading me into the wilder parts of the garden. Where the things that rot go. The compost pile is in the center of the clearing, a large wooden fence built all around it. I make my way to the fence and climb up on the lowest rung. I turn the pail upside down, dumping the food in. There are maggots as long as my fingers wriggling in the soil. There are so many that it looks as if the soil itself is moving, heaving up and down. Breathing. Sacrifice taking on new life.

I turn away from the mound before I feel the retch forming in my mouth, walking back the way I came. I am cleaning the goblets and silver offering plates in the kitchen when I hear Erica's laugh. I turn off the water and listen. I shut off the kitchen light and stand very still. She wasn't on the list of volunteers for the night. Her laugh is mingled with someone else's. It's low, seductive, and the man is aroused. I can taste it in the way he breathes in before he speaks. His laugh is a galaxy of blue with specks of darker blue in nimbus clouds. Hers is the white of winter, a cold slash in the dark. It's Jonah. And Erica. I close my eyes and my soapy hand closes around the moon locket hanging from my neck.

"Come on," she croons. I can see their bodies framing the doorway to the Paula shrine. Goddess of the light. I watch as Erica caresses the side of Jonah's face, watch the way his body sags toward hers.

Thief.

"That Marchosias shrine is in the best spot in the church. Paula deserves it more." She places a kiss by the side of his mouth. "Think about it. All that rotting meat and food in the best place in the church? Paula demands sweet things, perfumes and incense."

Jonah is uncomfortable, but he doesn't move away when her mouth finds his. As he is a priest of the blood gods, I can imagine his discomfort at the way Erica has framed her argument.

"Marchosias is a great goddess. She belongs in that shrine and she has followers, even a priestess in the making." My heart catches in my throat at his words.

Erica sucks air between her teeth. "Do you mean that puny Sorha? If that's the priestess that Marchosias chose, then I can see why she's going to lose that shrine before she can even be dedicated." Jonah moves away from Erica, but she doesn't seem worried.

"You like her. I can tell. She has that old quality to her. Like you." Erica presses her palm to Jonah's chest. "But you know how we operate. We'll see who wins the spoils of war."

She enters the shrine as Jonah walks away from her. I turn on the kitchen light, turning the water on again. The silence in my mind is deafening. I finish washing and drying the plates, bringing them up the stairs with me. The church is quiet as I make my way to my shrine. I put away the dishes, finish cleaning the stone beneath Marchosias' feet. Gone is the contented look. Now her head is lowered, her muzzle furled, revealing sharp teeth. I tip some of the jasmine oil over her head and on her feet. It fills the shrine with its aroma.

"Well, that's a change." I whirl around and Erica is at the entrance to the shrine, her long, dark hair in a low ponytail. Her dark eyes look over Marchosias and there is almost a tinge of envy in them. "If only most of her offerings smelled as good as that oil."

I say nothing and continue to wipe down with the oily rag. She moves into the shrine, kicking the pail at the foot of the statue.

"You should stop." My voice is clear, strong. Every cell in my body is vibrating to some distant hum. I feel it radiating from the statue, inside of me. "Please stop," I say again.

I'm not sure if it's the 'Please', but suddenly, Erica is in my face, her long finger in between my eyes.

"You have no business being a priestess! You and this abomination have no place here. She'll be out of here before the end of the month and you with her. There isn't another church giving the cult of the Fallen a chance."

Her smile is sharp.

I know she isn't lying. I know the power that she and others hold in the church. I move faster than I feel. I pick up the ceremonial blade, slashing it across her throat as arterial blood sprays me in the face. I wind my arm back, bringing it forward with all the force I can summon, finally burying the blade in her stomach.

Her face is a mask of confusion but only for a few moments. I drag her by the hair and place her bleeding neck at the statue's feet. There is so much blood that it pools around the statue, dripping down the altar, all over the shrine floor. The blood creeps along the marble, turning the green lake black.

When the pools of blood stop moving, I hoist the body on my back, carrying it out into the garden. With a shovel, I make a place for her beneath the mountains of maggots, and watch as the moving earth and garbage cover up her limp body. There is no trace of blood in Marchosias' shrine the next day. Erica's body is not found and Paula's shrine is destroyed that same night. The goddess is found crumbled, teeth marks along her white neck, her eyes hollowed out. When I look at Brother Jonah now, as helplessly as ever, I don't look away when our eyes meet. My ears and lips burn, but I don't look away.

"Nyarlathotep" by Shelby Denham

QUEEN OF A NEW AMERICA

WENDY N. WAGNER

THE LITTLE GIRL hunkered down to study the beetle, its shell a shimmering rainbow of colors like the ones she'd seen on the mud puddles beside the street. She was only six, but she had already learned that beauty could exist in places others would fail to look. She dropped a stick in front of the insect to force it to turn aside and make its colors play in the light.

A part of her mind went to sleep then. She did not remember when these moments occurred, although they happened more and more frequently as she grew taller and cleverer and more self-sufficient. Her brown eyes went blank for a second and then lit bright with some sharp intelligence that hadn't been there before. They narrowed at the beetle. It was no royal scarab, no sacred icon, but only some ordinary creature. All the creatures of this continent were *ordinary*. It pained her to know her soul was bound to this tedious, ill-bred, and utterly mundane place.

At home, there would be magic. She settled down on the sidewalk, allowing her thoughts to stretch out and fill the small mind she occupied. She spent so much time hiding, keeping herself small to keep from breaking the child's tiny brain. She had never been good at restraining herself. Once, she had killed a thousand guests at a state dinner, just to see if she could. Her lips twitched at the memory. Murder was a mere frivolity to a woman such as herself, Queen Nitocris, who had challenged the gods in the great necropolises of Egypt, and won out over life and death.

The smile vanished. Death, yes, she had vanquished. From the dead, she had made herself an army of creatures, hybridized beings whose disparate strengths were held together by her husband's embalming art and her own will. She hardly needed his skills, not with powers like hers. From her own embalmed body, she had captured her soul and held it to roam of all of Egypt as she pleased.

Until the interloper came. Thinking about that magic-less chicaner made her momentarily lose her grip on the host. The little girl moved to stand up. For a second, Nitocris's view of the iridescent beetle went gray as she began to dissolve into the depths of her borrowed mind.

She snapped back, wrenching the girl's consciousness into a prison of waking sleep. Sweat dampened her armpits and pain throbbed behind her eye. Damn, but the girl was strong. Since the illusionist had carried Nitocris out of Egypt and into this dry, drab America, she had almost forgotten the thrill of wrestling with another magical talent. In a place of less science and more emotion, the child could have been a real threat.

Nitocris recrossed her legs beneath the hem of her ruffled blue skirt and noticed the beetle moving slowly away from her. She scooped it up and lifted it to eye level. Deep within her, the child whimpered as the bug ran up her brown arm with prickling feet. The undead queen squelched her host's complaint. The little one would be in charge of their body all too soon. Nitocris would have her pleasures now.

Beautiful things had always been her love and she had missed them after her death. Her subjects had filled her tomb with all her most glorious treasures, but over the centuries, tomb robbers had carried them away. She had plenty of ways to punish them, of course. In the hidden parts of her tomb, her mummies were always at the ready, their jackal teeth and nimble ape fingers ready to rend and tear the flesh of her enemies. But they always returned to her shabby and dirty, her minions' linens unraveling in the wear of battle and the track of time.

Her treasures, too, lost their luster. Golden urns returned dented. Jewels were chipped. Her carefully preserved and gilded cats were ground into dust and mixed with wines Nitocris wouldn't have served to even her coarsest slaves. Even the once-great nation of Egypt had become a dirty, sad place. The energy ran out of it, drained like the nation's fortune into its conquerors' pockets.

Poverty and filth had weakened her. She understood that now. She scowled at the beetle, which stopped in its tracks. Its antennae trembled. Nitocris hated to recall herself in that weakness, but she had come to understand the source of her magical power and her own formidable will, and now that understanding had become its own kind of strength. Like removing the bandage from a festering wound in order to encourage healing, she could now allow herself to remember the moment she laid eyes on Harry Houdini.

He had come to her tomb on the kind of necropolitan tour so popular in those days. He wasn't a handsome man, but there was something mesmerizing about his eyes, something that drew her to him, that practically compelled her to slip inside him. But his mind! She shuddered to remember it. Such a painfully logical mind. It nearly smothered her. It drained the energy out of her before she could even begin to mount an escape. She fought back with mad dreams and strange headaches, but without the power of the old ways for her to draw upon, his will had dwarfed hers.

And then he'd brought her here, to America, where his logic had grown stronger and her own magic had dwindled. Even after he died, she hadn't found freedom, but had instead been drawn into the mind of the sleeping man in the hospital room next door. An engineer, as it would turn out. She poked at the beetle with a small finger, enjoying its nervous scrabble away. Here in America, everyone was so rational and scientific, their spirits pathetically small. She hadn't gotten a whiff of magic until this child's birth.

It had been a stroke of luck, being in the same place as the girl, the first good fortune she had found in centuries. Ever since, she had been soaking up the child's magic like a tender plant growing in the benevolent warmth of a hothouse. She had found just enough strength to escape the previous mind she'd been trapped in and make her way to the infant, allowing herself to be swallowed up by the tiny, developing brain. Slowly, so slowly, her mind and will unfurled from the years of psychic imprisonment. She could almost taste her freedom—and then she would have this lovely body to enjoy once she crushed the mind inside. If she could only find a bit more magic to draw to herself, the process would go faster.

The tinny thumping of drum and bass distracted her from her pleasant ruminations, and a car pulled to a stop in front of her. She eyed it warily. Green and yellow pennants waved on the dented front bumper and the young men inside nearly overflowed the shabby thing. This was a quiet street, but close enough to three fraternity houses to make the mother of the host child forbid the child from playing here in the front yard. One of the boys leaned out the back window, a brown glass bottle clenched in his hand.

"Hey, nigger!" He tipped back the last of the beer and then lobbed the bottle her way.

She threw up her arm, but the bottle struck her on the forehead hard enough to rock her backward. The bottle bounced off, clinking on the sidewalk. The car revved its engine and then screeched away. Someone inside whooped with delight and the sound sent her arm hairs up in prickles.

Nitocris stared after the car, taking in the red-white-and-blue bumper stickers and the back window full of unintelligible Greek letters. If her husband hadn't turned to dust five centuries before, she would have begged him to wrap those boys in linen and rub them down in natron. Such hatred! Such feeling! It was nearly as powerful as the fear and hatred her people had once given their gods. These boys were the kind of Americans she'd missed while she was trapped in the skulls of magicians, writers, engineers. Now that she'd tasted it, she realized it surrounded her, energy-rich and delicious as blood. What she'd sucked at beneath the sands of Egypt was nothing compared to this fresh power source.

The screen door banged open. "Baby girl, what are you doing out here? You get away from that street."

The host child's mother. The tedious old bag would drag her back into the realm of the swing set and the toy ponies, and Nitocris would be pressed back into the unthinking part of the child's mind. It was like being bludgeoned to sleep by stupidity. But today, she thought perhaps she wasn't as bothered by the thought. Today, perhaps sleep would bring rest, recovery, strength. She stretched her awareness after the boys and felt the pulsing throb of distant energy.

"I'm coming, Mom," she forced herself to answer. She eased the beetle back onto the ground.

The child's mind fluttered at the edges of consciousness, called by the presence of the mother. The little girl had registered a little of the pain of the bottle striking her head and fear made her fight Nitocris's control harder than usual. Nitocris had to whip a mental hand across the girl's awareness. She staggered a little and a hot explosion of pain made Nitocris squeeze shut her eye.

"You'll pay for that," she whispered. She grabbed a tiny tendril of her newfound energy and gripped the girl's will cruelly. An idea struck her. Nitocris forced the girl's hand back out to the beetle and scooped it from the sidewalk. The girl's wrist trembled as Nitocris wrestled the creature closer and closer to her face. Nitocris could not restrain a tiny giggle.

The beetle's legs tickled her lips for a second and then she brought her teeth together in a warm burst of bitter goo. The girl choked and gagged. Panic let her burst out of Nitocris's control.

"Mommy!" she screamed.

Nitocris slipped into the darkest corner of the girl's mind. Let the girl rail and cry. Let her know fear. Nitocris was coming for her.

The Queen closed the eyes of her spirit and basked in the knowledge of a new America, ready for her to tap.

THE OPERA SINGER

PRIYA SRIDHAR

THE COLD HAD blown in early on Sunday morning, too early for the fall. People shivered in their purple-and-black sweatshirts; so did Circe. She had taken to pushing her wheelchair, as a form of unofficial rehabilitation. She had managed to get it to the music school's practice buildings this time.

"You can't practice here," the security guard said, after Circe's wheelchair had gotten stuck in the door. "You're not a student."

Circe first stood up and got the chair out of the door jam. She then placed her fists on her hips and faced the woman in a pressed khaki uniform. Time had weathered Circe's dark skin, so that she had permanent circles under her eyes and creased wrinkles streaking her face.

"I'm an employee here," she said, indicating the ID around her neck. "I was a professor. In vocal training."

"Are you on the staff now?"

"I'm retired," Circe said. "Had a stroke couple of years back."

"How sad," the security guard said. "But if you want to practice here, you need to get a sticker on your ID, like everyone else."

"Come on." Circe pointed at the empty rooms. "No one is practicing here now. I just wanted to test out my vocal chords. The doctors say I need intellectual stimulation."

The guard repeated herself and made it a point to help out Circe with her wheelchair. She grabbed the older woman's arm.

Circe finally sat down, biting her lip. Visions of pigs and flashing, sting-angry red swirled around in her head, and her fingers crackled with energy.

"Could you wheel me to the bus stop?" she asked. "It's such a long distance from here."

�֍

In the old days, sting-angry would turn a foolish mortal into a pig. The lady had flicked her fingers several times, so the colors would fly out and drown men while they were eating, until their skin sagged and hung out to dry off round, stupid faces.

Then rocks crashed onto barren earth and exploded in various shades of orange, indigo and yellow. Sting-angry red concentrated in pink flesh, writhing against wilted bones and helpless eyes. Power trapped within a stupid form.

Wait, vengeance. Wait. Colors released soon.

✖

Much later, Circe slipped into the auditorium office, and met with the graduate students there. They remembered her and gave her a sticker for her ID. It was a small, green sticker with the school year listed on it.

"You should practice on Fridays," her old student Sylvie said. "That's when the nice security guard Toby comes. He loves hearing people perform. All the newbie guards act more stuckup."

"Must be part of their training," Circe joked.

"Oh, yeah. They're mainly night students who think they can get a degree by doing less work." Sylvie scowled. "Usually a bunch of ghetto dudes who are compensating for something."

"I took night classes," Circe said. "When I first got married. That was the only way that I could get my degree, having to work another job."

Sylvie immediately backtracked and apologized, but there was nothing to forgive. She had innocent eyes, despite her encounters with harsh reality and having to battle extreme stage fright. Circe had mentored Sylvie for two years.

She straightened up in her wheelchair. Her posture had always been good, even for a singer. She had never had intense back pains, not like her friends who spent their days sitting in front of computers.

"Do you think I could try out my voice on you?" she asked. "It's been too long and I don't want to go all the way back to the practice room."

"Of course." Sylvie stood back a few paces, to give her old teacher room.

Circe drew in a deep breath. She made sure that her diaphragm expanded and contracted; at least the stroke hadn't affected that part of her body. Her throat throbbed with anticipation. She heard the accompaniment in her head, a gentle-but-fast piano tune:

Rejoice greatly, O daughter of Zion,
shout, O daughter of Jerusalem,
behold, thy King cometh unto thee.

She felt the years peel off her as if they were bits of old skin, the deeper that she dug into the tune. Her gray hair seemed to curl at the ends, as if she had just gotten a permanent. Circe hadn't gone to a stylist since her stroke and kept her hair at a short, curly bob.

He is the righteous Saviour,
and He shall speak peace unto the heathen.

Sylvie watched as Circe managed to stand, so that she could give her lungs more air, the much-needed air that they deserved for doing a good job. Her voice sounded powerful against the still, stale air in the office, defiance against Grandmother Time and what lay beyond wrinkles and wheelchairs.

"Rejoice, rejoice," she trilled, letting the notes sail up and down. "Rejoice, greatly."

As she dived into the repeated phrases, about the King coming to

Jerusalem, the linoleum floor seemed to harden into polished wood and the plain white walls fluttered into curtains. Circe was onstage, dressed in a wine-red dress and belting against an orchestra. There was one year when they had done an experimental song cycle based on a novel about ancient Greece and she had volunteered her services when the tenor had fallen ill.

Splatter splash, exile in Rome, wailing purple in mourning, the black in the water—

Circe stopped. She took a moment, to let her vision return to normal, and then sat back in her wheelchair. There was a heavy thud from that, as if she weighed five hundred pounds.

"I don't know how you do it," Sylvie gushed, after a few moments of silence. "How do you do it so effortlessly, remembering to have fun and all?"

"If I didn't sing, I would die," Circe responded, breathing in hard. "Making an effort is much less dire than testing my body, so I have to belt out when I can."

She coughed a bit. Sylvie looked startled and then concerned.

"Are you okay, ma'am? Do you need help?"

"No," Circe wheezed. She fumbled and found her inhaler. "Bad lungs, from years of smoking."

"You smoked?" Sylvie sounded horrified. "But you're a singer!"

"Tell me about it," Circe wheezed, after she gave herself several puffs. "At the time, my voice wasn't giving out, so I thought I'd be fine. It was a hard habit to kick, but I had to. I got pregnant."

"That's not what I meant. Your voice doesn't sound strained," Sylvie said. "I've heard smokers and usually, they're fighting to breathe or sound scratchy. You don't sound like that at all. You sound perfect."

Circe gave a crooked smile. She heard the good intentions behind Sylvie's words and her fingers remained still.

"I guess I was lucky."

✳

Evening faded into a rainbow of pain, of might. Mourning blue, to celebrate the return of a lady.

A certain apartment with yellow walls, peeling paint, and chipped glass. Plants dried into withering husks. Work uniforms rotted into torn threads.

A woman with a husky voice screamed. Her screams became higher-pitched as a beer bottle fell to the ground.

The neighbors heard the crash and ran to the door. Crashes and broken screams echoed against the walls, until the super came with a key. A beeping cellphone, the promise of sirens.

The open door revealed broken glass, spilled beer. A pig squealed within a pile of t-shirt and pajamas, tottering. Its flesh shriveled at one of the neighbors' touch.

✳

Sunday morning. Day of strolling to the park, drinking coffee and eating a slice of whole-wheat toast at a café. The doctors had said that caffeine helped with the aftereffects of stroke, so she made it a point to drink a cup a day.

Circe licked her fingers and turned a page of the newspaper, trying not to notice where she scorched the pages. The local opera company was having financial troubles, plagued by years of debt, a money trap of a theater that housed various pigeons and rats, and budget cuts from the city. Not to mention that sleazy investor who had embezzled funds meant to pay for the new makeup and wardrobe.

Buzz buzz, chalky yellow of betrayal, the timbre of sting-angry red against a black backdrop—

She closed her eyes. Circe had performed in that opera for about ten years, on and off, putting on makeup and belting out various solos and choirs. Several of her friends in the university orchestra played for the operas well, usually balancing sheet music and practice with crying babies and long commutes.

What's happening to us? She asked herself. *Why are we all getting old, losing our jobs, and having encounters with the Grim Reaper?*

The opera didn't deserve this crap. Everyone who belonged to it worked their butts off to make the shows work and to keep production on time. Now, new people were going to suffer the loss of potential careers.

She remembered one of the singers, an exchange student from Spain. Hector had been heartbroken because his girlfriend back home had attracted another boy's attention and, to put it in layman's terms, committed a form of adultery. It was a form of adultery because she and Hector hadn't married, so she had committed no legal wrong. But in terms of moral wrongs, it had torn him. Circe had introduced Hector to REM in hopes of comforting him. The singer had then asked her out to dinner several weeks later.

That had been a strange year. One of her friends called it "blossoming into awesome." Circe had been a gawky, myopic teenager with a slight belly, but that year, suddenly, guys looked at her and saw something prettier within it. Except she hadn't felt prettier on the inside:

Go and catch a falling star, get with (misbehaving!) child a mandrake root, tell me where all past years are (in your pocket, milady), or who cleft the devil's foot —

Circe started. The paper turned black beneath her fingertips. She took a deep breath and wiped her hands with a napkin.

That singer, well, she ought to look him up. It had been too long. From what she remembered, he had had a long career in Canada and then toured Europe before settling down with another local girl that had studied law. Why hadn't she followed up with him?

The meteor. Crash, choke, swirl—

She took another rattling breath. No one could forget the meteor. She certainly hadn't.

Circe finished her coffee. She left her usual tip for the waitress, who smiled at her and unfolded her wheelchair. Circe settled in, lost in memory.

✺

Rock shattering ocean, making frothy white splash, muddying blue and green into a great angry stew.

Old days meant visitors, choices, power. Old days gone with one crash, stars passing uncertainly.

✺

That night, they had all performed a children's version of Romeo and Juliet, the opera. After the performance, the cast and choir had gone out for drinks, in the local city. They had stayed up at that bar with the mirrors on every wall and the harpoons for decoration. Hector had tried to pull one of the harpoons off the wall and chase everyone around with it; Circe had laughed, since the harpoon was superglued to the wall, a glass of cucumber and gin in her hands. She had sat on a wobbly barstool, rocking back and forth, cackling like a young hen.

No one had anticipated the chunk of rock crashing through the roof. They had heard the wood splintering, and the thud as something large and grey collided with Circe's thigh. Her glass shattered against the floor as she fell and her fingers brushed the rock, hot to the touch.

Later, the paramedics said at worst, she had suffered a huge bruise, but no major injuries. Some newspapers took her photo and the morning papers had stories on "the blessing of God."

Circe limped that week and had needed a cane. She kept singing, because singing helped deal with the pain and the tingling within her fingers. People marveled that she attended all her classes and kept performing. Hector had drifted away, his dark eyes always gazing at her swollen leg.

Later, she started researching astronomy and even visited an observatory up north. The scientists there had taught her how they measured asteroids, even helped her find one sharing her name: 34-Circe.

"We think it's gotten smaller," one of the scientists said. "Infrared will have to confirm it, but it looks like it suffered a minor impact and loss some of its mass."

Circe turned and smiled at the scientist. The tingling in her fingers became pleasant now.

"Do you think it could've been the same asteroid that hit me in the thigh?"

"Highly improbable," the scientist said. "The odds that an asteroid with your name from the main belt got minor fragmentation, and the odds of that little chunk of rock drifting for dozens of light years only to crash on Earth and into that particular bar, are highly improbable."

"I wouldn't know," Circe had responded. "Math was never my best subject. And a rock one foot long is 'little'?"

"We measure in meters and yes. Asteroids are usually measured in kilometers."

Circe had accepted that, even though the aching in her thigh wouldn't. That bruise had only faded in recent years. Sometimes, it changed colors, depending on her mood.

�✧

Accept the rainbow, taste every color, power great, once meant for goddesses. Know your true form, the formless demands of life and eternity.

Stir herbs, stir angry, stir love. Brew potions, stroke others' flesh, embrace in years lost.

✿

Back in the practice room on a Friday; Circe had spent her days strolling in the park, calling her daughter just to hear Melody's voice. Melody lived in New York now, studying liberal arts, and she liked her independence. Circe knew that her daughter had cut off her long hair, settling for a curly crew cut.

Circe showed her ID to the security guard Toby, a smiling young man with beard stubble and dark skin like hers. He escorted her to one of the largest rooms, with a wall-sized mirror and a black piano. Toby brought her a music stand and asked if she wanted water. So different from the first security guard.

Pleasant persimmon orange. Light-green bobbing in a soft, gray wind . . .

Her fingers remained still as she prepared herself and started warming up. She was even able to press keys on the piano, to go into the simple chords. Her throat lent its power well to the occasion:

"Thy hand, Belinda, darkness shades me,
On thy bosom let me rest,"

Toby strolled around the corridors, listening to her and to the regular orchestra students—*just like Ulysses, righteous mud-brown armor minty-green swirled together to fight unraveling pink*—but Circe ignored him and the thoughts in her head:

"More I would, but Death invades me;
Death is now a welcome guest."

Except Death wasn't welcome in Circe's home. She hadn't welcomed it the day she and Melody had gotten into a nasty fight, the only night Melody had stayed up past midnight to work on a high school project due the next morning. *Trouble is olive green rotting in orange autumn—*

"When I am laid, am laid in earth, may my wrongs create
No trouble, no trouble in, in thy breast."

Her fingers had twitched terribly, but by then, Circe knew what could happen and so, she held back and screamed, instead. Melody screamed at her to go to bed, and Circe did, holding in all the rage and frustration that Melody was acting stupid. When her fingers wanted to lash out with sting-angry, Circe used a mirror.

"When I am laid, am laid in earth, may my wrongs create
No trouble, no trouble in, in thy breast."

The next evening, when Circe went out to lunch with a friend in the afternoon, the friend had noticed that her face was starting to freeze in odd places and her movements were becoming sluggish. By evening, Circe had ended up in the hospital, in Intensive Care.

"Remember me, remember me, but ah!
Forget my fate."

Late at night, rubbing her eyes and yawning, Melody came into the room. She had thought her mother was asleep and sat beside her.

"I didn't start earlier because you were talking about not wanting to live anymore, with no husband and a dead-end job as a professor with thankless students," Melody had spoken to what she thought was a corpse. "How could I focus on myself if I was worried about you swallowing pills or slitting your wrists?"

"Remember me, but ah!
Forget my fate."

As Circe recovered, Melody had started distancing herself, while helping her mother with household chores. She paid for her college application fees and relied on guidance counselors to choose good schools, far from Circe. It was as if she had built a fortress so that schoolwork mattered more than family, so that Melody could please Circe without either of them worrying about each other.

"Remember me, remember me, but ah!
Forget my fate."

Circe looked at herself in the mirror; she had lost weight since her stroke and the kind dimples that always appeared when she thought of Melody. She was wearing dark pants, so that you couldn't see the scar from where the asteroid had hit her.

Where did I go wrong? She asked herself. *How could I get angry at her for getting angry about what I was saying? Why would I want to hurt my own daughter? I love her.*

She continued singing, repeating the verses. Colors appeared in her head, wistful violet regret, gentle pale-orange, peach-pink longing.

Goddesses don't love their children, another voice said in her head. *They only protect them from death.*

I'm not a goddess, Circe told the voice that she knew belonged to whatever controlled her fingers.

You are now. You could be, if you wanted. You could have men like Toby fawning over you all the time. You could have servants carry you from house to house.

And then what? I'd start destroying everyone that crossed me, until they fought back and destroyed me, and what would I do? Circe reasoned. She stopped singing to think. *You came from an asteroid.*

You can't fight me forever. One day, I'll take over. One day, they'll writhe.

"Not on my watch," Circe said aloud. She aimed her fingers at the mirror. This one was larger than the small one she had used that night she had gotten angry; it would certainly kill her.

You're bluffing.

"And if I'm not?"

Silence.

"Thank you," Circe said. "One day, maybe I'll let you go to a stronger body. But do nothing with mine, okay?"

More silence.

She took a deep breath and resumed her practice. The lyrics echoed against the walls.

"Priestess" by Sara Bardi

SHUB-NIGGURATH'S WITNESSES

VALERIE VALDES

SISTER HONORIA AND I walked into the cul-de-sac, our skirts sweeping the asphalt, the clopping of our feet like castanets. I had a good feeling that today, my sisters and I would bring the Word to receptive ears. I fanned myself with one hand while the other held my black umbrella to shade me from the morning sun.

There were enough of us that each pair could approach a separate house at the same time. Ours had a dirty white automobile in front, and a bougainvillea that was all dry thorns. I saw a crack in the blinds, a pair of fingers. We stepped onto the porch and Sister Honoria rang the bell.

At first, there was no answer. People often pretended not to hear us, or that they were not home. A shadow fell over the peephole, so I knew we were being watched. We waited.

The door opened, revealing a young woman wearing a pinstripe suit and a nametag that read, "YOURLADIES BENITEZ" in block print. "Sorry, *señoras*," she said with a fake smile. "I'm leaving for work."

I smiled back at her. "We understand. But surely, you can spare a moment for the Black Goat of the Woods with a Thousand Young?"

"I don't have . . . " Her dark-red lip curled. "The what?"

"Shub-Niggurath, the Black—" I was politely interrupted by Sister Honoria's cough. I had gone off-script in my enthusiasm. "Are there mysteries in your life that do not have satisfying answers?"

"Well, I mean—"

I held up a pamphlet, the cover of which showed a young woman very like Yourladies, her chin cupped pensively in her hand, question marks floating around her head. Underneath were bulleted questions, which I gestured to as I spoke.

"Have you ever felt that no benevolent god watches over you?"

Her brown eyes narrowed. "Sometimes."

"Do you feel your life is insignificant? That you are a tiny ant in a vast, uncaring universe?"

"I don't know, like, maybe."

"Do you feel you have no real control and could be wiped out at any time by unknown forces more powerful than you can comprehend?"

She fidgeted and looked over my shoulder, likely at my other sisters. "Yeah, sure, whatever."

"Then you will be happy to know there are answers to your questions, if you dare to look." I flipped open the pamphlet. "The Magna Mater grants her worshipers the knowledge and power to ensure the propagation of her seed across the cosmos. Her children are the chapters of her ongoing revelation."

Her gaze shifted to the paper I held, its signs and sigils squirming from the attention. "Is this a joke? Are there, like, cameras or something?"

"Not at all." I offered her the pamphlet. "Read this at your leisure. There is a website on the back."

"*Pero*, like, what's the point?"

Sister Honoria chuckled, the sound coming up from deep in her chest like a cough. "There is no point to anything. No point at all."

That wasn't entirely true, but I wasn't going to contradict her.

"Okay, sorry, but I really have to go." The woman snatched the pamphlet and closed the door.

Sister Honoria and I walked back out to the street to join the others. Some were already returning to the forest behind the neighborhood's flimsy wooden fence, with or without victims for the blood sacrifice trailing behind them. Sister Lydia appeared to have eaten another dog, but there was no telling with her. It might have been a cat, or a man.

"Sister," I said. "Why did you not tell her that Shub-Niggurath grants immortality to her chosen?"

The gentle clopping of her hooves stopped and I turned to look back at her. She watched as the woman climbed into her car and drove away, narrowly avoiding a pair of us in her haste.

"Because," she said, "the wife of the Not-to-Be-Named-One owes us nothing. We exist to serve her and her children."

"*Iä! Shub-Niggurath!*" I said.

Sister Honoria resumed her walk, scratching her horns absently. "Besides, not everyone survives the ritual to become a *gof'nn hupadgh*. Being regurgitated is very uncomfortable."

"She did take the pamphlet, at least."

"Indeed. Let us continue our ministry until she joins us or goes mad."

The sun disappeared behind a wall of dark-gray clouds, bringing with them a storm that quickly soaked through our skirts. We trailed Yourladies to her place of employment, an old movie theater in a shopping center, with a bright, neon-lit lobby jangling with gaming machines.

The projection booth inside was deliciously dark compared to the sunny streets. After a delightful few hours of terrorizing her—making bloodcurdling noises, casting eldritch shadows into empty theater houses, revealing to her the true forms of the Twin Blasphemies and the untranslatable Sign—we finally wore her down and she brutally murdered her supervisor with a conveniently placed umbrella.

"You had to, of course," I assured her as we led her out to the woods. "Your tender sensibilities can only withstand so much stress under the weight of the vast, ineffable horrors of reality."

"*Pero*, like, what do I do now?" she asked, examining her bloody nametag, which read, "YOUR NITE."

"The only solution is to give yourself to the will of the All-Mother," Sister Honoria said.

We soon reached the trees, whose branches tore off our clothes so we could cavort naked with our sisters in the glorious darkness between tongues of lightning. Yourladies was hesitant at first, but she did love to dance. Soon, she was twirling and stomping with the best of us. We even let her keep the umbrella.

PROVENANCE

BENJANUN SRIDUANGKAEW

THEY SAY SHE has always been there, as old as the station's rust: its progenitor, birthing a series of bio-systems, auxiliary supports, rooms and ventilation, and plumbing. The incredible labor, the vast contractions, the ichor on the thighs. The lack of a midwife. Upon the completion of decks slotting into place and parks fertilized to prosperity, she became part of the station itself. There was no umbilicus, or else the umbilicus was never cut—she feeds the engines still or they feed her, reverse-birth where offspring repays the womb.

In this version, she is the mother and ancestor of us all.

We come to adolescence, then adulthood, in her shadow. At its blue-black edge, we decant new infants; within the netting made by her tendril hair, we wed; and in corners formed between her limbs, we hold funerals. From first breath to last, we inhale her salt.

I see her as oil on wood, two-dimensional. The artist was imprecise with her skin color, or perhaps meant to blend her complexion into the fluids of her sustenance. Her head is an impression, hairless, her features smudged on purpose. Shadow of fins and scales undulate about her flanks, and her nictitating membranes are lit by anemone blooms. She's something between *nak* and *nguek*, we say, though she's neither serpentine nor piscine—and in any case, lacks the beauty of either. If she has been dreamed up, it was by a strange, afflicted imagination.

I've seen her name spelled out, but nobody can pronounce it. We say Prathayayi—close enough—and so, our version of her name overwrites her the way our languages have been overwritten in different times, our history overwritten in different places.

Others define her by comparison to fable; I define her by what she is not. My negatives are empirical and exact—a crèche evaluator has plenty of time to squander on observation. These are some of the things she is not: a robot, a fish, a crossroad. She is not a story, a prop, a mannequin—something animates her after all this time, moves breath through her lungs and turns the valves of her aortae. Every day, we monitor her vitals, just to be sure.

This is what we must never try: to speak to her, to wake her up, to remove her from her tank.

To listen to her will, even for a moment.

✸

There is a trick of optics and lighting that makes the hothouse foliage appear to stretch without limit, the fruits fatter and brighter than they are, facsimile of the humid forests that our ancestors knew in that country shaped like an axe. In their days, they filled those forests and public parks with dolls animated to an appearance of sweet intelligence, shaped like *kinnaree* and *upsorn-sriha*. They would enchant visitors, sing, dance. They would pour roselle drinks in celadon cups while musicians dressed like *khrut* plucked the *jakhe* and played the *khim*.

In our day, we hold the blueprints of those dolls and dream of a future when we will have the time and resources to devote to their making. For now, every breath and circuit—every fistful of raw substance—is strenuously accounted for. No waste. No frivolity.

It is this thought that preoccupies my client when I find him. He is standing straight, back to me, in a circle of pebbles and murmuring plants. Glossy coveralls, young, dreadlocked: From his application, I have learned that he's a botanist and a mechanic, and that he wishes for a child of his own. "Khun Kittisak," I say, barely audible above the foliage.

Even then, he jumps as though my voice had carried a killing charge, frying synapses and cleaving nerves. "Doctor Sutharee." His breath is short, the rhythm of guilt. "Thank you for coming to see me."

He wears an optical implant in the left eye. In its indigo lens, the color of Prathayayi's tank, I catch a concave glimpse of myself, interpreted as a black skull with an insect's gaze. "It was no trouble. I was glad for an excuse to get out of my office. Shall we get started? I see you entered the most recent lottery, but withdrew. May I ask why? There won't be another one for thirty-seven months."

Kittisak stares at me, eyes blank with alarm. "This isn't the most private spot."

"No one else is in the hothouse, Khun Kittisak. I'm sorry if I seem brusque." I am not sorry, but people expect a modicum of manners. "But I find it best to establish everything clearly from the outset with a prospective client. Your qualifications are fine; I believe you will ably provide for a child. The issue of your withdrawal will, however, need addressing. In this matter, indecision would be . . . troublesome, yes?"

"I want to bear the child myself."

"That'll take surgery." I make a note to his file, not adding aloud that it'd be difficult to convince my superiors the operation is necessary. He can't convince even me and I'm his case worker. "You're unpartnered."

He nods, matter of fact. "By choice, but I couldn't find a volunteer, either, and it's as fair as any that I should carry the fetus."

(Pregnancy parasitic, childbirth a nightmare of Prathayayi pouring a tide of fluids and gore through orifices. Until the entire body is one great wound, organs worn inside out.)

My face does not change. When suicidal despair and grief of rejected clients is so common, you normalize emotional extremes and learn control of your expression. React to nothing. More decorous that way. "Won't you consider the more conventional way?"

"The more normal way, you mean." He touches his belly, as though already, it is seeded and gravid. "I do want to do it. Gives you a special connection, they say." A delicate cough. "It's how I was born."

"I sympathize." The lie is automatic, rolling off my tongue with the easy taste of familiarity. Fish and lime. "If your request for an operation isn't granted, would you settle for the other option?"

Kittisak's expression flickers. He would not. "I'll consider it. Mostly, of course, I want a child . . . "

"Yes, and outside a lottery, it'll be tricky. Still, your suitability profile is good and you have every reason to be optimistic." I dismiss his file, vision adjusting to the greenhouse, tendrils of light residual behind my eyelids. There have been no breakthroughs in visual interfacing for years and implant components can be recycled only so many times before they degrade. Barring miracles—survey drones happening upon asteroids full of convenient metals and silicates—in three generations, our descendants will be down to interfacing with the station by console. In six, we will cut our birthrate down by a quarter to fulfill the logarithm of survival. In eight . . .

Everything rots, save the corpse in the tank. Everything halts, save the tempo of her pulse.

�֍

When I see Kittisak again, it is in Prathayayi's shadow and he has come to cancel his application.

Nowhere on the station can we escape the sight or sound of her, the smell and chill of her flesh. Among us, there isn't a soul alive who has ever seen shore or beach, the glare of sun on wave. But we all know the sea. Not the surface of it, where water drinks light and gives back jewels, where birds are alleged to flit and flying fish dart. Instead, we know the sea from the other way around: inside its cold, colorless liver and, like deep-sea creatures, we are blind and full of teeth.

My office is directly beneath her gaze, surrounded by her the way blood is sheathed inside arterial walls. Nowhere else are we so close to her, temple to its god, offspring to progenitor. Perhaps that is why I'm less inclined than most to revere and believe: familiarity, contempt.

Inhaling the salt smell for so long, my body is of it, my brain sodium-white. It may also explain why I don't have much empathy left, by sheer proximity absorbing the qualities of the carcass, its amphibious indifference, its distance from humanity. Black glass and old metal and her.

On a cluster of compound lens, I catch sight of Kittisak. He is furtive, looking over his shoulder and sideways. When he looks up and sees me standing between him and the exit, he essays a smile. "Doctor."

"You appear to have withdrawn your request." My expression is neutral, though I don't step aside. "While that is entirely your right, I can't help but feel my time has been wasted."

"I *am* very sorry about that." Kittisak is favoring his left side. His face, half-lit, is swollen. A tender, slightly red cheek. Drowning his sorrows? He can afford a decent alcohol allotment. "My elder sister talked me out of it. Family, you know how they are."

"Mine doesn't override my most important decisions."

His smile capsizes into an aborted chuckle. "No, I don't imagine any-one overrides you much, Doctor, in any matter. I do apologize terribly."

I gesture at the door. "You don't plan to apply again."

This time, his laughter is clear and true, the brittle brightness of it seeming to scatter the shadows for a moment. They resolve, leaving us both again in neon saturation and high-contrast blots. "No, I don't think I will. This time, I am very sure—I won't blight your door or vision again. This has been an education."

Educational, though I can't imagine what lesson he's learned other than that he is an indecisive, overgrown child. Back in my office, I peel a cigarette from its case. Fragile, half the circumference of my thumb, rolled in scrap fiberplast: my only vice, whose rarity and price alone save me from self-destruction. The stench always staggers as the fiberplast singes without combusting. The same stench in my mouth, throat, lungs. My supplier adds the occasional pinch of hallucinogen for a charge, quick-acting, one part chemical and one part interfacing with implants. The mildest: I can't afford stronger and have no wish to become dependent, though I hear the most expensive sort can give you an extensive alternate life. When I lean back, the low ceiling warps and bucks, smoke turning to claws. The desk softens to leathery flesh, the floor to pulsating quicksand. A gravitational peace, as of sinking.

Habit makes me flick on a monitoring channel for the womb-beat to accompany me into chemical haze. A quarter of the chambers down there are occupied by embryos in various states of gestation, tadpoles with frenzied hearts. The lottery is meant to treat all applicants equally, but in reality, it's of course more than luck. Fitness to parent. Relative wealth. Politics. Even the range of available genetic material differs; not all options are accessible to applicants with lesser claims.

I don't see the chambers in person often and have watched the decantation process just twice. The most alien moment of our existence: newly born infants are so animal when they first howl, so strangely inhuman when they are calm. It's better after they are cleaned—watching them emerge from amniotic fluids has always unsettled me—but even then, the nursery is full of small, inscrutable creatures with amorphous minds undefined by thought or geometry. Once, our forebears integrated behavioral modules into the uteral chamber to prime for socialization and language, but that piece of civilization has been sacrificed for survival. Like so much else. Soon, even the hothouse will go: It's long been thought of as more decorative than efficient, that one spot of color in all the station, and food will turn to nutritional efficiency rather than things with crunch and flavor.

There must be more than the endless din, the susurrus of salt, the shadow of Prathayayi that spares nothing. But if that exists, a possibility of a condition beyond the decay we know, it, too, has been lost.

When I flex my hand, webbing tautens wet and green between my fingers. A byproduct of the cigarette and a recurrent fantasy—half-subconscious, half-intent. Sometimes, I dream of the tank breaking, the corridors filling, and all of us turning to scales and fins. The babies spreading their limbs in starfish metamorphosis, infant fat shedding and gums hardening in their mouths, tiny fingers and thumbs replaced by eyes. An easy existence severed from endocrine burden, an echinoderm bliss without future or past.

The comedown is rarely predictable. As often excruciating as exquisite, this time barely a ripple, so much so that when the alarm trespasses on my vision, I mistake it for a drugged residue. There are still fins on my throat and my table is still half-submerged, sodden with seaweed. I know it's not real because the hallucination goes only so far; I smell nothing but office damp and nicotine cocktail. The alarm seems distant.

That pleasant languor eventually breaks, timed toward the end of my shift. Monitoring channels lets me know that nothing amiss happened—that trespassing notification was a glitch, after all. To be conscientious, I run an inventory check. Supplies fine, womb-chambers calibrated, no sensor tripped.

Habit again, on the way out, to look on Prathayayi. Always the same, larger than life. In the crèche, we can only see one part of her at a time: a lineless finger pressed against a window, a black cheek under a floor tile, wrist curving along a corridor. The side of a breast pressed against the shell of the maintenance hub, luminescent.

The fable of sightless hermits groping to tell the shape of an elephant and so we are.

When the first death happens, I don't hear of it until the autopsy.

People die all the time on the station, some easier and quicker than others. We all live badly, in poverty of flesh and spirit, but in the segment furthest from the crèche and Prathayayi's pulse, they live poorer than most. An officer asking me in comes as a surprise.

The Inspector has no use for preamble. "The deceased recently applied for a crèche license."

I glance at the profile she sent me, displayed in the corner of my vision. "He requested entry into the lottery, then withdrew before the results."

"I'd like to show you what his body is like. It's rather shocking, but your opinion would be of value."

"I've seen shocking," I say, without thinking but not untrue. Being alive is shocking.

When I last saw the deceased, he was losing his hair, middle-aged and skin cut close to the bone. He'd gained some flesh since. While I'd hardly call his state sanguineous, there's a radiance to his face that one associates with good health. Clear, supple skin, lustrous hair, features lax in repose.

The rest of him inspires a less-hopeful prognosis. He lies on the slab in a state of disassembly, severed limbs cleaned and laid out like spare parts. More parts than can be accounted for one body and some of them the wrong size. A small, stumpy leg. A tiny foot the size of a cowrie shell, as though his vivisection had been mixed up with that of a doll. "What are those?"

"They were inside him. A fetus in third-trimester development. Or rather," the Inspector corrects herself, "parts of a fetus. As though he was pregnant, but, since he lacked a uterus, the fetus was . . . distributed."

"That's a *very* silly idea, Inspector."

"So it is. You work at the crèche," she says, as though the crèche is a secret temple where impossible sorcery and unlikely biology occur. "You'd have a better idea of what might have happened than I do."

I try to make out whether she's being sarcastic or engaging in some strange interrogation technique. "I really don't, Inspector. The rare times we've approved manual birth, we first make sure the bearer is equipped for it. If I must stage a guess, an unlicensed surgeon and an implant-gone-wrong seem much likelier." I sketch in the air, no shape in particular but a gesture that, to the layperson, seems erudite. "To keep his youth or what else, who knows? It was certainly not going to get him a baby."

She lets me go: The Inspector doesn't seriously believe me a suspect— the crèche logs would corroborate my assertions and I lack either motive or means—but she seems disappointed that her only lead has no better to offer than dry speculation. In any case, none of it has much to do with me. A freak death of a freak condition; it happens to other people and not even in the vicinity of where I work or live.

Back in the office, I meet with a colleague and we discuss the matter briefly, the way we would handle gossip. None of us spares any great feeling for rejected applicants, united in a remote disdain for those desperate to parent. To add to the load of the station, to test the survival coefficient.

Schedule clear for the rest of my shift, I seek solace in another cigarette. This time, I remember little of what I see, though I retain the impression of headless newborns crawling and struggling to assemble themselves.

When lucidity returns, I find myself among the chambers.

No panic: My senses are still drug-glazed and everything shimmers in high contrast, the blackened metal of womb-capsules, the eye of Prathayayi. We'll never know why the station planners put this room here, directly facing that half-lidded eye. A scleral well without pupil, reflecting nothing. Not the wombs, the lights, not myself. Before this gaze, nothing exists.

A seam in the glass that I wouldn't have noticed without the hyper-focus of the comedown. The outline of it suggests a panel cut out and welded back in place with intricate care, the work of hours. When I press my ear to it, I almost expect a submerged, gurgling voice. All I hear is my cardiac meter reverberating back, seismic.

I recall the last time security logged an alarm. The hour is about right. There's a risk I am wrong, but I'll take it. My request is answered in the affirmative.

✳

Kittisak's shadow precedes him, distorted, but coming into view, it is more than just his shadow. He totters as though carrying an unfamiliar weight. The bloat on him has nothing to do with muscle growth or bad diet run amok—distributed fetal development, the Inspector half-joked. He kneels by the spot I pressed my ear to ten minutes ago, breathing onto the glass. Mesmerized.

"Khun Kittisak."

As before, his breath catches and he freezes, electrified by his own guilt. "Doctor," he begins, "I can explain this."

"Which part can you explain? That you've been sneaking in here, or that mysterious and—apparently—fatal condition?"

"Those who deserve her gift safely carry to term."

I glance sideway at the immense, inert eye. "Yes," I say mildly, "that sounds very sane."

"This is how we were meant to be and our children will live forever." He sweeps his arms outward. "There's no sunlight here; do you see? We need only to make. We need only to break the glass. The perfect seedbed in which the next Y'ha-nthlei must inevitably flower, in which *we* will be reborn."

"I have no idea what you just said." Nor was I aware the human throat could pronounce those sounds. "Attempting to reproduce without a license is illegal, Khun Kittisak."

"You don't *understand*, Doctor. I'm in total control of my faculties. If you listen and pay attention, you can hear her too. You would see."

A gun emerges from his hand, its passage smooth as an egg's. His aim drifts low, meant to wound, slow to squeeze the trigger as though he has all the time in the world. And against me, he does. Maybe he plans to explain himself while I bleed, persuade me to his viewpoint over the aria of my pain.

Unlike me, the Inspector is armed; unlike him, she does not hesitate, is quick to fire, and interested in no rhetoric save that of the bullet.

He goes down, a rupturing of more than just flesh, more than his own. A fetal arm or hand, maybe even a head. When the Inspector's subordinates take him away, he is weeping, clutching at the tiny limb dangling from his open wound. Numb to the pain but vulnerable to the grief. When they operate on him, I wonder how many they will find, those parasites attached to that willing host.

I stay behind, as does the Inspector. She commends me for my intuition and quickness of wit; I pay her only half my attention, the other half drawn to the wombs. But they remain as they are, ordinary and in order, much as the carcass is. Nothing has changed. Nothing will change. We march inexorably toward a certain end.

A silhouette that evokes my cigarette haze, for a moment, one of the fetuses seems finned and scaled, a sleek tail curled in on itself.

"Doctor? Is there something wrong?"

In the tank, that shadow has vanished.

"No, Inspector," I say quietly. "Everything is just fine."

T'LA-YUB'S HEAD

NELLY GERALDINE GARCÍA-ROSAS

Translated by Silvia Moreno-Garcia

THE FIRST THING that rematerialized was her head, vomiting with a death rattle. Then, as she regained her breath, her arched body began to appear. Slowly, the luminous vapor she seemed made of, turned into flesh until it collapsed on the floor. The long black hairs, drenched in vomit and sweat, adhered to her face painted red and black.

"What did I do wrong this time, Tonantzin? How did I make a mistake, Mother?!" T'la-yub asked in a scream when she was able to stand on her feet.

But there was no answer. Why should there be? So, she half-closed her eyes and held the amulet with such strength that its borders made her left hand bleed.

Then she said the words which, though they came from her mouth, sounded as if they had been said in a very deep place. Then T'la-yub's entire body turned into blue light. Then into nothing.

✻

We came to the Mictlán, the place of the dead, which the ancient people called Xinaián, because my grandmother had a vision.

287

"They say there, far north of the great Tenochtitlán, is the land of the dead. Farther than the mountains which encircle that city of water. Farther than the place of the herons and the deserts where the ancestors of the people who live here come from. There, where live the red people who adore the other eagles. There lived our families before Quetzalcóatl used his bones to create humanity and Cihuacóatl cried for us. There remains a door which we must watch because we are the key," Grandmother had said, the *pulque* gushing from her trembling lips, when she slipped from her prophetic trance.

"Rest, grandmother. You are no longer strong enough to speak so much to the gods," I said, as I held her hands. She was freezing.

"May no one have heard you, girl. Where we go, the gods rule and they will speak to you with their forked tongues. There, you shall learn the hidden words of duality and also, how to hide and change shape as we have done since we arrived in this world. There, you will be guardian and lady, spectre and goddess, T'la-yub. From there, there is no return. *Iä! Iä!*"

Despite this terrible promise, I agreed to travel with her because, in some way, I was certain she would not enter the underworld as a living being and that someone must prepare her body for the journey of death.

The preparations for our departure were quick and silent. We hung from our shoulders the rolls of *petate* and from our waists the gourds with *pulque*. We released the animals. We left the house without a lock. Nobody, alive or dead, returns from Mictlán.

We walked through many unknown paths for countless moons until we arrived at the place where the hills meet: the entry to the underground kingdom, the door of my family. I remember that the dogs howled as if they meant to announce our arrival at the place which was once the home of our ancestors.

My grandmother died the next day and she began her descent, like all the dead.

I cleansed her body. I tied it with papers full of praises for the gods and I placed a green stone inside her mouth—the jade of Mictlantecuhtli Iä! With a bit of food, I managed to attract one of the dogs that moved around the hill, a lean, reddish specimen that seemed to accept, docile, its destiny as a guide.

On the fourth day, I set fire to the funeral pyre.

✳

Her grandmother had told her that it was a metal which came from beyond the stars, which had fallen like scorching rock and that the gods had indicated how it must be carved.

"In dreams, Grandmother. You always knew everything thanks to your visions. But the gods do not speak to me. They don't tell me what I'm doing wrong," muttered T'la-yub. The scars the artefact had left on her left hand were healing and had already turned into a circular callus.

The amulet was of a green so dark it was almost black. On one side was engraved the image of a great serpent and on the other, a strange creature that agitated its eight arms ominously.

"Why did you give it to me if you would die without it? Why would you bring me here to leave me alone, making conjurings I do not comprehend?"

✳

Four years it takes for the dead to descend through the nine lands of the underworld and arrive at the abode of the lords of death. They say some forget the journey and remain here with the ancient people without being able to recall if they are alive or dead. They say they become specters without a will, slaves. I have seen them walk laboriously through golden streets. I have also seen them guard the entrance of the places that here they call amphitheaters, but which are nothing more than the place with blinding gray mist and obsidian wind that mutilates the dead.

I was in the amphitheater. I saw how those who were once alive tried to escape and reach the chamber of the lords of death where the sun rests at night. I saw, too, through the mist, a woman who wore a skirt of snakes. Her hands and feet had very sharp claws, and from her neck hung a necklace made with human hands and hearts, which covered her flaccid breasts.

"I am Tonantzin, your mother, the Mother of All," said Coatlicue, who gave birth to the moon and the stars when she noticed I was looking at her. "I am the one the ancient people called Yig, for I am also father. Here lies the mystery of duality."

As she spoke, one of the ones who is neither dead nor alive came close with his obsidian knife and decapitated her with one stroke. A thick and blackish liquid spouted. It reeked. Two great serpents slid from the neck to substitute the old head.

"Life and death. The lands of the surface and the underworld. To make a whole, you need two parts and two parts, though distant, will always be a whole. You have done nothing wrong, Daughter. The body is also a whole that is formed of duality," the serpents said. "Search for the man with red hair on his face and his head. He will be your crimson dog. Throw him on the pyre when you begin your own descent."

The serpents intertwined their forked tongues and disappeared into the gray mist.

I begin the journey of death being alive still. I descend to Mictlán protected by my mother Coatlicue, who showed that the art of dematerialization is the instrument of duality. I understand, at last, my grandmother's vision.

I look at the amulet: The two gods exist as one. I think that everything functions like this: in pairs, in dualities. I paint my face: one half-red, the other black. I dress in a skirt of snakes and a headdress of feathers. I am Cihuacóatl, the serpent woman. But I am also Mictecacíhuatl, lady of the dead.

I hear them come to drag me into the amphitheater where the mist blinds and the wind cuts like a knife: the last step before the arrival at the abode of the gods.

The doors open. The wind slices my cheeks. I half-close my eyes, though I can see nothing. I begin to salivate. I arch my back. My mouth already tastes like vomit, but I manage to pronounce the words that come from most deep, from the mouths of the gods with a thousand tongues who are not of this world.

Everything is blue.

※

The decapitated body of T'la-yub guards, by night, the door of her ancestors, which leads to Mictlán. Walking in dreams, she presents herself to the ashes of her grandmother. In the eternity of the mound, the time of dreams is not the same as the time of death.

In the principal chamber of Mictlán, time is also different. In the *tzompantli* of the lords of death, there is eternally a new head. The long black hairs writhe like tentacles. Her red-and-black lips sing to receive the dead, who, at last, have finished their tortuous journey. She kisses them like a mother and makes them rest in the same bed where the sun sleeps.

The head of T'la-yub opens her eyes, which are the stellar eyes of Mictlantecuhtli. They see everything and see themselves in them. The light of the stars is born and extinguished in that same instant.

"Lovecraft" by Sara Bardi

ABOUT THE AUTHORS

LAURA BLACKWELL is a writer, editor and journalist. She was raised in North Dakota, where the snow and dirt mingle, and become "snirt." Her publications include *PC World*, *Strange Horizons*, *TechHive*, and various speculative fiction anthologies. You can follow her on Twitter @pronouncedlahra and visit her website at www.pronouncedlahra.com.

NADIA BULKIN writes scary stories about the scary world we live in. She is more a fan of Hole than 311. It took her two tries to leave Nebraska, but now she lives in Washington, DC, where she tends her garden of student debt sown by two political science degrees. You can read her other Lovecraftian work in the anthologies *Sword and Mythos*, *Letters to Lovecraft*, *Lovecraft's Monsters*, and *The Mammoth Book of Cthulhu*—or visit nadiabulkin.wordpress.com.

SELENA CHAMBERS writes twenty miles south of the Black Lagoon. Her fiction has appeared in a variety of venues, including *Mungbeing Magazine*, *New Myths*, and *Yankee Pot Roast*, and in anthologies such as the World Fantasy-nominated *Thackery T. Lambshead's Cabinet Of Curiosities*, *The New Gothic*, *Steampunk World*, and *The Starry Wisdom Library*. Her non-fiction has appeared at Tor.com, Bookslut, WeirdFictionReview.com, and *Strange Horizons* (where she was also the articles senior editor for two years). Her first book, the Hugo and World Fantasy-nominated *The Steampunk Bible*, was co-authored with the award-winning Jeff VanderMeer. She blogs irregularly at www.selenachambers.com.

ARINN DEMBO is a prize-winning author of SF, fantasy and horror. Her fiction and poetry have appeared in *The Magazine of F&SF*, *H.P. Lovecraft's Magazine of Horror*, *Weird Tales*, *Lamp Light Quarterly*, and various anthologies. Single-author books include a military science fiction novel, *The Deacon's Tale*, and a collection called *Monsoon and Other Stories*. In addition to a long career as a writer in the entertainment industry, she holds degrees in anthropology and classical archaeology, fields which often provide grist for the mill of her horror stories. Follow her on social media or visit her website, www.arinndembo.com, for more information.

JILLY DREADFUL completed her Ph.D. in Literature and Creative Writing at the University of Southern California. She's the founder of The Brainery: Online Speculative Fiction Workshops + Resources. She's currently an associate editor of *NonBinary Review* and *Unbound Octavo*, and her major work includes *Light & Power: A Tesla/Edison Story*, a chamber opera with music composed by Isaac Schankler. Together with her writing partner, KT Ismael, she will be releasing a serialized fiction podcast that takes the feminist emphasis on friendship from *Parks and Recreation,* and mixes it with a Lovecraftian strangeness—stay tuned for it at blueprintandengine.com.

Former film critic and teacher-turned-award-winning horror author **GEMMA FILES** is probably best-known for her Weird Western Hexslinger series (*A Book of Tongues*, *A Rope of Thorns*, and *A Tree of Bones*, all from ChiZine Publications). She has also published two collections of short fiction, two chapbooks of speculative poetry, and a story cycle (*We Will All Go Down Together: Stories of the Five-Family Coven*, CZP). Her next book, *Experimental Film*—also from CZP—will be released in November 2015.

NELLY GERALDINE GARCÍA-ROSAS is a Mexican writer who just moved to the UK. She lives in South Yorkshire with her husband. There, she misses her cats more than anything in the world. Her stories have appeared in anthologies like *Future Lovecraft* and *The Apex Book of World SF 3*. She can be found online at www.nellygeraldine.com or tweeting mostly in Spanish @kitsune_ng

AMELIA GORMAN is a computer science student living in Minnesota.

LYNDSEY HOLDER enjoys long walks on the beach, eating too much chocolate, and writing paranoid fiction. She's currently writing a novel that is part pulp noir, part eldritch horror, and part teen detective.

PANDORA HOPE has a BA in English and has worked as a copywriter, science writer, editor and runologist when not moonlighting as a *volva* (a Norse witch). She has recently begun to write fiction and her first short story, "The Ferry Man," appeared in *Interzone* (January 2015). She is currently working on a novel set in the same world. Pandora credits Lovecraft's "The Rats in the Walls" as responsible for her first experience of night terrors and, paradoxically, a lifelong affection for rats. She lives in Australia with her partner and what may well be Melbourne's only rat-friendly Norwegian Forest Cat.

INKERI KONTRO is an award-winning Finnish short story writer who lives in Helsinki. Physicist by day, writer by night, she writes mostly science fiction and Finnish Weird with a touch of horror. She has published stories in magazines such as *Kosmoskynä* and *Tähtivaeltaja*, and her English debut was in *Strange Horizons* in 2014.

PENELOPE LOVE is an Australian who has written extensively for the tabletop role-playing game *Call of Cthulhu*, including contributing scenarios to the award-winning *Horror on the Orient Express* campaign. Her Cthulhu Mythos short stories have been published in *Cthulhu's Dark Cults, Madness on the Orient Express,* and *Tales of Cthulhu Invictus*. Her work also appears in the award-winning anthologies, *One Small Step* and *Belong*. Her story "A Small Bad Thing" was first published in *Bloodstones* and reprinted in *The Year's Best Australian Fantasy and Horror 2013*.

SHARON MOCK's short stories have appeared in publications including *Fantasy Magazine, Clarkesworld* and *The Mammoth Book of Steampunk*. She lives in California and can be found online at sharonmock.com.

Despite the warnings of her family that studying science would warp her tender mind and shrivel her womb, **PREMEE MOHAMED** completed degrees in molecular genetics and environmental science, and has used those disciplines to pursue the improvement of mankind's lot, somewhat ineffectually, for over a decade. When not performing mad science, she blogs regularly, tweets less regularly, paints, draws, writes, worries about the supernatural, and annotates her paperback copy of *The Necronomicon*.

EUGENIE MORA is a writer of fanciful, occasionally creepy, sometimes sweet, stories. In her spare time, she makes a science of hating walks on the beach, bird and TV-watching. Considers herself a music ninja. Professional reader. Passionate troublemaker. Food aficionado. Wine practitioner.

ANN K. SCHWADER's most recent collection of dark verse is *Twisted in Dream*. Her next collection, *Dark Energies*, is forthcoming from P'rea Press. Her fiction and poetry have recently appeared in *Black Wings IV*, *Searchers After Horror*, *A Season in Carcosa*, and elsewhere. She is a 2010 Bram Stoker Award finalist for her dark SF verse collection *Wild Hunt of the Stars*.

RODOPI SISAMIS lives and writes out of Brooklyn, NY, where she raises Hellion triplets, and lives with a dog and a cat. When she isn't devouring books, or running after children, she can be found spinning tales of romance and dark fantasy. "Cypress God" is her third contribution to an anthology.

Specializing in dark fantasy and horror, **ANGELA SLATTER** has won five Aurealis Awards, been a finalist for the World Fantasy Award, and is the first Australian to win a British Fantasy Award. She's the author of, among other things, *The Girl with No Hands and Other Tales*, *Sourdough and Other Stories*, and *The Bitterwood Bible and Other Recountings*. Forthcoming from Jo Fletcher Books is the novel, *Vigil*, and its sequel *Corpselight*.

PRIYA SRIDHAR has been writing since fifth grade, a year after her mother forbade her from watching television all day. This led to several published short stories, one of which made the Top Ten Amazon Kindle Download list, and Alban Lake publishing her novella *Carousel*. She invites readers to read her blog a Faceless Author at pseudonymousfictionwriter. blogspot.com.

BENJANUN SRIDUANGKAEW writes love letters to strange cities, beautiful bugs, and the future. Her work has appeared in Tor.com, *Beneath Ceaseless Skies*, *Phantasm Japan*, *The Dark*, and year's bests. She has been shortlisted for the Campbell Award for Best New Writer and her debut novella *Scale-Bright* has been nominated for the British SF Association Award.

MOLLY TANZER is the author of the Weird Western, *Vermilion,* and the forthcoming historical novel, *The Pleasure Merchant.* Her debut collection, *A Pretty Mouth,* was nominated for a Sydney J. Bounds and a Wonderland Book Award. Her short fiction has appeared in other Innsmouth titles such as *Historical Lovecraft* and *Fungi,* as well as other venues such as *The Book(s) of Cthulhu, The Book of the Dead,* and *Children of Old Leech.* She lives in Boulder, Colorado with her husband and a very bad cat. When not writing, she enjoys mixing cocktails, hiking in the Rocky Mountains, and experimenting with Korean cooking. She tweets @molly_the_tanz, and blogs—infrequently—at mollytanzer.com.

E. CATHERINE TOBLER's short stories have appeared in *Clarkesworld, Lightspeed,* and *Beneath Ceaseless Skies.* Her first novel, *Rings of Anubis,* is now available. Follow her on Twitter @ECthetwit or her website, ecatherine. com.

MARY TURZILLO's 1999 Nebula-winner, "Mars Is no Place for Children," and her *Analog* novel, *An Old-Fashioned Martian Girl,* are recommended reading on the International Space Station. Her poetry collection *Lovers & Killers* won the 2013 Elgin Award. She has been a finalist on the British Science Fiction Association, Pushcart, Stoker, Dwarf Stars, and Rhysling ballots. *Sweet Poison,* her Dark Renaissance collaboration with Marge Simon, was a Stoker finalist. *Sweet Poison* is on the 2015 Elgin ballot. She's working on a novel, *A Mars Cat and his Boy.* She lives in Berea, Ohio, with her scientist-writer husband, Geoffrey A. Landis.

VALERIE VALDES earned her BA in English at the University of Miami, with minors in creative writing and working too many jobs. She still lives in Miami with her husband and his miniature doppelganger. Valerie took the brakes off her roller blades because they only slowed her down.

WENDY N. WAGNER is the author of *Skinwalkers*, a Pathfinder Tales novel inspired by Viking lore. Her short fiction has appeared in many successful anthologies, including *Shattered Shields*, *Armored*, and *The Way of the Wizard*, and magazines like *Beneath Ceaseless Skies* and *The Lovecraft eZine*. She is the non-fiction editor of *Women Destroy Science Fiction!*, which was named one of NPR's Best Books of 2014. She lives in Oregon with her very understanding family.

ABOUT THE ARTISTS

SARA BARDI is an illustrator and conceptual artist born in a port town that she likes to consider the Italian equivalent of Innsmouth. Her illustrations have been featured in Italian and international publications, indie games and animated series. She first came across H.P. Lovecraft's fiction during her high school years and got totally enthralled by his uncanny universe. Because of her precocious love for gothic themes and heavily Disney-influenced artistic background, Sara always liked to portrait dark characters under a gentler light and show how even the 'cute' and unsuspected ones can be ruthless foes. In 2013, she began to serialize a webcomic titled *Lovely Lovecraft,* which explores HPL's cosmic horror through the eyes of fearless kids and Eldritch Gods that could probably use a hug.

SHELBY DENHAM was born and raised in Oregon where she was often inspired by the comics and movies she loved. She recently moved to Florida to work for the Mouse, but that doesn't keep her from illustrating the macabre.

SARA K. DIESEL is an award-winning digital artist working in Pittsburgh. Her work reflects her passion for all things science fiction, fantasy, and surreal. Using combinations of vivid color, her artwork contains an illuminated quality otherwise lost in traditional mediums.

LISA GRABENSTETTER draws inspiration from artists of the Symbolist movement, from Art Nouveau, and from contemporary fantasy and comic book illustrators. Working primarily in ink, graphite and watercolor, and the occasional hand-pulled print. A 2008 graduate of The Cleveland Institute of Art, Lisa has a BFA in printmaking and a minor in drawing. See more at magneticcrow.com

KAREN ANN HOLLINGSWORTH is a fantasy children's illustrator and fine artist living in the Chicago area. Working either in the notoriously unforgiving media of watercolor and colored pencil or simply in black-and-white, she strives to invoke a sense of magic and wonder in every image. Visit her website and see for yourself: Wrenditions.com.

C.L. LEWIS is a fantasy artist. She was born in Tampa, Florida. She began drawing monsters and dragons when she was four. Cindy's family moved to Mt. Carmel, Illinois during her high school years. She attended Wabash Valley College, winning a degree in art and numerous awards. Her professor and family, especially her father, encouraged her to continue developing her talent. In recent years she has undertaken numerous commissions, including tattoos, book illustrations and paintings. Her work is in many residences throughout the United States, Canada, and the United Kingdom. She resides in Toledo, Ohio, with her husband and five cats.

PIA RAVENARI is an artist and writer living in Western Australia. Her artwork expresses a constant ongoing fascination with natural history, archetypal fables, sacred tales, modern mythopoeia, and the challenging aspects of humanity. She's worked as an illustrator of book covers and internal illustrations in the past, across a range of subjects, and was nominated for a Ditmar award in 2014 for her cover art for *Prickle Moon* by Juliet Marillier. She prefers traditional mediums over digital, and her staples are pen, ink and pencils.

LIV RAINEY-SMITH specializes in the superannuated art of hand-pulled xylographic prints. She designs, cuts and prints her original woodcut editions in Portland, Oregon. Her publications include *Arcanum Bestiarum*, from Three Hands Press, and *Starry Wisdom Library*, from P.S. Publishing. She is a regular guest and Pickman's Apprentice competitor at the H.P. Lovecraft Film Festival. She serves as Art Show Liaison for the Esoteric Book Conference in Seattle, Washington and volunteers with Print Arts Northwest. Rainey-Smith received her BFA from the Oregon College of Art and Craft in 2008.

DIANA THUNG makes comics. Her graphic novels include *Captain Long Ears* and *August Moon*. She lives with her two dogs in Sydney, Australia.

KATHRYN WEAVER is an illustrator and writer whose work has previously been published in *Apex Magazine*, *The Toast*, and *Lackington's*. She lives in Minneapolis with her girlfriend and two birds. Her portfolio can be found at kathrynmweaver.com.

ABOUT THE EDITORS

SILVIA MORENO-GARCIA's debut novel, *Signal to Noise*, about music, magic and Mexico City, has been called "a magical first novel" by *The Guardian* and an "elaborate symphony of awesome that defies simple definitions" by *Kirkus*. Her first collection, *This Strange Way of Dying*, was a finalist for The Sunburst Award for Excellence in Canadian Literature of the Fantastic. She has worked on several anthologies, including *Dead North* and *Fractured: Tales of the Canadian Post-Apocalypse*.

A saltgunning medieval historian and author of three novels, over forty short stories, a non-fiction book, and lots of articles, **PAULA R. STILES** is currently working on her fifth degree, in Historic Preservation Technology, when she's not editing everything on Innsmouth Free Press. She currently lives in eastern North Carolina with an elderly, flatulent dog and a clowder of alarmingly optimistic cats. You can find her on Facebook, Twitter @ thesnowleopard, and at thesnowleopard.net.

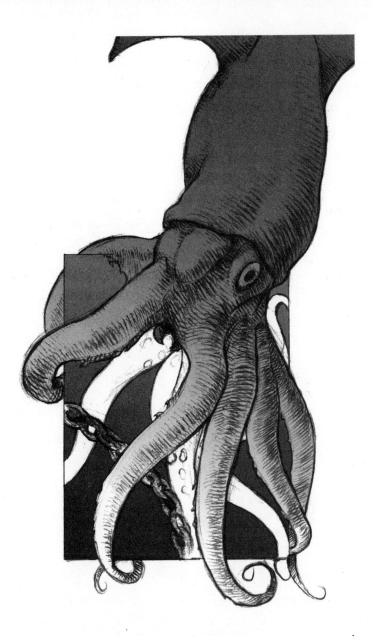

Money for the first publication of this project was raised via a crowdfunding campaign. During the campaign we utilized artist Lisa Grabenstetter's squid to promote *She Walks in Shadows*. We thought it would be fitting that it appear here to thank everyone involved with this project including backers, writers, artists, proofreaders, and associate creatures. It's been a blast.

ALSO FROM PRIME BOOKS

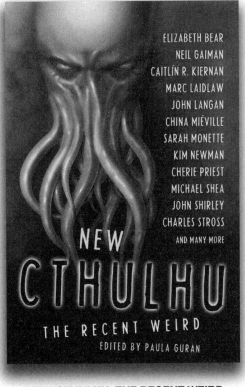

ELIZABETH BEAR
NEIL GAIMAN
CAITLÍN R. KIERNAN
MARC LAIDLAW
JOHN LANGAN
CHINA MIÉVILLE
SARAH MONETTE
KIM NEWMAN
CHERIE PRIEST
MICHAEL SHEA
JOHN SHIRLEY
CHARLES STROSS
AND MANY MORE

NEW CTHULHU
THE RECENT WEIRD
EDITED BY PAULA GURAN

NEW CTHULHU: THE RECENT WEIRD
528 Pages | $15.95

Praise for *New Cthulhu: The Recent Weird*

"For fans of Lovecraftian fiction and well-wrought horror." —*Library Journal*

"Guran smartly selects stories that evoke the spirit of Lovecraft's work without mimicking its style." —*Publishers Weekly*

"It's a pretty impressive line-up, with nary a clunker to be found. . . . You don't have to be a Lovecraft fan to enjoy this anthology . . . You'll find alienation, inhumanity, desperation, cruelty, insanity, hopelessness and despair, all set against the backdrop of a vast, unknowable universe filled with vile, indifferent monstrosities. You'll also find beauty, hope, redemption, and the struggle for survival. What more can you ask for?" —*Tor.com*

"I highly recommend this collection . . . If you have even the slightest interest in contemporary horror fiction, you'll want to try this one on for size!" —*BookGuide*